THE UNKNOWN SPY

The RING OF FIVE

THE UNKNOWN SPY

Eoin McNamee

WENDY
LAMB
BOOKS

Text copyright © 2011 by Eoin McNamee
Jacket art copyright © 2011 by Scott Altmann

All rights reserved. Published in the United States by Wendy Lamb Books,
an imprint of Random House Children's Books, a division of Random House, Inc.,
New York. Originally published in paperback in Great Britain
by Quercus Publishing Plc, London, in 2011.

Wendy Lamb Books and the colophon are trademarks of Random House, Inc.

Visit us on the Web! www.randomhouse.com/kids
Educators and librarians, for a variety of teaching tools, visit us at
www.randomhouse.com/teachers

Library of Congress Cataloging-in-Publication Data
McNamee, Eoin.
The unknown spy / by Eoin McNamee. — 1st ed.
p. cm.
Summary: Danny Caulfield's quiet Christmas break from Wilsons Academy, the school for spies, is shattered by gunshots and a heartrending discovery about his parents, and he is called back to Wilsons to prepare to go undercover to protect the Treaty Stone that keeps peace between the Upper and Lower Worlds.
ISBN 978-0-385-73820-0 (trade) — ISBN 978-0-385-90713-2 (lib. bdg.) —
ISBN 978-0-375-89950-8 (ebook) — ISBN 978-0-375-85470-5 (pbk.)
[1. Fantasy. 2. Spies—Fiction.] I. Title.
PZ7.M4787933 Un 2011
[Fic]—dc22
2010052152

Printed in the United States of America

10 9 8 7 6 5 4 3 2 1

First Edition

For Finbar and Caitlin

THE UNKNOWN SPY

*T*he countryside around the old house was dark and silent. The night was cloudless, and stars glittered in the icy sky. The previous few days had seen the first snowfalls of the year, and the snow lay heavily on the fields and woods. A fox's tracks led toward the frozen lake on the grounds of the house, but not a living thing was to be seen, all the wild creatures huddled in burrow or nest against the cold.

The house was very old and might have appeared uninhabited were it not for a single light burning in a window just under the eaves. It was the kind of light you saw when you were out late and had a long way to go and were cold and hungry so that you imagined a cozy bedroom with a fire burning in the grate.

Only the sharpest-eared of creatures would have heard the sound, as if a faint breeze rustled across the land, and only the sharpest-eyed would have seen the bright stars dimmed for a moment. Yet in their beds the wild animals stirred and whimpered in their sleep. Something evil was abroad in the cold night. On the topmost branches of a tall pine tree overlooking the house there was a sudden flurry, the strong branches bowing down and dumping their load of snow on the ground.

The branches sprang back. Now, instead of being weighed with snow, they carried a different burden. A tall stooped figure stood in the tree—a man, perhaps, with long gray hair and eyes that burned yellow. A man and yet not a man, for from the middle of his back sprouted a pair of long feathered wings. The fierce eyes were fixed on the single light burning under the eaves of the house. The creature had risked much to be here. There was a solemn treaty forbidding him and his kind from crossing the border between the Lower World and the Upper, where he now stood, and he could not be sure of the consequences if his presence was revealed.

But the prize was great. The boy was the only one who could unite the Two Worlds. The winged creature and his companions had tried once to turn the boy to evil but had failed. Stubborn values of friendship and loyalty could not be overcome. But this time they would succeed.

The creature's name was Conal. Once he had been a winged Messenger, an envoy who came and went between the Two Worlds in time of peace. But he had been corrupted and had become a member of the Ring of Five, the greatest spy ring that had ever existed. Together with his three companions, he had sought the fifth member of their fellowship, without whom their powers were incomplete. They believed they had found him in Danny Caulfield, a boy with a pixie-like face and different-colored eyes—the marks of the Fifth.

The Ring had watched from afar as the boy had begun

to train at Wilsons Academy of the Devious Arts, the school for spies. He had been a natural, discovering in himself almost at once a gift for treachery, a part of him that longed for the thrill of secrets and betrayal. He had resisted it, but that only made the moment so much sweeter when Danny finally turned his back on friendship and love and embraced the dark world of mistrust. He had regretted that choice and escaped the Ring, but now they sought him anew.

Conal shifted his weight on the branch and spread his wings. He had found the boy. It was time to consult his colleagues. The forces of darkness were gathering, but Danny's protectors had chosen well. Conal could see the untidy nests in the bare trees around the house. The ravens would be sleeping, but he couldn't risk being seen by them. The great wings flapped once; Conal launched himself gently into the frigid air and was gone.

AGENTS

Danny lay in a warm little room, a Nintendo DS closed on the bedspread beside him. That was the problem, he thought. Once you had been a spy, your life in jeopardy every minute, when one false slip meant betrayal and perhaps death, then a computer game seemed very tame. But that wasn't his main worry.

He had come home for the Christmas holidays from Wilsons Academy to find that his parents were their kind but absent selves. As usual, they were hardly ever home. Danny had thought they might appreciate him more since they hadn't seen him for three months, but if anything, they were gone more often. Even on Christmas Day (after a morning of present opening under the tree and a delicious turkey dinner) his father had received a phone call and ten minutes later his car swept out of the driveway. As he'd dashed away, his wave to his wife and son was cheery, but Danny had seen the fatigue around his eyes.

That night he and his mother had sat by the fire, his mother reading and eating chocolates, Danny watching a Christmas film. It was almost too good, Danny realized, to have her to himself for a whole evening.

"Goodness," his mother had said, "I can't remember the last time I had a chance to just sit and read."

"I haven't watched a film in ages," Danny said.

It's a Wonderful Life. She smiled. "I was half watching it over your shoulder. It was my favorite when I was your age."

She stood up.

"Would you like some hot chocolate?" He nodded and watched as she stood to go to the kitchen. Even in a dressing gown, her hair tied up, she was elegant. She paused beside him, her hands resting gently on his hair. There and then Danny almost blurted out the truth about where he had spent the last three months. His parents thought they had sent him to a boarding school called Heston Oaks. Instead he had been virtually kidnapped and spirited off to Wilsons.

When he'd arrived home for the holidays, he found that someone—probably Brunholm, the devious vice principal of Wilsons—had constructed an elaborate cover story for him, complete with fake letters sent home saying what a wonderful time he was having at Heston Oaks. Part of Danny ached to tell the truth, but he thought that he wouldn't be allowed back to Wilsons, and he could not bear the thought of not seeing his new friends again. That was what he told himself, anyway, although he wondered if the part of him that loved secrets and shadows was the real reason for his silence.

"Have your hot chocolate, then clean your teeth and get to bed," his mother had said, moving off. Danny had grinned inwardly. Imagine telling a member of the Ring of Five, the most terrifying group of spies ever known, to brush his teeth.

While his mother made the chocolate in the kitchen, he had looked at the family photographs on the mantel. His mother and father were tall and blond; he was short and dark. He'd never questioned this when he was younger, but the physical differences between him and his parents was starting to trouble him. What if . . . what if they weren't really his parents?

"Here you go." His mother had handed him a steaming mug. Her smile made him feel what he'd missed in the past, and what he was going to miss in the future when she started to go out every evening again.

But that worry was for the future. For the moment Danny had enjoyed his mother's company, enjoyed pretending to be asleep when she came in to check on him before she went to bed, enjoyed all the normal things other children took for granted. If only this could last forever, he'd thought.

But of course it hadn't. Three days after Christmas he'd woken to find a scribbled note from his mother on the kitchen table, saying that "I've gone out for a few hours."

That had been forty-eight hours ago, and still she had not returned. She had stayed away overnight once or twice before, but she had always phoned to let him know. Danny had tried both of his parents' cell phones, but they had been turned off. There was plenty of food in the house, and he was used to being on his own, but still he was lonely and worried. They might not be my real parents, he thought, but they're all I've got.

For the tenth time that evening he went to the window and stared out at the snow, untouched for miles around. This time he knelt down and squinted into the distance. He could see a far-off light on the road—a car! Small at first, but growing rapidly. He blinked and looked again. There was another set of lights behind the first, moving just as quickly. How could both drivers keep up the pace on the icy road? And why were they going so fast? There could be only one reason for the speed. He opened the window a little and his heart dropped. From the lead car he could make out the throaty growl of his father's Mercedes. It dropped a gear, and Danny heard the second car do the same. His father was being chased!

Danny pressed his head against the windowsill. He tried to remember something from his spying classes that would help. The two cars would be at the house in minutes. He had to think! What had he learned? Concealment! The approaching car would need to be hidden.

He ran down the stairs two at a time, grabbed a broom from the closet and turned off the hallway light before opening the front door, so that he wouldn't be seen. The cold made him gasp. The car engines were clearly audible now, the roar of the Mercedes and the smooth powerful hum of the following car. Danny ran around the side of the house, skidding on the hardened snow. He flung open the garage doors and ran back, broom at the ready. It would be a close thing.

The Mercedes was coming round the last corner flat-out, fishtailing, and it flattened a small sapling. His mother was behind the wheel, her face pale. His father was in the passenger seat, head flung back. Danny didn't have time to absorb the information. He gestured franti-cally with the broom. His mother looked at him in shock, then instantly understood. Spinning the wheel, she threw the car into a long, graceful slide, then straightened. The car sped through the backyard and into the garage. Danny slammed the big doors. As fast as he could, he brushed away the tire tracks, running to the front of the house and finishing the last track just as the second car rounded the corner. If it hadn't been for the fallen sapling he would have been caught in the headlights, but the beams pointed mo-mentarily across the frozen fields. Danny looked around wildly. No cover near, except for the shadow of the stairs to the front door.

The car slowed, then stopped. A door opened. Foot-steps crunched in the snow. Danny crouched in the small shadow by the door. He knew from Concealment classes at Wilsons that you could hide almost in plain view if you didn't move a muscle. Movement drew the hunter's eye. Danny didn't dare look up. The whites of his eyes in the darkness would give him away. The footsteps stopped; then a harsh female voice spoke.

"They are still in front of us! Fly, Sasha, fly like the wind!" The pitch of the engine rose as the car door slammed shut. The tires spun, then gripped, sending an arc of snow high into the air. As the car picked up speed, Danny risked a glance. There were four men and one woman in the car, all tough-looking, and Danny found himself shrinking back into the shadow.

He gave the car a full minute to clear the house, then leapt to his feet and raced to the garage. The door was open, and he saw light from the kitchen. As he ran toward the light, he looked down. The virgin snow at his feet was spotted deep red. When he reached for the door handle, he found it smeared with blood. The door swung slowly open.

His father was slumped at the kitchen table. His mother was bent over him, but as the door creaked, she spun around. To his shock Danny found himself staring down the barrel of a large and deadly-looking revolver. His mother's hair had fallen over her face and there were streaks of oil and blood on her cheek, but her steady brown eyes did not falter. Slowly the gun was lowered.

"Are they gone?" Her voice was brisk and commanding. Danny stared back before nodding dumbly. Where was the elegant, remote woman who had sat by the fire beside him a few days previously? This new mother wore no makeup. Her black jeans and top were streaked with mud.

10

"Don't stand there gaping," she snapped. "Help me. Quick. Get him under the arms."

Danny moved to do as his mother said, questions flooding his mind. As he reached her side, he opened his mouth to speak, but a glance silenced him. He looked down at his father for the first time. The man's face was pale and his breathing was quick and shallow. The shoulder of his shirt was sodden with blood.

"Heave!" his mother said. Together they got him onto the kitchen table.

"The bullet's gone into his shoulder and taken some fabric from his shirt into the wound," she said. "We have to get it out. Now." Danny looked at her blankly.

"We need to get a doctor—hospital . . . ," he stammered.

"No time," she said. "Besides, they'll be watching the hospitals. There's a box in the top drawer of the writing desk. Get it."

Danny ran for the box. It was a steel case that he had never seen before. He handed it to his mother. She flipped it open. Inside were surgical instruments and several vials of liquid. She opened one of the vials and poured something onto a cloth. She held it over his father's mouth. "Breathe deeply, Agent Stone," she said. "We need to put you out."

Danny watched as the cloth covered his father's nose and mouth. Agent Stone? But there was no time to quiz his mother. The man was out cold now, his breathing shallow.

Danny's mother took a scalpel and what looked like a

11

pair of pliers from the case. With one swift stroke she cut through the flesh around the bullet wound.

"I'll hold the wound open," she said, "you reach in for the bullet and the piece of fabric."

Danny gulped as she pressed the pliers into his hand. He wasn't squeamish, but he'd never carried out kitchentable surgery before, particularly when the patient was the man who was supposed to be his father. As he hesitated, the man groaned again.

"We have to do this, Danny," his mother—or whoever she was—said. "Please." She met his eyes, and this time there was something of the person Danny remembered in them. He gulped and nodded.

Danny closed his eyes. When he opened them again, he was looking down into an open wound, blood everywhere, muscle and sinew exposed.

"Quickly!" Danny could feel a trickle of sweat run down his back. He lowered the tips of the pliers toward the wound. The matted piece of shirt fabric was clearly visible.

"Now!" He plunged the pliers down and grasped the fabric. In one quick movement he removed it and dropped it on the table. Now for the bullet, the small gray slug deep in the wound . . .

"You'll have to dig for it." As if in a nightmare Danny reached into the wound. He had to grope and twist to extract the bullet. It seemed to take hours. When he was done, he slumped back into a chair and stared numbly as his mother efficiently bandaged the wound.

"Go into the drawing room," she said, her voice gentler now. "I'll finish here."

It was almost an hour before she joined him. She handed him a mug of hot chocolate. She had showered and was wearing a dressing gown. She sat down beside him and looked into the fire.

"He's sleeping now," she said. "He should be okay."

"You called him Agent Stone," Danny said. "Dad."

"Did I?" She looked thoughtful and a little sad. "Funny the things that give you away."

"You're not my real . . ." The word stuck in Danny's throat.

"Mother? No, though sometimes I feel like I am. A lot of the time, in fact."

"Well, if I'm not your son, then who am I?" His voice rang harshly in his own ears.

"That," she said, "is complicated."

"Is it?" Danny said sarcastically. He was trying to be tough, but his heart was hammering in his chest.

"I'm afraid so." She sighed and hugged her knees. "He said it was time to tell you. Past time."

"Tell me," Danny said, his voice cracking.

"You were given to us as a mission, your . . . Agent Stone and I."

"A mission?"

"To protect you and . . . well, watch you."

"In case of what?"

13

"This is very difficult," she said. "We don't really know why. We were just given a mission. Your father—"

"Agent Stone," Danny interrupted.

"Don't be too hard on us, Danny. We've worked night and day for many years. To guard you, but also now to find out why! We were given much support over the years by unknown hands, but we do not know who has been helping us. There is danger—you saw what happened tonight."

"Who are they? The attackers?"

"I don't know. We were recruited anonymously, and now we can't get in touch with those who hired us. All we have now is you. . . ."

Danny held up his hand. No more. There was too much to take in. This woman looking at him was a stranger. What right did she have to ask for understanding? He got to his feet.

"I'm going to bed," he said.

"All right," she said. "We can talk again in the morning."

"Perhaps," Danny said. "Good night."

She watched him walk away. It was too much for a boy of his age to bear, she thought, and he shouldn't have found out like this. Still, she could talk to him in the morning, explain in more detail so that he might begin to understand.

"Good night," she called after him; then, under her breath, her lips barely moving, she formed the word "son."

* * *

Danny tossed and turned, words racing through his head. "Agent Stone." "A mission!" Deep down he had long suspected that the people he lived with were not his real parents, but now, faced with the knowledge that he was right, he was in turmoil. After several hours he fell into an uneasy sleep in which he dreamed he was back at Wilsons Academy, sitting in Ravensdale—the strange village canteen—with his friends, and then lying in bed in the Roosts—the dormitory—trying to ignore the voice of Blackpitt, the school announcer, who organized the students' day. *Cadet Caulfield, Cadet Caulfield!* the voice in his head said. *Go away,* Danny moaned in his sleep, but the voice did not go away.

"Cadet Caulfield!" Danny sat bolt upright. It really was the voice of Blackpitt, coming from behind the bed! Of course—the Radio of Last Resort! The radio had been given to him on leaving Wilsons so that the school could contact him as needed.

"Awake at last," Blackpitt said through the little transistor radio, sounding faintly amused. Somehow Blackpitt always knew what you were doing. "Please hold for Master Devoy."

Sleep fell away. Devoy was the head of Wilsons and a master spy. Why was he calling? Danny threw back the bedclothes and sat up.

"Cadet Caulfield." Devoy's tone was smooth and untroubled, but Danny knew that he had trained himself to show no emotion. "I am sorry to disturb you at this hour of the night, but it is urgent that you return to Wilsons immediately. Fairman the cabdriver will pick you up in

15

twenty minutes. I am sorry to interrupt your holiday, but this will not wait." The Radio of Last Resort crackled and went silent.

Twenty minutes! Danny grabbed a bag and started to stuff clothes into it. He half smiled before taking a battered-looking overcoat from the back of the door. It smelled musty and looked old-fashioned, but it had many hidden secrets.

Ten minutes later Danny was in the foyer. He peered into the living room. The woman who had been masquerading as his mother had fallen asleep on the chair beside the fire. He tiptoed down the hall to the downstairs bedroom. The man who had said he was Danny's father was also asleep, his face gray. He looked terribly unwell, and Danny had to resist the temptation to go over to him, perhaps whisper something in his ear. But it was better this way. Better that Danny leave without saying good-bye.

He opened the front door and closed it gently behind him. He walked down the long avenue bordered by bare lime trees. The night was still starlit, but there was a faint gleam of dawn to the east. His feet crunched in the snow and the cold nipped at his ears and nose, but the battered old coat kept him warm.

He heard a rattling engine in the distance. It grew closer and closer. Danny put down his bag and leaned against one of the lime trees. A cab drew up and the driver leaned out. He had deep-set eyes and big yellow teeth. "Get in," he growled. Danny climbed into the back. As the cab jolted forward, he leaned his head against the headrest. He was on his way back to Wilsons, the only place he now belonged.

Master Devoy stood at the window of his office in Wilsons Academy of the Devious Arts, looking out at the wind-tossed trees of the forest that fringed the huge rambling building. He was a tall thin man with a smooth unlined faced. Seated in the room behind him was Marcus Brunholm, a swarthy figure with a large mustache and darting brown eyes.

"You agreed, my dear Devoy," Brunholm said, "that the best course of action would be to bring Danny back to Wilsons immediately. His location in the Upper World is no longer safe."

"Yes, of course I agree," Devoy said. "So why send him back into danger?"

"Because we have no choice! Who else can we send?"

"If he is caught it will be seen as breaking the treaty. It will bring war. Our job is to guard the Upper World, not unleash mayhem on it."

"And what if the Ring of Five find the Treaty Stone first, Devoy? If they find it and break it, then there is no treaty. As you know, the treaty between the Upper and Lower Worlds is inscribed on the Stone and is dependent on it. There are other risks. I only hope the boy can be relied upon. He is a true spy. He has the smell of treachery on him."

"I won't allow it," Devoy said.

"You will allow it," Brunholm said, getting up and

approaching Devoy, looking into his face, so close that his luxuriant mustache almost brushed Devoy's skin. "You will allow it, because you have no choice."

"What about his parents?"

"Parents?" Brunholm shrugged. "You mean the paid agents hired to guard him? They know nothing of his relationship with Wilsons. I made sure of that. They are expendable. Let Conal and the Ring have them. The Ring can torture them until their eyeballs pop out of their skulls, they'll learn nothing."

THE UNKNOWN SPY'S WIFE

Danny had tried to stay awake as the snowy fields lightened, illuminated but not warmed by the rising sun. But the air in the cab was warm and fuggy, and before long he'd fallen asleep. He slept as they hurtled along, Fairman guiding the cab through the barren lands that lay between the Upper and Lower Worlds. Few people knew the routes, and Fairman was the only one permitted by treaty to use them. Once there had been comings and goings between the Two Worlds—the angels in old paintings were in fact messengers—but war had broken out, ending only with the negotiation of a harsh treaty that promised death to those who broke it. A key term was that there be no more movement between the worlds. The Upper World was too vulnerable to attack by the Lower and its deadly army of Cherbs, who, like Danny, had pointed faces and different-colored eyes.

Danny didn't wake until they were on the road leading to Wilsons, Fairman perhaps intending it to be that way. The route through the barren lands was his; he probably didn't want some little spy nosing it out and recording it for future use.

Danny stared as Fairman wound up the Wilsons driveway. The main building towered above the cab. There were turrets and buttresses and blind windows and complicated angles, all in a mixture of styles. Statues of nymphs stood in niches and gargoyles peered down from the roofline. There was snow on the ground here too, and great icicles hung from the eaves. Danny looked across the gardens to the Roosts, the dormitories built on iron legs that rose high into the trees. A thin thread of smoke rose from the girls' Roosts. He wondered how many of his friends were there—all of them, he hoped, since they were mostly orphans and had nowhere else to go.

Fairman stood on the brakes, so that Danny banged his head against the seat in front.

"Ouch!"

"We're here," Fairman said. "Get out."

"What do you do when someone pays?" Danny muttered, getting his gear together. "Do they ever get please and thank you?"

"Folks pay a high price to ride in this cab," Fairman said, baring his teeth in an unpleasant grin. "Please and thank you don't mean nothing to them."

Danny shivered. He didn't want to think what price

they paid. He got out of the cab and watched it speed off, then turned to look at the school, imagining himself to be alone. But in fact, several pairs of eyes were studying him. . . .

Brunholm watched with satisfaction from the Third Landing; his plans were unfolding nicely. Above his head, in a niche once reserved for the statue of the goddess Artemis, stood the siren, Vicky, mischief bubbling in her pretty eyes.

So the Fifth is back, she thought. I wonder who would pay for that information. And high above the siren's head, perched on a crumbling gable, the black eyes of a rook gazed steadily down.

Danny thought about going over to the Roosts and meeting his friends, but he wanted to know why Devoy had summoned him back early. For nothing good, he thought sourly, particularly if Brunholm was involved. He went into the entrance hall. Unusually, there was no one behind the desk. Danny was uneasy. The porter, Valant, was always there. Danny went to the desk and rang the bell, but there was no response. He was about to turn away when he heard a groan.

He went behind the counter. Valant lay on the floor, eyes fluttering, his hand to his head, where a large bump was starting to rise.

"What happened?"

"Hit from behind," Valant groaned. "Took me like I was an amateur. I just heard a movement behind me, then lights-out." He sat up, fingering his head. "I must be getting old."

"Why . . . I mean, what . . . ," Danny started to ask, but Valant's eyes had already gone to the great board above their heads.

"Keys," he said grimly. "He was after keys and he got them."

Danny looked up. There was every kind of key under the sun on the board, from little padlock keys to great ornate iron dungeon keys. It was said that only Valant knew what they were all for. The porter got to his feet and set off down one of the corridors.

"He knew what he wanted and he got it," he repeated over his shoulder.

"Which did he take?"

"The key to the Unknown Spy's room. His wife was staying with him. If she's abroad in Wilsons . . ."

Valant didn't have to finish the sentence. The Unknown Spy and his wife had been undercover for so long that their minds had given way under the pressure. They could not remember who they had been, or what lost mission they'd been on. Everyone they met was a potential enemy. You could reason with the Unknown Spy to some extent, but his wife shot first and asked questions later. Last time she'd been on the loose there had been several serious injuries.

Valant hurried down the corridor, with Danny following. The door to the Unknown Spy's room stood open. Danny made for it, but Valant stopped him. He took an old-fashioned flintlock pistol from his inside jacket pocket and cocked it, then, beckoning to Danny, crept slowly forward.

The room was in darkness, the way the Unknown Spy normally kept it, but Danny dug in the pocket of his trench coat . . . he was sure he'd found one in there before . . . and there it was, a battered metal torch. He flicked it on. The beam showed that the room had been ransacked: drawers emptied, furniture slashed open, its stuffing strewn across the floor. A body lay on the carpet in front of the empty fireplace.

"Here," Valant said, thrusting the gun into Danny's hand. "Keep your eyes peeled. Whoever did this can't be far away."

The porter went down on one knee beside the body. It was a woman. Her face was lined and her gray hair tumbled over her shoulders, but Danny could tell that she had once been beautiful. As if reading his thoughts, Valant sighed.

"Ah, that so much beauty should end like this. She's dead."

"Who is she?"

"No one knows her real name. She is the wife of the Unknown Spy. When they came here many years ago she was like a queen, regal and haughty and quite, quite mad. Look."

From her back protruded a knife with a strange metal handle forged in the shape of a raven.

"The ravens have a part to play in everything. In death as in life," Valant said, straightening. There was a flutter near the ceiling and a dark shape glided out the door. "Nothing happens here that they don't know about."

"Could they not tell us who did it?" Danny asked.

"Spell a name out in twigs or fly to the place where the person lives?"

Valant shook his head. "The ravens do things for their own reasons, not for ours," he said. "And a dead human means no more to them than a dead bird lying at the side of the road does to us. No. The urgent thing now is to find the Unknown Spy."

They found him five minutes later. He was sitting on a bench in the shrubbery, muttering to himself. He did not look up as they approached.

"She was dead when I found her, stiff and cold," he said. "She was dead when I found her."

"Did you see anyone?" Danny asked. The Spy glanced up, then leapt to his feet.

"You!" he exclaimed. "They told me . . . they said . . . what did they say . . . ?" His voice trailed off. Danny and Valant continued to question him, but he would not say anything else.

Valant shook his head and took the Unknown Spy gently by the arm. "I am very sorry for your loss. She was a rare woman." The Spy raised his head and a single tear ran down his cheek. "We had better wake Master Devoy and give him the news."

Half an hour later Valant, Danny and the Unknown Spy stood in the Spy's room with Devoy and Brunholm. Devoy was wearing a suit, but Brunholm had on an extremely loud floral dressing gown, which looked incongruous beside the cold dead body.

24

"Call McGuinness," Devoy said. "We have a murderer in our midst."

"I've already done it," Valant said.

"And I wasn't far away." They all turned to see the Wilsons detective in the doorway behind them. McGuinness was wearing a raincoat. His gray hair was cropped close, and he had the air of having seen everything bad that people could do to each other so that nothing surprised him. He took in the scene with an expert eye, then knelt to examine the body.

"Well?" Brunholm growled. Danny resisted the temptation to tell Brunholm that even McGuinness couldn't solve a crime in two minutes, but McGuinness merely fixed the vice principal with a thoughtful expression.

"There are two main possibilities: first, that someone wanted to murder her, and second, that she stumbled across someone ransacking the room."

"Looking for what?" Brunholm exclaimed.

"Yes indeed, looking for what," Devoy said, in a musing voice.

"For that, I'm afraid you'd have to ask the Unknown Spy," McGuinness said.

"Or find out who he really is," Danny heard himself say. The others turned to look at him.

"Well, if we find out who he is, maybe we can find out what the killer was after."

"Makes sense to me," McGuinness said.

"Yes, well," Brunholm said, "you can get on with working down the normal channels, full resources of the college available to you, no stone left unturned, et cetera, et cetera."

Danny eyed him. The slippery Brunholm didn't seem too enthusiastic about finding out the Unknown Spy's real identity.

Devoy turned to Danny as if seeing him for the first time.

"Ah yes, of course, young Caulfield. Well, at least you have arrived safely. I must speak to you later. It's breakfast time now, however, and I'm sure you're hungry. Most of the pupils have gone home for the holidays, but there are still a few here with whom you are acquainted. Skip along to Ravensdale and have something to eat. I'm sorry that your first hours back have been so distressing."

In spite of the shocking sight of the dead woman, Danny was in fact very hungry, and he was delighted to take himself off to the little village called Ravensdale, some of whose houses had been converted into canteens for the pupils. He made his way along a maze of corridors, remembering to look out for signs indicating the way, such as the ravens painted on the floor pointing south. When he reached the curtained entrance to Ravensdale, he took a deep breath before entering.

He found himself on an ancient street with old houses on either side. Above his head a raven cawed. Otherwise nothing moved. He glanced at the names on the house doors as he walked: THE JEDBURGHS. THE KAMIRILLA. If you walked to the top of the deserted street you would find a gallows. But Danny wasn't going that far. He saw a door with CONSIGLIO DEI DIECI on it and gratefully plunged in. The Consiglio was his assigned dining place.

The first thing to greet him was the smell of frying bacon. The second was squabbling voices.

"You'd eat it if it was a blood sausage," a thin raggedy-looking boy with wings was saying to a pale-faced girl whose prominent incisors made her look like a vampire.

"Leave Vandra alone, Les," said a blond girl with a slightly absent look on her face, while a dark-haired boy with sallow skin studied a piece of bacon suspiciously.

"Er, I'm back," Danny said. The reaction was instant. The blond girl ran over and threw her arms around his neck, covering him in crumbs and butter. Les, the winged boy, leapt up with a huge grin on his face, while Vandra, who was a physick, a healer with a vampiric appearance, bared her incisors in a smile that if you didn't know her would be truly terrifying. (Although if anyone had been looking, they would have seen a hint of color creep into her cheeks at the sight of Danny.) Even Toxique, the trainee assassin, thrust the piece of bacon he had been studying into his mouth so that he could shake hands with Danny.

Dixie, the blond girl, disappeared and reappeared at the other side of the table beside the physick, who glared at her crossly.

"Do cut that out, Dixie."

"I can't help it; I'm excited. We didn't know if you were going to come back," Dixie explained to Danny.

"I wasn't sure myself," Danny said. "Devoy sent for me to come back early, I still don't know why."

"I see blood," Toxique said suddenly, "blood and death."

27

Toxique had the Gift of Anticipation and could often tell what was just about to happen.

"Give it a break, Toxique," Les said.

"Honestly," Vandra said, "I thought you'd gotten over all that blood and death stuff." Toxique looked abashed, but Danny grasped his arm.

"You're right," he said quietly, "there *is* blood and death in the air." He told them about the Unknown Spy's wife.

"Blimey," Dixie said, "things have a habit of happening around you, did you ever notice that?"

"Least it makes life interesting," Les said. "It's been pretty boring around here since the holidays started and everyone went home."

"Boring, boring, boring." Dixie rolled her eyes.

"Christmas was nice," Vandra said. "Devoy got us all presents, as usual, and we had a nice meal."

"Except the meal was in Brunholm's rooms," Les said. "Toxique was convinced the man was going to poison the lot of us. We had to listen to Brunholm sing 'Good King Wenceslas.' Not for the fainthearted."

"The lady was murdered," Toxique said quietly. "We need to find out who did it, and why. Could be one of us next."

"He's right," Vandra said. "If Devoy brought you here early, then something's up, and the murder could be connected. We must put our heads together and think about it."

"Perhaps not solve the murder," Danny said. "Mc-Guinness is working on that. But if we could find out

28

about the Unknown Spy and his wife, who they really were . . ."

"Good idea," Dixie said brightly. "How?"

"We need to get a look around the Unknown Spy's room," Les said. "Stands to reason there's got to be answers there."

"Danny isn't doing that today," Vandra said. "Look at him—he's out on his feet."

"Here," Les said, sliding a dish of bacon, sausage and fried egg toward him. "That'll set you up."

"Whoops," Dixie said, "how was your Christmas? Never thought to ask."

Danny stuck a fork into a sausage and took a great bite, as much to avoid answering Dixie as from hunger. He was aware of Les watching him with concern. When finally he'd finished eating and they were all walking together down the Ravensdale street, he found Les beside him.

"Are you okay?" Les asked. "Did something happen at home?"

"No, nothing," Danny said; then, seeing Les's skeptically arched eyebrows, he admitted, "Nothing much, anyhow. I don't want to talk now. I'll tell you when I've had a chance to think about it."

"Fair enough," Les said. "In the meantime, we'll get you back to the Roosts and let you have a bit of a nap. Things could get a little busy around here. If Devoy sends for you I'll hold him off."

They emerged from Ravensdale into the main building and took a side exit into the gardens. The snow lay thick and undisturbed on the lawns and shrubberies. The air was cold and stung Danny's lungs when he breathed, but it felt fresh on his tired eyes. A robin alighted on a snowy twig near them and followed their progress across the gardens. When Danny saw the treetop dormitories in front of him, he had a sense of belonging, a sense that increased when they climbed up the stairs and the warm, fuggy odor of the place hit his nostrils (as did, it has to be said, a faint aroma of boys' socks). The iron stove in the center of the room glowed dull red. Danny sank down in his bed gratefully.

"See you later," Les said with a grin. Danny took his shoes off and pulled the blankets up around him. He knew he should undress, but the bed was soft and the room was warm. An image of the woman who had pretended to be his mother drifted into his head, but he pushed it away bitterly. She had no claim on him now. This was his home, and his friends were his family. Within minutes he was fast asleep, the room around him quiet and peaceful.

Far away, in the house Danny had left, it was also quiet, but it could not be said to be peaceful. All morning the woman Danny had known as his mother had felt a sense of dread that she could not account for. There was no sign of the car that had chased her and her partner the night before. The countryside was dead silent, the cold lying on it like a weight. The ravens had left that morning, as they always did, to scavenge what food they could find.

Agent Stone was sleeping peacefully. The woman had

given him antibiotics and some morphine for the pain. She sat down at the fire, her eyes grainy with fatigue, her heart heavy. She could not remember a time when she hadn't been on duty, all to do with Danny. She was Agent Pearl now, but once upon a time she'd had a real name— she had been Alison, a young woman with a life and ambition. The ambition had led her to this job, a vital job, she had been told. But for many years now she and Agent Stone had had little contact with their mystery employers, apart from checks in their bank accounts every month and emails every so often with terse instructions.

Danny, she thought tiredly, remembering the look of utter betrayal on his face that morning. At the start Danny had been only a job, and he had been an easy child to look after. But he had become more than a job. Tucking him in at night, cooking for him, worrying about him when he was out of her sight . . . sometimes Agent Pearl started to think of Danny and Agent Stone as her real family. She felt a pang of guilt. If that was the case, then she hadn't been a very good or attentive mother.

She sighed. Months earlier she'd been told in an anonymous email that Danny was to be going away to school and she was not to ask any questions. But she couldn't help wondering where he'd gone. He had seemed changed when he came home for the holidays, more confident, and yet unsure, like someone who had been handed a great responsibility but didn't know what to do about it. What were they doing to him? Where was he now?

A fiercely protective feeling swept over her. Danny

thought he had left home secretly, but Pearl had watched from her bedroom window as he walked away from the house toward Fairman's waiting taxi. Her heart had ached to see him go, and she had longed to call him back, yet she knew that wherever he went, he would be safer than he would be at home.

A sudden fall of soot down the chimney made her jump. She frowned and went to the window. The countryside was empty, the snow untracked, yet the ominous feeling had grown.

She went to the kitchen and took a revolver from her handbag, checking to see that it was loaded. She went to Agent Stone's room. He was sitting up in bed looking haggard, a gun in his hand.

"You feel it too," she whispered. He nodded. Stone was the brains of the partnership, the one who had worked so hard trying to draw together the complex pieces of Danny's history. He had found himself in many dark and dangerous places over the years.

"Check outside," he whispered.

Carefully Pearl went down the corridor, unlocked the back door and stepped out, gun in hand. The crunch of her feet on the snow was too loud, her grip on the revolver too fierce. The hairs on the back of her neck were too tight. Yet nothing stirred; there was no sign of danger. Forcing herself onward, she made a full circuit of the house, peering into the garage and the toolshed. When there was nothing more to search, she let herself back into the house and went to Agent Stone's bedroom.

"Nothing," she said. "I can't see anything."

But she hadn't looked up when she was outside. It was probably just as well that she hadn't, that she had not been caught in the open, for she would have been cut to shreds. They were waiting for her. If she had glanced over her shoulder, there would have been no time to scream. Lining the eaves of the house, like a flock of loathsome vultures, wings folded behind their backs, were Conal's Seraphim, their eyes cold and their bright metal blades by their sides.

Agent Pearl locked the front and back doors and closed and bolted the wooden shutters upstairs and down. She stood in the hallway, looking around for other possible entry points. Her eyes were drawn to the huge window at the stair return, a beautiful stained-glass version of the *Eve of Saint Agnes,* the cold light setting its colors afire. As she looked, the colors appeared to darken, dim and suddenly go out. With a huge crash the window splintered into a thousand pieces, and there in place of a window stood a man—was it a man?—tall, very tall, with lank gray hair and burning yellow eyes. Pearl felt her insides turn to water as she saw two huge wings spread wide on his back.

She backed away and the Seraphim Conal threw his head back and emitted a terrible shriek of triumph. He launched himself and glided forward, more of the creatures taking his place in the window.

Before Pearl had a chance to raise the gun, Conal had her pinned against the wall. She could feel his weight against her chest. His eyes were burning and his breath was cold and foul.

"Where is he?" Conal said. "Where is the boy?"

She heard a shot, and over Conal's shoulder saw one of the Seraphim falter in the air, then plunge to the ground. Conal spun around. Stone stood in the bedroom doorway, pale and bloodstained, the gun in his hand. Pearl ducked under Conal's wing and ran to her partner. The air of the hallway was full of wings, great swooping blades that would stun her if she collided with them. She reached Stone. Together they backed into the doorway. Despite his wound, Stone's eyes were bright with excitement.

"What are they?" Pearl gasped.

"Seraphim!" he said. "The old books talk about them, but I never thought they really existed. This changes everything."

The Seraphim had landed and were standing in a crescent facing the agents. Pearl recoiled from the threatening figures.

"Where is the boy?" Conal growled again. "Where is the Fifth?"

"He's not here," Stone said. "You won't find him."

Conal gave a signal. Half of the Seraphim took to the air and sped up the staircase. Others made for the ground-floor rooms. There was great crashing and rending as doors were burst open and rooms searched.

"He isn't here," Pearl insisted, "and we won't give him up to you."

"You think not?" Conal sneered and took a step closer. Pearl raised her revolver, but as she did so the shutters in the bedroom behind them splintered into a hundred pieces and a tall female Seraphim entered and flung a spear. It struck Stone a glancing blow on the forehead. He cried out and fell to the ground.

"How many bullets do you have in that gun?" Conal taunted. "Six? Do you think you can kill all of us? Throw down the weapon and give yourself another few hours of miserable life. Others have survived the Ordeal of Memory; you might too!"

The female Seraphim had a ghastly grin on her face. Another spear thudded into the wood of the door. Pearl whirled round and in a second the female was on her, her wings flapping about Pearl's face, hands like talons gripping her arms and a rancid smell overwhelming her. She felt consciousness start to swim away, but as it faded she heard a cry.

"The ravens! The ravens are coming!" As she sank into oblivion, she wondered why the Seraphim should be so afraid of the ravens.

THE BUTTS

Danny woke at lunchtime, feeling ravenous. He went out onto the balcony of the Roosts and looked down to where his friends were using a battered old sled on the slope behind the shrubbery. A door to the side of the building opened and a group of what at first looked like pensioners came out, dressed in woolly hats and ancient-looking tracksuits. They peered around anxiously as if afraid of being watched; then a small female figure emerged from the door.

"All right, ladies and gents," she cried out in a shrill voice, "you know what to do. Remember, it's Wing Hygiene Week!"

Grumbling, the group unfolded rather dusty wings and began flicking snow into the feathers and rubbing them together. Danny grinned. The Wilsons Messengers were elderly and very self-conscious about their wings.

"They would die of embarrassment if they knew they were being watched," a quiet voice said. Danny turned. The head of Wilsons had been standing quietly against the wall of the Roosts.

"Master Devoy." Danny was taken aback.

"I thought I'd let you sleep," Devoy said, "but now there is an urgent matter we must discuss. First of all, was anything different during your stay in the Upper World, any untoward happenings?"

Untoward? Danny felt a stab of pain as he remembered his mother's face, but he put the thought away.

Danny told Devoy quickly about how his father and mother had been pursued home under fire and how his father had been wounded. He didn't tell the headmaster that he had learned that his parents were agents. People don't have to know everything about me, he thought.

Devoy nodded.

"The fabric of things is starting to come apart. I hope your parents are safe." Danny looked at him, startled. It hadn't occurred to him that they would still be under threat.

"I'll see you at five in my study. Some things should not be talked about in public."

Danny watched Devoy descend from the Roosts and cross the snowy lawn. A sudden gust of wind blew across the surface snow, and Devoy disappeared within the minisnowstorm as if he had never been there.

* * *

The four cadets played in the snow all afternoon, using the sled, building a snow effigy of Brunholm and throwing snowballs at Vicky the siren when she appeared at the lawn. The siren climbed out of reach and bestowed a small cold smile on them. Danny wondered if it was altogether wise to provoke her. Vicky was very beautiful but also very malicious, and she had a long memory.

But they didn't care. There was a sense among them that soon there would be little time for being silly and playing games, and they were determined to make the most of it. There was a great freedom in having the school to themselves with no teachers or other pupils about, and this too would not last. It took Vandra to point out to Danny that it was almost five o'clock. He threw a few last defiant snowballs, but in the end he put his head down and trudged off as the others headed to Ravensdale for muffins and hot tea.

Brunholm was waiting in the hallway to take him to Devoy's office. He took off at pace with Danny running to keep up. They went through the silent Gallery of Whispers and through a maze of corridors, up past the library of the third landing and on to the treacherous stairs to Devoy's office, where Danny kept an eye out for piano wire—Devoy was fond of stringing it at neck height to catch unprepared visitors.

Master Devoy's office was decorated with spy paraphernalia from through the ages, such as miniature cameras and poison-tipped umbrellas. Devoy looked completely at home in it, a spymaster of the old school.

Danny sensed the tension in the room the moment he entered. Although Devoy had trained himself to appear absolutely emotionless no matter what the circumstances, the manner in which he turned from the table was a little too swift, his greeting a little too warm. He regarded Danny for a moment, then shook his head.

"You learn too quickly, young man. You have sensed my anxiety. And yes, I am anxious, and for good reason. More than anxious. I believe the Ring are moving with speed and aggression. Everything we have worked for is in jeopardy."

Devoy lifted a deadly stiletto from the mantel and tested the point with his finger.

"They intend to break the treaty and take over the Upper World," Brunholm said, smashing a fist into his palm a little too vehemently, Danny thought. Was he acting?

Devoy whirled around, the stiletto pointed at Danny.

"The Treaty Stone itself is discovered! The whole foundation of the Two Worlds is at risk."

Brunholm had found his way to Danny's side, so close that Danny could feel hot breath on the side of his face.

"There is a kingdom called Morne," the vice principal said, his voice low and hard, "a part of the Lower World that exists in the Upper. The Stone is kept there for safety. But no longer. The Ring have discovered it."

"We must have it, Danny," Devoy said. Danny stared

39

at him, his eyes fixed on the stiletto in the headmaster's hand. "We must!"

"Why—why me?" Danny stammered. "I mean, you have experienced spies."

"Yes," Brunholm said, "but none who have lived in both the Upper World and the Lower. One must travel through the Upper World to reach Morne. Your experience there is vital. Believe me, boy, if there was anyone else I could send—an adult—you would be drinking cocoa at home."

"The under-sixteens were exempted from the treaty, in anticipation of happier times when students could cross over," Devoy said. "The kingdom is placed in the Upper World to protect it, to keep the enemy out. Once you are there, it will require all your skills as a spy to get to the Treaty Stone before the enemy."

"I don't understand why the Ring wants the Stone. Either there is a treaty or there isn't," Danny said. "What's to stop them from attacking the Upper World?"

"The treaty written on the Stone is binding under pain of death enforced by the Dead. You remember your oath in front of the Dead, Danny?"

Danny shivered. He remembered taking his oath as a spy, the voices whispering around him. He had no doubt that the owners of those voices would hold him to his word.

"The only way to break the treaty is to smash the Stone. That's what the Ring want to do, and we must stop them," Brunholm said. "If the Stone is broken, all rules are gone."

Then Devoy spoke. His voice changed into something remote, majestic, in a way, like the light from distant stars that have been cold and dead for many years.

" 'Here is the treaty writ in stone. Here is the bargain sealed in blood. Death to the faithless. Death to the oath breaker.' "

"That is written on the Stone," Brunholm said. Danny shivered. Who did they think he was, to send him to steal such a thing?

"You will not go alone," Devoy said.

"You will have companions," Brunholm said, "all your little pals except that tyke Knutt." Seeing Danny's mouth open in protest, Devoy interjected.

"It's the wings, Danny. How can he go openly in the Upper World with wings?"

"We don't have time to argue over trivialities," Brunholm said gruffly. "Too much is at stake."

"And yet we cannot rush into things without careful preparation, as much as time permits," Devoy said. "Go back to your friends. Say nothing!"

Devoy looked resolute, ready to face danger, but as Danny turned to leave, he noticed a bead of blood on the man's finger where the stiletto had pricked it.

Danny went down the stairs deep in thought, avoiding the gaps by instinct. The mission itself was enough to take in, but knowing that he would have to leave Les behind worried him even further. When he got to the school hallway his friends were waiting.

"Well," Dixie said eagerly, "are we going on another mission?"

"I think so . . . ," Danny said.

"Leave him alone," Vandra scolded. "He's probably been told not to say anything."

"I bet it's a tough one," Les said. "Here. I thought you might be hungry." He pressed a large hunk of chocolate cake into Danny's hand. "I don't mind what the mission is," he went on, "as long as we do it together—isn't that right, Danny?"

"As long as we're together," Danny said, the words out of his mouth before he realized he'd said them. He felt a dark little thrill at telling the lie, and groaned inwardly. No matter how hard he fought it, betrayal was in his blood.

"One thing at a time," he said, changing his tone, making his voice brisk and businesslike. "Vandra's right. I can't discuss the mission. But we have our own mission tonight—to learn the identity of the Unknown Spy."

In daylight, solving the murder of the Unknown Spy's wife by finding out the couple's true identities had felt like a straightforward matter. Now that the cadets were safely tucked up in the Roosts with a cold wind stirring the trees and the promise of further snow in the air, it didn't seem such a good idea. Nevertheless, the boys met the girls on the balcony as arranged.

"Maybe we should leave the crime-busting to our ace detective, Mr. McGuinness," Dixie said, suppressing a yawn.

42

"No," Danny said, "it's too important."

"He's right," Vandra said. "We can't just let a murderer prowl Wilsons. Any one of us could be next."

By common consent, Toxique had not been included on the mission. He was hypersensitive to death, which was often useful, but he couldn't help calling out at every hint of danger—moaning on about death and blood, as Dixie put it—which made them all nervous.

"Who's on point of entry?" Danny asked, the term coming to him from a lesson forgotten until now.

"I am," Les said. "There's a cellar door under the corridor to the Unknown Spy's room. I've already picked the lock. We're ready to go."

They set off down the stairs of the Roosts, moving silently in single file. Danny looked round his small team with approval. They were all dressed in dark clothes, high collars or hats pulled down over their eyes so that they could not be easily seen or identified. They carried a variety of equipment—there were flashlights and lockpicks hanging from belts. During the previous term they would never have been so well prepared. Danny hadn't realized they had absorbed so much of what they had been told in class.

They kept close to walls or other shelter, moving warily and stopping to check their surroundings. When they got to the cellar door, Les quickly whipped off the padlock, the others forming a watchful semicircle around him. When he had finished, they all moved swiftly to enter, as if a part of the night had detached itself and flowed darkly through the small door.

Inside the cellar Danny lit a small flashlight and hooded it with his hand. Les indicated the direction they should go with a nod, and the others followed.

The cellar opened onto a dank little corridor dripping with water, little ferns growing from the walls.

"You sure you've been here before?" Vandra whispered.

"Yes," Les said, "but you know what this place is like."

It was always hard to find your way reliably in Wilsons. The corridors and staircases had a way of seeming to change direction, of not leading to the same place from one day to the next. You had to look out for clues as to what direction you were going in—but in this damp passage there were none. They walked on for five minutes, an uneasy feeling growing that they weren't getting any nearer to the room of the Unknown Spy.

"It was dead easy today," Les said. "I saw the cellar door under the Spy's window, I popped the lock, and a manhole just inside led to the corridor outside his room."

Danny shrugged. "It doesn't matter, Les. We'll follow this for a while and see where we end up. Sometimes I think the building itself is like an old spy, full of secrets and tricks and dead ends. Maybe we're being led toward something else."

"Yuck," Dixie said, trying to brush a spiderweb from her hair, "maybe it's leading us toward the biggest spider's nest in the world. Feels like it, anyway."

On they trudged, the tunnel walls getting older and older. Here and there were carvings, figures in relief or

44

etched into the stone. Though it was impossible to make out the faces depicted, to Danny there appeared to be a cruel turn to some of the features, making him secretly glad that they weren't visible.

The cadets were just about to turn back when it happened. A sudden burst of air struck them, growing from a cold gust to a howling arctic gale. Danny felt ice sting his flesh like needles and frost form on his lips. Vandra cried out in pain and Les cursed in the distance. The cold was so intense that Danny's flashlight dimmed and went out, then fell from his hand. In the howling of the wind they heard whisperings, dread voices speaking words that they did not understand but that were full of fear and loathing.

Danny was aware of shapes around him, haggard white faces with empty sockets where eyes should have been. At first they appeared without bodies, but then the bodies formed, frost bodies, hideously mutilated, with gaping spaces where hearts should have been, bellies rent open. They surrounded him, and he could feel hands clutching at his old raincoat, plucking at the fabric. With sudden terrifying force the hands were inside his coat. He gasped as sheer naked fear gripped him. The hands were strong and sinewy and freezing, and they would grab his heart from his chest and leave him lifeless and mutilated while they gorged on his warmth and life. He fell back onto the ground, consciousness fading. In the distance a light flared and he heard a voice cry out,

" 'Ware old ghouls, 'ware!" Then blackness came over him and he knew no more.

*   *   *

Danny woke up in a warm room, lying on a neatly made bed. There was a smell of hot chocolate, and when he raised his head he saw his companions sitting round a fire with blankets over their shoulders, sipping from steaming mugs.

The room was plain and tidy, everything in its place: shirts folded perfectly on a shelf, a single polished silver trophy on the mantel, some military decorations in a frame on the wall. He looked up to see Valant watching him, concern on his face.

"If you're wondering where you are, you're in my quarters," Valant said. "You're damn lucky to be alive, wandering down in the Butts on your own."

"Sorry," Les said with a weak grin. "That was my idea, actually. Thought it was a bit of a shortcut."

"Thought you would avoid my beady eye in the hall-way, more like," Valant said. "However, no harm was done."

"Who—or what—were they?" Vandra asked.

"They were ancient spies and traitors. The Dead of Wilsons. The Unquiet, they are called. You met them when you took your oath."

"They were horrible," Dixie said, "full of holes and all."

"I suppose some of them were horrible," Valant said. "The fact is that in medieval times spies were hanged, then drawn and quartered. They had their entrails and sometimes their hearts cut out and held up in front of them."

"You'd be a bit shook up after that," Dixie said.

"They wandered the earth, haunted by their own cries of agony, unable to rest," Valant said.

"But . . . they found their way to Wilsons," Danny said slowly, "the only place in the Two Worlds where their treachery does not render them outcast, where they can have peace from their own screams."

"Very impressive," Dixie said.

"I could hear it," Danny said, "in their voices."

"They gathered around Danny," Vandra said. "We thought they were going to kill him."

"Really," Valant said. "I thought you had just stumbled across them by accident—they are inclined to roam the Butts a bit. They seem to like it there. Has that dungeon feel, I suppose."

"What are the Butts?" Danny asked.

"The secret passages that connect all the different parts of Wilsons—*if* you know what you're doing, which obviously you four do not. I wonder why the Unquiet took a fancy to Danny here."

"I don't know," Danny said. "All I remember is that they were cold, very cold."

Danny remembered the chill, sinewy hand that had reached under his jacket. He reached into his jacket to feel the place where it had touched him, and to his shock, his fingers closed around a small parcel wrapped in what felt like oilcloth.

"Is everything all right, Mr. Caulfield?" Valant was looking at him curiously.

"Yes, yes, fine," Danny said hastily. "I just thought for a moment they'd taken off with my heart."

As his friends laughed, Danny hastily tucked the package into a more secure place. Was it underhanded not to tell his friends that the ghost spy had put something into his coat, or was he merely being cautious? He told himself that he was being cautious, but a part of him felt sneaky. It was one of the things he hated about the spy side of himself, the way he always had to mistrust his own motives.

"Are you going to tell Devoy about this?" Les asked Valant nervously. "It'll be a Third Regulation offense at least."

"What were you doing in the Butts?" Valant demanded. "Tell the truth!"

"We thought we could help find the killer of the Unknown Spy's wife," Vandra said. Valant looked at her sternly.

"If I smelled a lie you would be in Master Devoy's study before your feet could touch the ground," he said after a pause, "but I believe you, and I think that Master Devoy has enough to worry about without adding a bunch of amateur detectives to the list. Now, if you're feeling a little less chilly, I suggest we get you back to the Roosts before you are missed."

"Er, how do we do that?" Les asked.

"Here," Valant said. "I think I can entrust this to . . ." His eye swept over the four, barely pausing at Dixie and

Les, dwelling for a while on Danny, then landing on Vandra with a thoughtful look. ". . . our physick here, who has a trustworthy if rather melancholy look."

He handed her what looked like a glass ball.

"What is it?"

"A precious thing," Valant said, "so I'll expect you to take care of it. If you want to find your way back through the Butts, then tell it so."

Vandra gave him a dubious look and turned to the glass. "The Butts," she said shortly, as if it was a trick. But the glass started to cloud over immediately. It turned a murky brown, then a drippy gray, and a network of paths appeared on it.

"Where are we?" Dixie said, poking her head over Vandra's shoulder. Straightaway five tiny figures appeared in the top left-hand side of the globe, enclosed by the walls of a room. The lines on the map showing the Butts shimmered and moved as Danny and his friends watched, sometimes merging with each other, sometimes turning back on themselves.

"No wonder we got lost," Les said. Dixie said nothing. There was something eerily beautiful about the map and the tiny silvery paths. She stared at it, the light reflecting in her blue eyes until they shone like sapphires.

"Just follow your progress on it while you're down there," Valant said, "and you'll find your way out."

"What is it?" Dixie breathed.

"A Globe of Instant Positioning in Ephemeral Places," Valant said.

49

"A Globe of Instant . . . *G-I* . . . a GIPEP!" Dixie said brightly.

"If you must," Valant said, a little wearily, "but if you have to shorten it, I'd be more inclined just to refer to it as a Globe. Now. Off you go."

"It's a very precious thing," Danny said. "How come you're giving it to us?"

His question sounded more suspicious than he had intended, and Valant looked at him a little oddly but answered reasonably enough.

"Because you may need it in the future. Now go!"

"Aren't you coming with us?" Vandra said.

"You were resourceful enough to get into the Butts in the first place; I believe you can manage without my assistance. The Unquiet will not trouble you when you have the Globe. I am surprised that they approached you at all. Normally they are very shy. Perhaps they sensed your uncertainty."

Danny fingered the package in his jacket and wondered if that was in fact the reason.

Despite a few false turns, they found their way back. Vandra guided them through the dripping tunnels of the Butts, which, though they still appeared to be made of solid stone, twisted and writhed in the Globe in a most disconcerting manner. In twenty minutes they were out in the gardens, the wind whipping the snow into their faces. Walking single file and holding on to each other, they made it back to the Roosts.

They split up on the balcony, the boys going into their room and the girls into theirs. Bone weary, Danny and Les lay in front of the stove and told Toxique what had happened. Toxique's nostrils flared at the mention of the Unquiet and Les groaned.

"Please don't start going on about blood and death and all," he said.

Toxique gave him a dark look.

"You must be roasted sitting there with your coat on," Les said to Danny.

"I'm fine. The Unquiet touch left me really cold," Danny said, but in fact he was afraid the oilcloth parcel might fall out if he removed his trench coat. Another lie— he could feel himself at the center of a web of untruth.

Later, when the others were asleep, he took out the parcel and unwrapped it. It was a piece of canvas folded in half, then folded twice more. The material was old and appeared to be bloodstained. In the middle was a ring. It was made of gold, and etched on its surface was an intertwined "S" and "G."

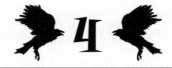

THE BEETLE OF TRANSMISSION

Devoy and Brunholm left the cadets alone for the next two days, and they spent their time in the Roosts, by common consent ignoring the main building. For some reason the danger they had faced from the Unquiet looked even more terrifying now that it was over. Although they spent a lot of time together, in many ways they were separate. Danny struggled with the fact that Les would have to be told he was not going on the mission. And behind everything was the thought of the parents Danny did not have.

On the third morning they were awakened by a familiar voice.

"That's right, campers," the voice said, "term starts again tomorrow, so let's see a little enthusiasm! Breakfast in ten minutes, and a First Regulation offense for stragglers—let's go!"

"Put a sock in it," Danny muttered.

"I heard that, Cadet Caulfield, but your ungracious remark cannot dim my renewed passion for life at Wilsons Academy of the Devious Arts."

All that day the other pupils drifted back, full of stories about the holidays—trips taken, parties thrown. But there were also tales of worried adults gathered together in groups, talking intently, and some pupils said that their parents had employed security guards.

It was in this atmosphere that the summonses arrived. First Danny was called to Devoy's office. He returned silent and downcast, and when Dixie asked him what had happened he snapped at her.

"No need to bite my head off," she said, but then her summons came. She also was silent and unapproachable when she came back. Next it was Vandra's turn. Les greeted her when she came in, but she walked straight past him, her face set.

"What's up with you lot?" he said. "You'd think somebody had died or something."

But no matter how much he asked, none of them would tell him what had taken place. He went off on his own, muttering. Danny watched him go. There was an old summerhouse in the woods where Les went when he needed to think, and Danny reckoned that was where he was going.

Les didn't come back until teatime and sat at the far end of the table in their house in Ravensdale, trying to look unconcerned.

After tea, Danny walked back to the Roosts on his own, his thoughts troubled. He wished Devoy would move ahead with the mission. He needed action. As he approached the stairway to the Roosts, a figure detached itself from the shadows. Danny's hand went to the pocket of his trench coat, but there was no need. It was the detective McGuinness.

"Glad to see you're wearing the coat," McGuinness said approvingly. The coat had once belonged to the master spy Steff Pilkington, and although shabby, it had many strange and wonderful qualities. It wasn't exactly fashionable, and Danny wouldn't have been caught dead in it in the Upper World, but slipping it on every morning had become one of the few reassuring routines he had in the unreliable world of Wilsons.

"Did you find out anything about the Unknown Spy's wife?" Danny asked.

"My investigations are making some progress," McGuinness said, "despite the presence of some freelance investigators muddying the waters." Danny felt his face turn red.

"However," McGuinness continued, "there is something you might be interested in. Come with me."

The detective led the way back into Wilsons and down the corridor to the Unknown Spy's room.

"He has taken temporary lodgings with Master Devoy," McGuinness said. "The killer left no clues, but as to your idea about finding out the Spy's identity . . . look."

He handed Danny a calendar. There was nothing

unusual about it that Danny could see until he noticed that the fifth day of the month was circled. He flipped through the calendar. The fifth of *every* month was circled.

"And there are many calendars, decades of them," McGuinness said. "Look at this." He held up a copy of *Spy News (Incorporating Covert Times)*. Every time the number five was printed on the page, it had been circled or underlined or had a question mark beside it.

"Everything's the same," McGuinness said, holding up a shirt on which the size—5—was circled.

"My guess is that he's trying to remember something, and that something has to do with the Fifth."

The detective's wife, Cheryl Orr, was a spy and had helped Danny escape the Ring. Danny realized that McGuinness knew everything about his being the fifth member of the Ring of Five.

"Me?" Danny said.

"Yes. He has no memory of his life before Wilsons, but something appears to be gnawing at him. Every time he sees the number five a thought is stirred, but he can't quite grasp it. It's not much to go on, but until we find what the killer was looking for . . ."

Danny walked back across the lawn to the Roosts. Before he got to the bottom of the ladders he saw Dixie and Vandra. They were obviously waiting for him.

"What is it?" he said. They drew him aside into the shrubbery.

"What did Devoy tell you today?"

"I'll tell you what he told us," Vandra said furiously. "We're to pretend that we've fallen out with Les, that we're not friends with him anymore."

"It's for his own good, and for yours, he says," Dixie added bitterly. "I said we're friends and Brunholm puts this sneery face on and says it's about time we learned that spies don't have friends. That it will be a valuable lesson for us."

"We're going on a mission and leaving Les behind," Vandra said miserably.

"I know," Danny said, having had the same brusque lecture from Brunholm and Devoy. One part of him was relieved that the secret was in the open. Another part was irritated that he was no longer the only one who knew.

"Well, what are we going to do about it?" Dixie asked.

"I don't know," Danny said. "There's something wrong about the way they're going about it. They're saying that it's best that Les not get too attached to us, because we're going away."

"But when did Brunholm start caring about hurt feelings?" Vandra said.

"Exactly," Danny said. "So what is he up to?"

"I don't care what he's up to," Dixie said crossly, "I'm not going around pretending that Les isn't my friend. I'm going to tell him everything."

And without waiting for the others, she started up the staircase to the Roosts. Vandra and Danny looked at each other, then ran after her. Dixie disappeared, reappearing at the top of the stairs.

"It's really irritating when she does that," Vandra said, breaking into a run. Dixie waited for them, then burst through the door. Les was standing on the other side and Dixie took a step back in surprise.

Les looked at each of them in turn, then burst out laughing.

"What's so funny?" Dixie demanded.

"Your faces," Les said. "I was going to let you say your bit, but I couldn't keep my face straight, the way you burst in."

"We were just going to say—" Vandra began.

"I know what you were going to say," Les interrupted. "I've been listening to you for the last ten minutes."

"How?" Danny said.

"Reach into the left-hand pocket of your skirt," Les told Vandra. She did so with a suspicious look on her face, then withdrew her hand, looked at it, shrieked loudly and jumped back. From her hand fell a small black object that started to move slowly away from them.

"Don't step on it!" Les cried, moving forward rapidly and scooping it up.

"Ugh!" Vandra said. "What *is* it?"

"It's a Beetle of Transmission."

"What on earth is that?"

"You need two of them. The hearer has one and the listener has the other. Look. The hairs on their bellies vibrate in time to our voices. When one beetle vibrates the other picks it up, and it comes out as sound."

Half fascinated and half repelled, Danny, Dixie and Vandra stared at the beetle, which Les held upturned in

57

his hand. As Les spoke, the dense hairs on the device's underside rippled in time to his voice.

"You put the other one to your ear and you can hear what's being said near the other one, as long as it's not too far away, of course. Here."

He took another fist-sized black beetle out of his own pocket and handed it to Danny. Danny took it gingerly, feeling the hard shell cold against his hand, the legs moving against his palm. He turned it over and saw the little hairs on its belly rippling.

"Put it to your ear," Les said, holding the other beetle to his mouth. Trying to quell his feeling of revulsion, Danny put the beetle to his ear, shuddering as the hairs touched his ear. Les whispered into the beetle's belly, and Danny jumped as he heard his friend's voice clear as day.

"I know what you're up to. . . ."

Danny's surprise was quickly followed by annoyance. What did Les mean? He couldn't know all Danny's secrets. . . .

But when he lowered the beetle from his ear and saw his friend's cheerful open grin, he felt ashamed.

"I could hear what you were talking about down below. You're going on a mission and they don't want me to go with you."

"You don't sound upset," Vandra said, puzzled.

"You don't have wings, otherwise you'd know," Les explained. "There's always stuff you can't do. The whole point of being a spy is that you don't stand out, right? This must be a mission in the Upper World, so it's only logical that you can't have a boy with wings."

"We reckon there's more to it than that," Vandra said. "Brunholm is up to something."

"He's always up to something," Les said with a shrug.

"The Upper World," Dixie said. "Super, absolutely super!"

"Can't have that many physicks up there either," Vandra said, touching one of her incisors self-consciously.

"It's all right, Vandra," Danny said. "You'll look perfectly normal, or almost—I mean, there's lots of variety in girls. . . ."

"When you're in a hole, stop digging," Dixie said. Danny saw tears in Vandra's eyes.

"But none of them are as beautiful as the Wilsons girls," Danny said.

"Yeuch!" Dixie said. She pulled a face, but Vandra beamed at him.

"We'll make a deal," Danny said. "When Brunholm's around we'll ignore Les. It'll keep Brunholm onside, and maybe we'll be able to find out what he's up to."

Behind them the door opened and Toxique came in. There was no point involving Toxique. His doom-laden pronouncements were completely out of his control, and he was likely to talk out of turn at any moment.

"Girls shouldn't be in here," Toxique said shortly, and went over to sit heavily on his bed.

"Girls don't want to be in here," Dixie said, turning with a flounce. "Smells of boy!"

She walked out, followed by Vandra. Danny sat down beside Toxique.

"What's wrong?" he asked gently. Toxique was the

only pupil who had stayed at school over the holiday even though both of his parents were alive. His father thought it would harden him up. Toxique's family were professional assassins going back many generations, and the heavy burden of following in their footsteps had fallen on Toxique's shoulders. His father believed that he lacked the necessary ruthlessness and didn't hesitate to tell him so in frequent letters.

"Another letter," Toxique said glumly. He pulled it from his pocket and read.

" 'For generations this family have been the assassins of choice when the termination of a king or prime minister has been called for, though we were not too proud to end a peasant's existence if required. Our service has always been discreet and efficient. Our profession is as essential to the smooth functioning of society as that of a lawyer or an architect. . . .' "

"I get the idea," Danny said, "but it's just the normal stuff, surely?"

"Well, that is, but listen to this: 'No one in our family has ever reached the third term of his or her first year at Wilsons without carrying out at least one termination. This happy tradition is in danger of being broken, and I am sure that even you do not want the burden of being the first failure. Please choose your subject and carry out all necessary steps to maintain the tradition by the end of term.'

"He wants me to bump somebody off," Toxique said in despair. "What am I going to do?"

"When did this come?" Danny asked.

"Four days ago. I haven't been able to concentrate on anything since."

"Let me think about it," Danny said. "We'll sort it out. I promise."

"You mean that?"

"I do," Danny said, wondering what he had let himself in for.

"The door is going to open in a few seconds," Toxique said absently, "and some faces you won't want to see are going to walk in."

To Danny, Toxique's Gift of Anticipation was much more valuable than his being an assassin. He was never wrong—and this time, unfortunately, was no exception. The door opened and their classmates Smyck and Exspectre walked in, the first boy tall and thin, the other small with large dark-rimmed eyes that made him look, as Les said, like a bush baby.

"We're back. What's wrong with Toxique?" Exspectre said.

"Probably assassinated that freak Dixie by mistake when she went invisible," Smyck said with a laugh.

"Leave it out, Smyck," Les said.

"If you picked him for your 'subject,'" Danny said to Toxique, "I think I'd side with your dad. Sometimes family tradition is a good thing." Toxique gave a wan little smile but his gaze rested thoughtfully on Smyck, long enough for the tall boy to look uncomfortable and hurry off.

"I was only joking," Danny said. "You do know that, don't you, Toxique?"

* * *

Twenty miles away, on the other side of the channel of water that separated Wilsons from its enemies, Conal the Seraphim stood in front of three others. On the left was Rufus Ness, the leader of the Cherbs, a brutal character with a cunning look who, like Danny, had one brown eye and one blue. On the right stood a glamorous woman in a red dress. She was smiling, but Nurse Flanagan's smile did not touch her eyes. In the middle stood a man of medium height with a gentle, almost chiding smile on his face, as if he was a teacher who had found a child doing something bold but was waiting patiently for a reasonable explanation. He was Ambrose Longford, the leader of the Ring.

"You fled because of a flock of birds?" Ness said incredulously.

"Not birds," Conal said, his yellow eyes glittering menacingly. "Ravens!"

"They *are* dangerous," Longford said to Ness. "More than you know."

"Surely not so dangerous that they should send our Seraphim fleeing with their tails between their legs," Nurse Flanagan said with a little laugh.

"They make a poison with the filth from the bottom of their nests and coat their beaks with it," Conal said. "It is deadly."

"Particularly to Seraphim," Longford added. "The avian part of their genetic make-up is particularly susceptible to the poison. You did the right thing, Conal.

Imagine what would have happened to the treaty if the countryside of the Upper World had been littered with the corpses of Seraphim," he told the others. "Would you be casting doubts on the courage of the Seraphim then, or would you be running for your lives with the whispers of the Unquiet in your ears, Rufus?"

"Perhaps it was the intention of the ravens to undermine the treaty," Nurse Flanagan said, again with that little laugh that had no real amusement in it, "to portray us as treaty breakers and leave us at the mercy of the Unquiet."

"Perhaps. Were they there to guard Danny, or were they using him as bait to lure us into an attack? We will probably never know. All I can say is that the ravens will have to be watched in this matter."

"The real problem is that we did not capture the boy," Rufus Ness said impatiently.

"Yes, Rufus, but I have been thinking, there's more than one way to skin a cat."

"What do you mean?" Ness demanded.

"Wilsons will have worked out by now that we are seeking the Treaty Stone."

"Why would they think that?" Nurse Flanagan said, examining a highly polished nail.

"Because they know it is the only way we can destroy the treaty and invade the Upper World. If the Treaty Stone is found and broken, then the treaty ends."

"The Upper World will be ours for the taking," Rufus Ness said with a satisfied grunt.

"The problem is that the Stone is held in the Upper World. We are not permitted there," Conal said.

"And you failed in your first secret mission to the Upper World anyway, so there's no point in trying that again," Nurse Flanagan said smoothly, drawing an angry glare from Conal.

"Enough," Longford said. "Squabbling will not bring us the Stone."

"What will?" Conal said.

"Not what, but who?" the leader said. "I know how Devoy's mind works. He will want to find the Stone and hide it from us. So he must send someone who is permitted in the Upper World and is used to its ways."

"The boy!" Ness said. "He wouldn't dare send the Fifth."

"He might not, but Brunholm will persuade him that the Fifth is the only person for the job. Doubtless he will send that ragtag group, the physick and the blond girl and that miserable Messenger boy."

"Are they not barred by the treaty?" Nurse Flanagan said.

"There is a loophole. Those who drew up the treaty did not think that anyone under the age of sixteen was a threat, and at the time there were children to be moved from the Lower to the Upper World, so they are exempt. Another reason why Danny Caulfield is the obvious choice."

"I see," Nurse Flanagan said. "So what is your plan?"

"If Danny succeeds in stealing the Treaty Stone, then we must get it from him. We have planted the seed of treachery in him. With the right persuasion, he will join us and bring the Stone with him."

"You sound very sure about that, considering that his friendship with the others won out over us the last time. He did not betray them," Conal said sourly.

"We went about it the wrong way before. We must make sure that his friends abandon him. He will feel betrayed, and that in turn will make him betray them. Then he will join us and the Ring of Five will be complete— and will hold absolute power!"

A POISON DART

Danny, Vandra and Dixie stood in Devoy's office, each of them intent on the master's words, each heart beating fast. Brunholm turned to the wall behind him and swept aside a cloth, revealing a map. The cadets moved closer. It was a Living Map. Even though it was pinned to the wall, the rivers flowed with threads of real water, clouds scudded across the skies, and smog hung over the towns and cities.

Brunholm pointed to a mountain range, its peaks white with snow. A blizzard was moving across the range from north to south, coating pine forests at the base of the mountains with more snow.

"The mountain kingdom of Morne," Brunholm said, whipping a giant magnifying glass from under his cloak and holding it up to the map. Through it they saw large stone buildings perched on a crag on the western flank of one of the mountains. Snow-covered gardens and terraces ran down the face of the crag until they reached forbidding cliffs on three sides.

"To the outside world it is hidden so it isn't interfered with. By the treaty Morne is allowed to accept scholars from the Lower World, so you will travel there as students. Danny, you will go as a student of the history of the Lower World. Our young physick can go as a student of medicine, and you"—he turned to Dixie, who was watching him with an expression that managed to be eager and vacant at the same time—"you can go as a student of . . . something or other."

"How do we find it?" Danny asked.

"It is a Kingdom of Unreliable Location," Devoy said, "and therefore moves from mountain range to mountain range. At the moment it is in the Carpathians, but we expect it to move soon. We'll keep you informed.

"Now, that is enough for the time being. We will have more detailed instructions for you in the following days. In the meantime, I hope I do not have to tell you not to speak of this to anyone."

Danny stared at the dark buildings of Morne. Part of him feared its stone walls and high narrow windows; part of him longed to learn its secrets. Vandra had to pull him away.

*   *   *

That day the Unknown Spy had been allowed back into his room for the first time since the murder. Valant had cleaned it thoroughly, but it wasn't the same. The spy sat behind his desk in the darkness. He had forgotten many things, but he had not forgotten his wife's face. He sat there until darkness fell, his eyes unseeing. He had often sat like this, feeling that there was a great secret just out of grasp, if he could only reach back into his memory. Now there was nothing but his sorrow.

He heard a careful click. He had not forgotten the sound of a lock being picked and stealthy feet entering a room. He reached for the drawer where he kept his revolver, but when it slid silently open he felt in vain in the empty space. Valant had removed it. A voice spoke in the darkness, a high-pitched, hissing voice—he could not tell if it was male or female.

"You do not need your pistol; I do not intend to harm you."

"Who are you?" the Unknown Spy said. His voice was calm. He had been in a thousand dangerous situations in his career.

"That is of no consequence. I have information for you about the death of your wife."

"What information?" The Unknown Spy's voice was cold. Was the creature in the dark responsible for his wife's murder?

"I did not kill her, but I can identify the killer for you."

"Why would you do that?" There was a curious whining sound in the darkness—his intruder was laughing.

"A belief in justice, perhaps?"

"I don't think so."

"No. You are right. A belief in revenge, then." The wheezing laugh had stopped.

"Let me have my revenge. Tell me," the Unknown Spy cried, "and then leave me to it!"

"Very well," the voice said. "The boy with the wings, the Messenger Les Knutt, killed your wife."

There was a shuffling sound in the unlit room. The door clicked again. The Unknown Spy was alone in the darkness.

"Wow," Vandra said, "easy!"

"Yes," Danny said, "get into a kingdom that moves about without warning, steal the Treaty Stone while pretending to be students and get out alive, presumably chased by the kingdom's army. Dead easy."

"Lay off the snarky tone," Dixie said.

"Sorry," Danny said, looking contrite. "Every time I meet Brunholm he puts my teeth on edge."

"I can't wait to see the Upper World," Dixie said excitedly, disappearing and reappearing in the corridor ten feet ahead of them.

"Hey," Danny said, pointing out the window. They were looking down onto a hidden inner courtyard that was rarely used and only visible from that window. Four elderly Messengers stood in the courtyard. The winged Messengers had flown between the Two Worlds carrying information before war had broken out. Once the treaty had been signed and the Two Worlds divided, the Messengers were no longer needed. Some had gone over to the enemy and had become the Seraphim. The others had fled to Wilsons, and rather than face the fact that they were no longer needed, they had decided to treat their old life as something to be ashamed of. So much so that unless it was absolutely necessary, they never flew; flying was regarded as vulgar and their wings as burdensome.

"How come Les is the only young Messenger?" Dixie asked, the thought suddenly popping into her mind.

"As far as I know all the other young Messengers died of disease and hunger during the war. The ones that are left are too old to have children," Vandra said.

Four Messengers stood in the square, including Gabriel, once an aerial ace, but now earthbound like the rest. Or was he? Danny and his friends crouched to watch as Gabriel rose into the air, flew around the courtyard once at a leisurely pace, then casually performed a loop the loop before landing in front of the others. With varying degrees of success the three others, two respectable-looking lady Messengers and an absentminded male, imitated him.

"Let's go down there," Dixie said.

"No," Danny said, "they'd be embarrassed."

But Dixie wasn't listening. She smiled at Danny, then disappeared, reappearing in the courtyard right beside Gabriel, who leapt so far into the air he had to use his wings to give himself a soft landing.

"Quick," Vandra said, "there's a door. Maybe we can smooth things over."

When they got to the courtyard one of the female Messengers was complaining bitterly to Gabriel.

"You promised all this would be highly confidential. 'Oh no, Gertie, no one will ever see us!' Now we'll be the laughingstock of Wilsons!"

"Steady on, Gertie old girl," the other male Messenger said.

"It's all very well for you to talk, Waldron," Gertie said.

"Gertie," the other female said sternly, "you have to remember what all of this is about."

"We were caught unprepared the last time the Cherbs attacked," Waldron said. "We only escaped by the skin of our teeth. We must have at least one attack squadron if they come again."

"Even if the others don't agree," Gabriel said.

"We won't tell anyone, honest," Danny said.

"Oh no!" Gertie exclaimed. "More of them!"

"Isn't that the boy they said was the Fifth?" Waldron exclaimed.

"Really?" Gertie said, peering at Danny. "He's not very impressive, is he?"

The other female Messenger, a small, careworn-looking creature in a frayed cardigan, appeared to be lost in thought, moving her wings in little circles and talking to herself. Dixie was watching her as she took two small jumps from the ground before rising a few feet into the air and gliding back to land. Dixie applauded.

"Not quite as good as the old days, my dear." The lady Messenger smiled and did a little curtsey.

"Why are the Messengers so embarrassed about flying?" Dixie said.

"Most of them are blithering idiots," the lady replied with a snort. "They'd rather sit around and knit or something."

"What would you prefer?" Dixie said.

"To have a go at the enemy, attack from out of the sun so they don't see you coming and knock the tar out of their filthy Cherb hides."

Dixie looked suitably impressed by the bloodthirstiness of this outburst. She stuck out her hand.

"Dixie Cole." The lady Messenger took her hand and wrung it with unexpected strength.

"Daisy McEachen. Absolutely charmed to make your acquaintance. If I ever need a tail gunner I'll give you a shout—you'll sit on my back when I'm flying and cover my back. Always nice to have a human crew member on board."

Dixie looked delighted at the prospect, but Danny was distracted. A small piece of stone had dislodged from the parapet far above their heads and fallen at his feet. There was a flicker of something black on the rooftop. Was someone sneaking around up there?

Danny grabbed the people nearest to him—Vandra and Gertie—and drew them into the shelter of the wall beside him. Before he could shout out to the others, something flew through the air. Daisy, who had just risen into the air, gave a little gasp, cartwheeled and fell to earth. Gertie screamed. Vandra and Dixie reacted quickly, moving swiftly to try to observe the attacker.

Danny ran to Daisy. Her eyes were closed and she was breathing shallowly. A sinister-looking dart tipped with black and red feathers was buried in her arm.

"Vandra!" Danny called out. The small physick ran to his side. Gabriel had recovered from the shock and was rising cautiously into the air, his eyes alert. Vandra examined the dart, then knelt and smelled Daisy's breath.

"Smells of marzipan," she said grimly.

"Is that bad?" Danny said.

"Means the dart is tipped with cyanide," Vandra said. Her face, ordinarily pale, turned deathly white, and her hand shook a little.

"Vandra," Danny said, "if it's too dangerous, you don't have to . . ."

"I do," Vandra said. "I am a physick." Danny knew what she meant. A physick was a healer who healed by drawing the patient's illness or poison upon themselves. Vandra would have to draw the cyanide on herself. Her body was strong—physicks had physical gifts that enabled them to deal with disease and toxins. But there were no guarantees, and there was no protection against pain.

Vandra bent her head, her incisors protruding. She drew the dart from Daisy's arm and plunged her teeth into Daisy's shoulder, just above the wound. She stiffened, spasms running through her body. Danny looked on helplessly. Behind him he heard a shout. A figure dressed in black was running across the rooftop, beside one of the huge crumbling chimneys.

"Gabriel," Danny said, "can you get me up there?"

"Put your arms around my neck!" Gabriel said.

Danny embraced the Messenger's frail neck, wondering if the body beneath him would bear his weight. Danny had once flown on the back of Conal, the Seraphim, who had borne him easily, but Seraphim were strong. Aside from being elderly, Gabriel was weakened and his muscles atrophied from disuse.

Gabriel's back seemed to bend as Danny climbed on. There was a strong odor of mothballs from his jacket, but his wings were surprisingly powerful and bore them upward with great beats. When they got to the level of the roof, Danny could feel Gabriel tiring. As they cleared the parapet a snowy gust drove them across the rooftops, Gabriel desperately fighting against it. The swirling wind carried them out over the edge. Gabriel faltered and Danny lost his grip. For one sickening moment he clung by one hand to the collar of Gabriel's coat, his legs dangling over a drop of a hundred feet.

With an enormous effort Gabriel was able to get Danny onto his back again, but the wind forced them across the roof, blowing snow from the slates in great whirling clouds around them.

"Can you land?" Danny shouted over the howl of the wind.

Gabriel's answer came in gasps. "Too much . . . turbulence . . . can't see landing spot." Neither did he see the great redbrick chimney rearing up in front of them. With an impact that drove the breath from their lungs, they struck and started to fall. Danny braced himself, but they landed in a drift of snow that had piled up against the chimney breast.

Gabriel groaned and tried to shake snow from his feathers. Danny leapt to his feet.

"Are you all right?" he said. Gabriel nodded. "Stay here, then." Danny looked around to get his bearings. The rooftops of Wilsons were vast, great peaks and troughs rising and falling. There were chimneys and buttresses with windows in them, doors that looked as if they had been locked and sealed forever. Clusters of aerials and dishes hinted at mysterious purposes. The chimney they had hit was the very chimney where Danny had seen the attacker. He cast around on the roof for footprints and found small neat tracks leading away. He began to follow them.

The attacker had been able to run lightly over the snow, but Danny found himself blundering, slipping into gullies and catching his shins on objects hidden under the snow. He tripped over a roof peak and slithered down the other side on his belly, landing chin-first on a patch of ice. He rolled over to find himself looking down the barrel of an ancient blunderbuss. The gun was held by a small red-bearded man wearing a parka. There was rope looped over his shoulder, and climbers' crampons hung from his belt.

"Getting very busy on the rooftops this morning. Unauthorized entry all over the place."

Danny got to his feet, eyeing the blunderbuss warily.

"I'm a pupil at Wilsons," he said. "We were in the courtyard down there and someone attacked us with a dart. I was chasing him."

"One of these?" the bearded man said, holding up a dart tipped with red and black feathers.

"Yes."

"He threw one at me too."

"Good thing it didn't hit you," Danny said. "It's poisoned."

"Is it?" The man raised an eyebrow. "So what makes you think you can come up here willy-nilly? These rooftops is highly organized places. You can't just be running about."

"Sorry," Danny said.

"There's lead flashing that's hard to fix and there's expensive copper sheeting and slates and tiles, not to mention the aerials. Looking after the roofs is a full-time job."

"I'm sure it's hard," Danny said, guessing that the little man looked after the roofs, "but they look like very well-cared-for roofs."

"Do they?"

"I've never seen better-looking roofs. Look at the way they're keeping out the snow," Danny said.

"Snow is difficult," the man said. "Causes expanding, and we all know what expanding leads to. . . ."

"Yes, of course," Danny said. "Expanding leads to . . . leads to . . ."

"Leaks!" the little man said. "The roof man's mortal enemy! Leaks and drips."

"Shocking," Danny said as the man lowered his gun. "And the attacker . . ."

"Gone," the man said shortly. "Must have had a key to one of the roof doors. That's the only way you can get up and down." There was a clattering, clanking noise from behind him. They turned to see Gabriel. The

76

Messenger had tried to take off and the wind had blown him into one of the clusters of antennae, where he had become completely entangled. The little man lifted his blunderbuss to his shoulder. Danny dived forward and knocked the barrel off target just as the roof man fired. The shot went harmlessly upward.

"What are you doing?" Danny cried.

"Look at my good aerial!" the roof man cried. "I haven't seen such a mess since the great storms of 'thirty-nine. Pesky birds!"

"It's not a bird, it's a Messenger!" Danny exclaimed as the roof man tried to reload.

"I don't care what it is, get it out of my aerials," the man grunted. With a supreme effort Gabriel wriggled free of the aerials and dropped to the rooftop in a tangle of wings and limbs. The roof man lowered his gun and clambered up among the antennae, straightening and redirecting them with care.

"Come on, Gabriel," Danny said, "we'd better get out of here. Sorry about your aerials, Mr. Roof Man."

"Come up here with nothing to do but make trouble," muttered the man. "Why can't they stay on the ground?"

"You didn't happen to see what the attacker looked like, by any chance?" Danny asked as he clambered onto Gabriel's back.

"Small and fast-moving was all I seen," the roof man said. "Too busy watching out for his darts to get a right look. Well rid of the likes of that off the roof."

Still grumbling, he did not look round as Gabriel half launched himself, half stumbled from the roof, then glided unsteadily toward the ground, lost for a moment in a flurry blown from a ledge. Danny could see the three Messengers and his friends below. Daisy was sitting up, supported by Gertie, but Dixie knelt beside Vandra, who lay pale and still on the ground.

The roof man moved to the edge and looked down at the small group. The cross-old-workman persona had vanished. The face that looked down was now cold and cunning, the eyes glittering with malice. He scratched at the ginger beard and part of it came away. He took one of the darts from his pocket. The physick had saved the Messenger from his poison, but if it had cost her her life, then it would have been a good day's work. Besides, the man had plenty more darts. "Plenty more darts," he said to himself in a voice that the Unknown Spy would have recognized. Then he turned and skipped lightly across the snow-covered roof.

AN OATH

Danny knelt beside Vandra. She looked dreadful, her pale face gone gray, her chest barely rising and falling and spasms racking her every few minutes while she grimaced with pain.

Dixie had gone to get Valant. They returned with two wheeled stretchers and lifted Vandra onto one. Daisy was able to get up onto the other by herself.

"The poor dear," Daisy said quietly, "she saved my life. I will not forget that."

Valant and Gabriel wheeled the stretchers quickly along the quiet corridors of Wilsons, then stopped in front of an ancient cage elevator. There was only room for the two of them and the stretchers.

"I will take them to the apothecary," Valant said. "You may visit the physick in the morning, not before. She needs rest and whatever assistance she can be given there."

Danny watched as the elevator clanked upward into the gloom. He didn't say anything to the others, but he was determined to find the person who had hurt Daisy and put his friend in danger.

They met Les coming across the lawn.

"What happened?" he demanded. As Dixie explained, she was interrupted by a quiet voice.

"Probably the same person who attacked the Unknown Spy's wife." McGuinness was leaning against a tree beside them, his coat fading into the color of the trunk so that he was virtually invisible.

"What makes you think that?" Danny said.

"These kinds of incidents are rare in Wilsons, and both required a close knowledge of the layout of the school, which, as you know, can be complex. Speed and cunning have characterized both attacks. And they have both been successful, or would have been, if not for the physick. This is a professional at work, make no mistake about it. The question is why? Answering the why of a crime almost always leads you to the culprit."

"Lead me to him," Les said angrily, "and he won't bother anyone ever."

"She'll get better, Les," Dixie said, putting her hand on his arm.

"You have to keep your eyes peeled," McGuinness said, lowering his voice confidentially. "Until we know what motivates this person, everyone is in danger."

"Time for tea," the school announcer Blackpitt said,

his voice booming from a speaker hidden in the tree, making them jump.

"It really is a wonderful day," Blackpitt said.

"What's he so cheerful about?" Les growled.

They went off to tea in a gloomy mood, not helped by the sniggering at the other end of the table from Smyck and the others, accompanied by warnings to each other to "watch the game pie" in case it was poisoned and the like.

After tea Danny found himself wandering on his own in the woods. Without thinking about it he made his way toward the summerhouse. The summerhouse had not been used for many years. Its curtains hung in tatters, but its old planks retained a sense of sun-warmed days and balmy evenings, and sitting there always lifted his spirits.

He'd brought a slice of cake from Ravensdale, and he wrapped himself in a blanket and sat on the window seat, watching the sun lower in the west, the bare black limbs of the trees silhouetted against it.

He wondered about his parents. He hated to admit it, but he missed them. They had always been there, and now there was nobody. They were secret agents, but who were they working for? Why did he have to be guarded? Danny already knew that he was the Fifth, the link between the Cherbs and ordinary people, and that the Ring of Five sought him as their missing member. Was that the reason? Did some secret service want to keep him from joining the Ring?

He sat in the summerhouse for an hour, his mind swirling. When he finally stood up, stiff and cold, it was dark. He felt in the pocket of his coat. The coat had many pockets that weren't immediately apparent. He found lockpicks, a comb, a pen with a secret compartment in it, a broken spy camera and a foldable grappling iron before he finally put his hand on the old-fashioned-looking but reliable flashlight.

As he pulled the flashlight out something clinked against it—the "S" and "G" ring he'd been given in the Butts. He studied it in the light. Who were S and G, and why had the hand of the Unquiet slipped this into his coat?

Returning the ring to his pocket, he started to walk back toward Wilsons, keeping the light shaded with his hand so that he wouldn't be too visible, not so much because there was a killer at large, but because he had started to acquire a spy's habit of secrecy. There were noises in the darkness, night creatures starting to move about, but they didn't disturb him. Then he heard something different—not like a badger scuffling in the leaves, but like people struggling. As he got nearer he could hear groans and panting from somewhere to his left. He switched the torch off and listened. A voice in his head told him to leave it, walk back to Wilsons, that it was none of his business.

I can't leave it if they're in trouble, he said to himself. And a quiet cold voice in his head said, *Go to whoever it is. Anybody about this time of night is up to no good. They might be useful to you!*

He put the torch back on, shading it again, then picked his way through the undergrowth, pausing every few steps to listen. Whoever or whatever Danny had heard was growing tired—the sounds had become feeble—but there was no sign that he had been detected. Then the noises stopped altogether. Instead, Danny heard someone sobbing. Whoever it was didn't sound dangerous anymore. Danny straightened and took his hand away from the torch.

He had found Vicky the siren. She had been caught in a trap and was hanging in a net from a tree branch. Below her, sharpened spikes had sprung from the earth. Whoever had set the trap had clearly taken no chances. Vicky's dress was torn and her hair was full of leaves, but when she saw the torchlight, without knowing who was holding it, she cried out in a breathy girlish voice.

"Oh, thank goodness, kind stranger! I have been caught in this dreadful trap. I was just getting some medicine for my poor sick mother and some evil person left this awful thing here. If you could just help me I would be so grateful. . . ."

"It's all right, Vicky. It's me." Danny angled the torch so it showed his face.

"Oh," she said, bad-tempered and sulky. "You. I suppose you lot helped Brunholm build these traps. My dress is ruined."

"No!" Danny said. "I wouldn't help Brunholm build something like that. Course I wouldn't."

"You wouldn't?" she said, surprised. "Well, maybe you could just step over here for a second and cut one or two strands of this net. . . ."

"Why would I do that?" Danny said, feeling the

cunning part of his brain taking over, deep in the forest at night with a trapped creature.

"I could do things for you," Vicky said with a coy smile. "I could help you."

"I don't think there's anything you can do for me," Danny said, pretending to turn away.

"Wait, wait, don't go, there must be something. If Brunholm gets his hands on me . . ."

Danny waited. Brunholm had been setting traps for Vicky for months, ever since Danny and Les had been fooled into releasing her from her cell in Wilsons.

"You're probably better under lock and key," Danny said. "All you do is make ships run aground on rocks by beguiling sailors."

"I've given up beguiling, honestly I have," Vicky said. "I've put all that behind me. I'm a very respectable siren now." She put on an innocent face, which Danny didn't believe for a moment.

"Besides," Danny said, "you'd promise me anything to get free and then you'd try to double-cross me."

"I swear I wouldn't. I'll take the siren's oath. The Unquiet come for you if you don't keep it." Vicky shivered at the mention of the Unquiet, and something about her reaction made Danny think her fear was real. As far as he could see, nobody joked about the Unquiet round Wilsons.

"Okay then, let's hear the oath."

"You have to tell me what you want me to do."

"I want you to be my eyes and ears when I need you, to find out any bit of information I ask."

"Is that all?" Vicky said. "You sure you don't want more? I could throw in some theft if you like. A little assault could be in the deal as well. . . ."

"No thanks," Danny said quickly, "the eyes and ears will do very well. Now, what about this oath?"

"Oh, the oath." The siren closed her eyes, put her head back like a child in school about to say a poem and began to recite in a high-pitched voice:

> *"This is the oath as siren I make.*
> *This is the oath I cannot break.*
> *The dead await the liar;*
> *The faithless burn in their cold fire.*
> *State your wish."*

"I want you to be a spy in the school for me when I ask you," Danny said. The siren listened gravely, then replied:

> *"Your wish for me you have said.*
> *I obey or will be dead."*

She opened her eyes. "That do?"

"That'll do."

"Well then, cut me loose!"

It was difficult to get Vicky out without dropping her onto the spikes below. Finally Danny realized that he still had the Knife of Implacable Intention, a knife that did exactly what its owner wanted of it. Vicky watched him closely as he weighed the knife in his hand.

"What are you going to do?" She eyed him nervously. For answer Danny threw the knife. It ripped through the side of the netting on the way out. The siren shrieked as she tumbled sideways out of the net, the tips of the spikes glinting in the torchlight beneath her. Describing a lethal arc in the air, the knife swung back toward her. She went silent as it plunged through the shoulder of her dress, pinning her to the trunk of the tree behind her.

Dangling from the tree, the siren examined the place the knife had struck. She fingered the ruined fabric and gave Danny a dangerous look.

"If you swing round to the branch on your left," Danny said, "you should be able to get down." Vicky did as he said, and just as she reached the branch the knife fell from the tree trunk into Danny's waiting hand.

"Don't forget," he told her. She looked at him through narrowed eyes.

"I won't," she said, and for a moment there was something strange, almost sad in her tone. Then she dropped from the branch and disappeared into the woods.

As he walked back to the Roosts, Danny didn't feel very good about himself. He had recruited a valuable ally and bound her to him, but the way he had gone about it felt dishonest and sneaky. He should have just released her. He had earned an advantage over her, but he had the worrying feeling that she might turn on him.

The forest path opened out into the lawns of Wilsons and the building sprang up in front of him. For all the danger lurking in it—the assassin, the Unquiet roaming the Butts, the devious games of Brunholm—the building looked welcoming with its many lights blazing, and Danny's heart leapt. This was where he belonged, he thought as he hurried toward it.

In another world, the woman whom he had once known as his mother fed another piece of broken furniture into the fire. She was afraid of going outside to get fuel in case the winged creatures returned. They had terrified her, no matter how delighted Agent Stone was to confirm his theory that there really was a Lower World. All she could remember was their burning eyes and their foul stench. During the attack she had fallen unconscious, but she had seen the Seraphim fleeing before the ravens, and she felt a little bit safer when she looked out the window at the ravens in their ragged nests in the bare trees outside. Most of them flew off to find food during the day, but some remained behind.

Agent Stone was getting better, but since seeing the Seraphim he had spent most of his time in the library, barely pausing to eat. Pearl was on her own during the day, and she spent hours in Danny's room sitting on his bed. For years she had pretended that they were a family, and now she felt she was being punished for it. She prayed that Danny was safe and that the Seraphim had not caught up with him, for surely they had been after him when they'd come here. And she hoped that, wherever he was, he would be able to forgive her.

7

PECULIAR GEOGRAPHY

The following morning Danny, Dixie and Les went up to the apothecary straight after breakfast. Vandra was sitting up in bed. She looked ill and her voice was faint, but, as Dixie said, "At least she had her eyes open." They only stayed for a short while. Vandra was always gloomy when she was recovering from poison, and barely responded to their questions. They knew she would get better as the days went on, and that was enough for them.

Classes had started, and the halls had been full of pupils when the group went up to the apothecary, but now they were deserted. Dixie looked at her schedule.

"Oh dear," she said, "we're late for geography!" Les and Danny glanced at each other and they all broke into a run. They tried to slip in quietly at the back, Dixie disappearing and reappearing at her desk, but it was no good.

The wooden-backed blackboard eraser whistled through the air, glancing off Les's head with a dull sound. A rattled Dixie disappeared from her desk but mistakenly reappeared beside the teacher's, where a flung textbook of *Bottomless Lakes of the Lower World* just missed her. Spitfire, the geography teacher, was brilliant at her job, and the pupils liked her, but she had a hot temper and didn't suffer fools gladly. Danny got a raised eyebrow, which meant that she would talk to him later.

"Now, class," Spitfire said, "back to the exam topic of this term—the geography and history of the Upper World."

It was odd sitting there listening to his world being described in the same way someone might describe a foreign country they didn't know very well. It was clear for a start that Spitfire had no idea what religion was. She said that people could only guess at what the strange buildings that dominated so many towns and cities were for, but that in some of them there were paintings and statues of Messengers, which meant that they may have been communication centers between the Upper and Lower Worlds before the treaty.

Spitfire turned the lights out and began to project some photographs and paintings of Danny's world onto a screen.

"Our limited contacts with the Upper World have enabled us to get some idea of what modern life is like there," she said.

The trouble with Spitfire's photographs was that there was no way of telling what era they were from, so that a photo of a modern building was followed by one of a steam train.

"The steam engine appears to be the only mode of transport," Spitfire said. "Unlike us, they do not have any automobiles."

Danny opened his mouth to say something, then closed it again. Spitfire had moved on to people. A black-and-white photo of a man in a top hat and tailcoat was described as wearing "everyday work clothing," whereas a girl in a bikini represented "normal leisure clothing" for women.

"What are you laughing about?" Les whispered as Danny snorted. A "typical schoolchild" wore a cap and shorts and carried a slingshot in his pocket. A picture of an airplane on the ground bemused Spitfire and Danny suddenly realized there were no airplanes in the Lower World.

"This would appear to be some kind of futuristic train," Spitfire said. She went on to describe the landscape.

"The climate is similar to our own, with cold winters and temperate summers," she said, apparently unaware of the existence of deserts and icecaps or all the variations in between.

"Must be kind of funny where you live," Les whispered, "what with no cars and wearing shorts to school and all."

Danny wanted to speak, but Spitfire's eye fell on him and he knew that this wasn't the time or the place to put her right. So he sat meekly listening to his instructor discuss signs of food shortages (skinny models on a catwalk) and indications that people were constantly spying on each other's communications (satellite dishes on houses). Spitfire obviously thought this last point very important.

"It's one of the reasons that Wilsons is vital to the Lower World. Spying is obviously regarded as central to the interests of the Upper World, and we must be ready if by any chance they should cross our borders."

Danny now realized that there were also no cell phones or televisions in the Lower World, never mind computers. He had never thought of the two places as being so different. He put up his hand.

"Please, do you know what a television is in the Lower World?"

"A tele-vision," Spitfire said. "No, please do enlighten us."

"It's like . . . a box, and moving pictures are beamed onto it. There are programs like—I don't know—the news and cartoons and drama."

"Really, Mr. Caulfield, such a vivid imagination," Spitfire said. "Actors being transferred into a box? I don't think so."

"Pull the other one, Caulfield," Smyck mocked him with a snigger.

"Does sound odd, Danny," Les muttered, looking a bit embarrassed for his friend.

"Sounds odd?" Danny looked at Les incredulously,

not wanting to point out that having wings was more than a bit odd, never mind being in a spy school with the dead running about in the basement.

"Now that we've all been most wonderfully entertained by Mr. Caulfield, perhaps we should get back to work," Spitfire said firmly.

After some more peculiar notions about the geography of the Upper World, Blackpitt announced the end of the class, giggling to himself as if he was enjoying some private joke.

"What is wrong with that man?" Les said. As they filed out of class, Spitfire told Danny and Dixie to stay behind. Les continued but looked back a little wistfully.

"Now," Spitfire said, unlocking a drawer in her desk, "this is top-secret. Mr. Brunholm requested that you be given this for your upcoming mission." She took out a tube and produced a scroll from it, unrolling it carefully onto the desk.

"There!" she said triumphantly. "The Upper World!" Danny stared. It was a map with a great splodge of land surrounded by flashes of blue. Mountains with snow-capped tops sat here and there, as did beautifully drawn groups of buildings with *Unknown City* written underneath them.

"Er, did you do this?" Danny asked.

"Yes," Spitfire said, beaming with pride, "it took many hours of work using all our available knowledge. What do you think?"

"If you don't mind my asking," Danny said, "when

was the last time someone from the Lower World went to the Upper World?"

"Well, I can't speak for the other side, the Ring and Cherbs," Spitfire said with a sniff, "but it's been generations since someone has *admitted* to going over. Fairman brings back bits and pieces, and I believe he's had a few illegal fares. Someone must have crossed the border, but no one admits it."

"I see," Danny said, thinking that it must have been a very long time since anyone either crossed or took a good look around them when they did.

"Take the map and study it well," Spitfire said, rolling it up. "Keep it safe. It could be deadly in the wrong hands."

Deadly in any hands if you relied on it, Danny thought. But he tucked the map under his arm anyway.

Classes continued as normal for the rest of the day: Poisons. Maths. Disguise. Danny and his friends were tired when they finished, but he knew he had to talk to them. He arranged to meet them in the infirmary after tea. He included Les even though he wasn't going on the mission.

Vandra looked a lot better, and she sat up in bed when Dixie said they'd been given a map of the Upper World.

"Give me a look!" she said. "I've always wanted to see it."

"But the thing is that the map isn't anything like the Upper World," Danny said. "That's what I want to tell you!"

However, nothing would quiet them but to open the map out on the bed and pore over the strange cities and snowy mountains, trying to guess how many people lived there and what they were like.

"It's . . . it's . . . completely different," Danny said. "Spitfire's information is all wrong. There are planes and cell phones and things like that!" They looked at him as if he was talking nonsense and went back to the map. It was hard to talk about cell phones to people who used beetles as listening devices.

They'll just have to see when they get there, he thought.

Vandra moved and grimaced with pain.

"Are you okay?" Dixie asked.

"Kind of," Vandra said. "It was a very strong dose of cyanide—I was only just able to deal with it. If it hadn't been pure, I wouldn't have been able to cope."

"What do you mean?" Les asked.

"If there had been any impurities in the poison, my system would have collapsed. That was professionally made. We're not dealing with an amateur here."

"No, we're not," Toxique said quietly. "You said the feathers on the dart were red and black?"

Danny nodded.

"Red and black are the colors of the house of Toxique. We use them when we want the victim to know who their assassin is. I'm not surprised that the poison was pure. The Toxiques make the purest poisons in their own workshops. It's a matter of family pride."

Danny was the first to see the implications of

this detail: someone was trying to pin the attack on Toxique.

"Does anyone else know about this?" he asked. Toxique nodded.

"Brunholm and Devoy would both know. Toxiques
have been coming to Wilsons for generations."

"Does anyone else know that you're supposed to assassinate someone this term?" Les asked carefully.

"And did anybody see you to provide an alibi for
when the dart was fired?" Dixie said.

"Dixie!" Danny cried.

"I'm only trying to keep him out of trouble," Dixie
protested.

"She's right, you know," Toxique said. "I went for a
walk in the woods yesterday afternoon. No one would
have known where I was. And yes, my father wrote a letter
to Devoy saying that there was no point in my training to
be an assassin unless I got to actually kill someone and
show off my skills. And now," he said, using his Gift of
Anticipation, "I'm in trouble."

The door burst open and Brunholm strode in. "I
heard about this dart, young man," Brunholm said. "The
colors of Toxique. I demand an explanation."

Toxique stood up. "I am aware of the incident," he
said with great dignity, "and I am also aware that the poison was probably manufactured by a Toxique, such was
its purity."

"So what's your defense, then? I know you are supposed to kill someone this term. Thought you'd try your
hand at a poor Messenger, is that it?"

"My defense is this: the lady is still alive," Toxique said.

"Meaning?" Brunholm said.

"Meaning that if the assassin had been a Toxique, she would be dead. A true Toxique never fails to kill."

"That's the point," Brunholm cried. "A true Toxique! But are you a true Toxique or a reluctant one?"

"Leave him alone," Dixie said. "Toxique doesn't tell lies."

Brunholm's eyes glittered dangerously. "I believe that punishment is called for in the family Toxique for failed assassinations?"

"Yes," Toxique said unhappily.

"And if your family feels that this was a failed attempt, then it is their duty to carry out such a punishment?"

"You know a lot about my family," Toxique said.

"Wilsons' library is full of books about the glorious history of the Toxique family," Brunholm said. "It is one of the most eminent names in the history of spies and assassins. They have never lowered their standards."

"Then you know the punishment," Toxique said heavily.

"Yes, and I know that it has been carried out at the mere suspicion of a botched assassination."

"That's true."

"What is the punishment, then?" Les said.

"Death," Brunholm said.

"Slow and agonizing death by poison," Toxique said.

"No!" Dixie said. "Specially when you didn't try to kill that Messenger in the first place!"

"When it comes to the family name," Toxique said, "fairness doesn't come into it."

"You'd better hope that they don't get wind of this," Brunholm said. "Or that we catch someone for throwing the darts."

He glared at the cadets, then turned on his heel and stalked out of the infirmary.

"Phew," Danny said, "he wasn't too happy."

"He better find whoever did it," Vandra said. "I'm not going to be up to sucking any more poison for a while."

Danny said nothing. He had seen Vandra shudder at the words "slow and agonizing."

Toxique lifted his head. "Devoy's coming this way," he said quietly. A few seconds later the door opened and Devoy entered and went straight to Vandra.

"The apothecary has informed me of your condition," he said, "and has said that you are not well enough to leave your bed yet, so I will be carrying out preparation for your mission in the infirmary. Mr. Toxique and Mr. Knutt, you will be good enough to excuse us?"

Toxique nodded and turned to go. Dixie squeezed his arm. Danny winked at Les, who gave him a thumbs-up as he followed the dejected Toxique out the door.

8

A CROSSBOW OF
EXQUISITE SENSITIVITY

"Now," Devoy said, when Les and Toxique had left, "we have received news of an incursion by Seraphim into the Upper World."

Danny didn't notice the quick look that Devoy cast in his direction before going on.

"This is evidence of their intentions with regard to the Upper World, and I think we can expect more of these raids, stretching the boundaries of the treaty to the limit. The Treaty Stone is no longer safe in Morne and must be removed. The matter is now urgent.

"The last report I have of the kingdom of Morne is that it is located in a place called Tibet. Is that name familiar to you, Danny?"

"Well . . . from books, yes . . ."

"Splendid, then it shouldn't be too hard to find."
Danny shook his head. Was there any point in saying that
Tibet was at the far ends of the earth to where he lived?
Or that it was a vast mountainous place where they spoke
a different language and where strangers might not be all
that welcome? But before Danny could decide, Devoy
strode to the door and wrenched it open. Danny's heart
sank. Les and Toxique were on their knees listening at the
door.

Devoy's voice was icy.

"Mr. Knutt. Mr. Toxique. Eavesdropping on a con-
ference of this nature is a Tenth Regulation offense, verg-
ing on the Eleventh. These are great matters of state!"

"What's an Eleventh Regulation offense?" Danny
whispered.

"I don't know," Dixie said, "but it must be terrible!"

"It's my fault, Master Devoy," Toxique said, hanging
his head.

"As if you were not in enough trouble, Mr. Toxique."

"It his Gift of Anticipation!" Les said.

"Meaning what?" Devoy demanded.

"I was just leaving the room," answered Toxique,
"when the gift told me that an untrue thing was about to
be spoken."

"An untrue thing?"

"I didn't know what it was at the start," Toxique said
miserably, "so I listened in."

"He only wanted to help," Les said.

"Silence!" Devoy said. "What was this untrue thing?"

"That the . . . the . . . kingdom of Morne was in Tibet."

"What do you know about Morne?" Devoy said.

"N-nothing, I never even heard of it before now. It's the gift. Things just come into my head."

"And what came into your head?"

"That the kingdom of Morne has moved to Ireland within the last few days."

"Ireland!" Danny said. "That's where I'm from, and it's a lot closer than Tibet."

"I see," Devoy said. "And is your gift ever wrong, Mr. Toxique?"

"Never," Toxique whispered.

"Then," Devoy said, "I have to thank you, and I will exempt Mr. Knutt from punishment as well, although I doubt his motives were as pure as yours. Please leave us now. I will know if you breathe a word about what you have heard here. And if it reaches my ears that you have . . ."

"No, sir, we promise, never!" Les said, grabbing Toxique. "Cross my heart and hope to die. Come on, Toxique. . . ."

Les half dragged the trainee assassin out of the room. The door slammed.

"Please, Master Devoy," Dixie said, "what is an Eleventh Regulation offense? I thought they only went up to ten?" Devoy gave her a long, considering look, then clapped his hands briskly together.

"Now. Back to our mission. Tell me about Ireland, Mr. Caulfield."

"It's an island."

"An island." Devoy frowned. "Do they have bridges or boats?"

"There's no bridge to Ireland, sir, but there are boats and . . ." Danny was going to mention the existence of airplanes, but he remembered how the Wilsons people had reacted to the mention of television and thought better of it.

"Wonderful," Devoy said. "I imagine it will be possible to steal one of these boats, or to bribe the ferryman."

"You could do that," Danny said, "but you could always just pay the fare."

"Pay the fare," Devoy said suspiciously. "You mean they would demand a terrible forfeit, perhaps a hold over your very soul?"

"Er, no," Danny said, "usually a few coins—well, banknotes, really."

"It's almost too easy," Devoy said. "It might be a trap."

"I don't think so," Danny said, thinking of the huge ships that crossed the Irish Sea every day carrying cars and trucks.

"We'll see," Devoy said. "It is a good thing that Morne has moved—in cold climates it usually covers its movements by creating snowy conditions, so look for snowstorms, or snow lying where it is normally rare."

Danny shook his head. They laughed when he

described a television set, yet they talked about a secret kingdom that moved from country to country without blinking an eye.

"You'll need local currency," Devoy said. "I gave Fairman some gold and asked him to change it for money from the Upper World."

A suitcase had stood unnoticed by the door. Devoy brought it over and opened it. Danny gulped. It was full of bundles of different bills—euros, dollars, pounds. There must have been tens of thousands in each currency.

"Is there a problem?"

"No, no," Danny said quickly, "I think it'll be just enough."

"Good," Devoy said. "Now we have to talk about infiltration. You will be traveling in with Fairman. The problem is, where to take you?"

"If we go as far as my house," Danny heard himself saying, "we can use that as a base and operate from there."

"That sounds reasonable," Devoy said, "but what about your parents?"

Does he know that the people I live with are agents? Danny thought.

"We'll say we're going on a study tour," Danny said. "They'll swallow that."

"If you're sure," Devoy said. "Now, for the next few days we'll be working on your new identities. In the meantime, are there any questions?"

"What does the Treaty Stone look like?" Vandra said.

"And how do we find it?" Dixie said.

"And steal it and carry it?" Danny said.

"Your questions are reasonable and I wish I could answer them, but the truth is I can't. The Stone is held in Morne, we know that for sure, and it will be protected. As to the rest, you'll have to find out by yourselves. Master Brunholm will give you all the information we have on Morne. Now. Go back to the Roosts and get a good night's sleep. From this moment on you are on alert for the crossing into the Upper World. The crossing is difficult at the moment, after the Seraphim incursion, and Fairman will not give us much notice when he decides to go."

The cadets were tired when they left the apothecary, but there was to be no rest. They got back to the Roosts at ten o'clock to find Toxique sitting on his bed moaning about blood and death and, down at the far end of the boys' Roosts, Smyck and Exspectre with satisfied grins on their faces.

"What happened?" Danny asked.

"Smyck," Les said with a moan. "He found out about Toxique and the family punishment and everything. He's threatening to tell Toxique's dad about the failed assassination attempt and blame it on Toxique. And to make it worse, Toxique's dad is coming to Wilsons tomorrow!"

"How did he find out?" Dixie said.

"It was my fault," Les said. "I left the beetles in my locker and forgot to lock it. Smyck took them and hid one under my bed. I was trying to make Toxique feel better about everything and Smyck heard it all!"

Danny swung around and looked at Smyck, who grinned and gave him a sarcastic thumbs-up. Danny strode toward him.

"Listen, Smyck," he said, "this is no joke. If Toxique's dad thinks he tried to assassinate someone and failed, then Toxique is in serious danger."

"Yeah, sure," Smyck said. "Toxiques, always going on about blood and death and stuff like that. I bet nothing will happen to him. Whoever heard of a family killing their own son?"

"Whoever heard of a family of assassins either?" Danny said. "You don't know what they might do."

"In that case," Smyck said, putting his face close to Danny's, "you'd better mind your manners, Caulfield, because the least squeak from all of you and I'm straight up to Toxique's old man to tell him how useless his son is."

"If you do that . . . ," Danny said, his fists clenched.

Smyck threw his head back and laughed. Danny knew he would have to be watched very carefully the following day.

After Danny got into bed he whispered across to Les.

"Les, we've got preparation for this mission tomorrow. Can you trail Smyck?"

"Course I can. Might mean missing a few classes, but I don't mind that!"

The following morning both Roosts were late for class. Blackpitt must have slept in, for he didn't wake them until half an hour later than usual. There was a chorus of displeasure directed at the unseen announcer, and he was snappish back.

"It's your responsibility to get up, my little chickens. I'm doing you a favor by calling you at all."

Danny and Les rushed off to Ravensdale for breakfast, snatching up cold toast and dried-out pieces of bacon, realizing with dread that their first class that morning was with Exshaw, who had been known to use lethal force against latecomers.

As the other students darted off to class, Blackpitt directed the mission team to Brunholm's quarters. There were startled and suspicious looks from the other students, who hadn't known about a mission. Les whispered a quick "Good luck" to his friends and took off at a run, dragging Toxique behind him by the hand.

Danny and Dixie climbed the stairs to Brunholm's quarters. They were in one of the oldest parts of the building. None of the dimly lit corridors were straight; mysterious doorways opened onto passages leading off to the side, disappearing into darkness. There were portraits of solemn men and women in black cloaks on the walls, some wearing masks or holding the edge of their cloak across their face to conceal their identity. As Danny and Dixie approached Brunholm's office, Danny noticed certificates on the wall, all belonging to Brunholm. A place known as the Institute of Advanced Surveillance was "pleased to note" that Brunholm had acquired a "distinction in miniature cameraship." There were awards for Advanced Concealment of Weapons and Intermediate Poisoncraft.

"Nice bunch of awards," Dixie said with a sniff as the passage grew darker, lit now only by flickering candles at great distances from each other. Finally they came to a door covered in quilted green leather. Above the door was a brass nameplate reading MARCUS BRUNHOLM, BRACS, TENS. Danny raised his hand to knock but the door swung open before he touched it.

"Very impressive," Dixie said. "It even creaked. I imagine we're supposed to be spooked out."

But Brunholm's parlor was spooky enough without ghostly creaking doors, Danny knew. He had sneaked into it with Les once before, and he recognized with a shiver the little jail cell where the siren Vicky had been held as part of one of Brunholm's schemes. The blowpipe and poison darts she had used were still on the wall, though now in a locked glass case.

"Kind of feels like Brunholm in here," Dixie said.

"I know what you mean," Danny agreed. The furnishings were dark and ornate with lots of velvets and leather. There were paintings of sickly-looking flowers and a smell of strong cologne.

"It's the kind of a room that if it was a person you wouldn't trust it, if you know what I'm saying," Dixie commented. Danny often couldn't follow Dixie's thought processes, but this time he nodded.

" 'Scuse me," Dixie said, patting her stomach. "That's what comes of bolting breakfast."

Danny hadn't heard the first sound, but it came again, a low moan.

"That wasn't me this time." Dixie looked around. "Where is Brunholm, anyway?"

Danny led the way to the corridor of teachers' bedrooms. Each shabby brown door had a nameplate.

"They all sleep here?" Dixie said.

"So they can keep an eye on each other, I expect," Danny said. "Here it is. . . ." They heard the moan from behind a door with MR. M. BRUNHOLM written on it. Danny knocked tentatively, then harder. The moaning got louder.

"We'd better go in," Danny said.

"Be careful . . . ," Dixie warned as Danny opened the door and put his head inside.

"Master Brun—" he began. In a tenth of a second his mind took in the scene. The floral wallpaper, the pink spread and the fluffy pillows plumped up on the bed. The cushioned headboard with a terrified Brunholm spread-eagled against it, frozen to the spot, his eyes fixed on something on the dressing table, the moaning coming from a mouth that he seemed unable or unwilling to open. Danny's gaze rested on the dressing table and the device that sat there, a silver machine about the size of a man's head with a horizontal bow on top, two silvery antennae springing from it. Instantly the antennae twitched and the whole apparatus swung toward him. He pulled his head back and slammed the door just as something struck it with terrible power.

Danny gasped, his heart racing. "What is that?"

Dixie was absently fingering what looked like the point of an arrow that had pierced the door from the other side. "By the look of this," she said, "it's a Crossbow of Exquisite Sensitivity."

Danny stared at her. "It's a what?"

"An automatic crossbow with a hair trigger. You set it

up and activate it. Once it detects the slightest movement from a target it fires a bolt at the source."

"That's why Brunholm was moaning," Danny said. "He didn't even dare open his mouth to call out."

"He's a dead man," Dixie said with an air of finality— and not much in the way of regret.

"We can't let him be killed by that thing," Danny said. "We need him for the mission."

"Is that all you need him for, Danny?" Dixie said, giving him a level look. Danny didn't meet her eyes. Brunholm was completely without scruples, sly and selfish. All the attributes you needed to be a truly successful spy. Part of Danny, the part he didn't like to acknowledge, had a sneaking admiration for Brunholm. And every time Brunholm betrayed somebody or let them down, Danny learned something.

"How many arrows does it have?" Danny asked.

"Lots," Dixie said. "Lots and lots."

"And how quickly does it move?"

"No you don't," Dixie said. "I'm not acting as a decoy for Brunholm."

"We need him, Dixie, whether you like it or not," Danny said, "and he will be grateful."

"Sure," Dixie said sarcastically, "he's always grateful and really nice about things."

Five minutes later Dixie pushed the door open and stood stock-still on the threshold. The crossbow's antennae twitched as though suspicious. Dixie winked at it. Almost faster than the eye could see, the crossbow whirled and fired an arrow straight at her. Dixie disappeared and re-appeared beside a leopard-skin dressing gown on a stand at the other side of the room just as the arrow struck and stood quivering in the doorframe.

"Every time she moves, you move," Danny shouted to the quivering Brunholm. Danny could see the interior of the room by looking at its reflection in the dressing-table mirror.

Dixie moved her hand and disappeared. The crossbow turned and fired, and Brunholm threw himself to the floor and edged a few desperate inches forward. Dixie's next move got him to the shelter of the bed, where he was able to crawl six feet without being detected by the crossbow. But in the meantime the machine appeared to have worked out what Dixie was doing. As she shuffled again and Brunholm gained a few more feet, the crossbow moved with incredible speed, so fast that Danny had to wait until Dixie had reappeared by the dressing table to see if she'd been hit or not. The next time she disappeared without moving at all, yet the crossbow was able to discharge a shot, as though it had read her mind. Brunholm was almost at the door. Dixie and Danny had agreed that her last reappearance would be at the wardrobe close to the door.

"Okay," Danny said to Brunholm, "one . . . two . . ." As he completed his countdown a thought flashed through his head. As the word *three* left his mouth, Danny grabbed a chair from the corridor and flung it into the air directly between the wardrobe and the crossbow. Three things happened very quickly: Dixie disappeared, Brunholm flung himself across the threshold, and the crossbow swung around and fired an arrow straight at the wardrobe where Dixie was about to appear!

Danny saw the next events as though they were happening in slow motion—Dixie appearing at the wardrobe, the arrow cleaving the air, its tip glittering. For a moment he thought all was lost, that the chair would fall too quickly. Dixie's mouth made an O as she realized what was happening; then the arrow struck the chair in one leg, carrying it away and slamming it against the wall. Quick as a flash Dixie disappeared and reappeared beside Danny, her breathing fast and shallow.

"It read my mind!" she gasped. "It knew where I was going to appear and it aimed for there!"

"Look at my chair," Brunholm growled. "Best Chinese lacquerwork on that chair."

"Don't say it," Danny murmured to Dixie. "Don't say it!"

Without a backward glance Brunholm strode toward the parlor, where he threw himself down in an armchair and, despite its being early, poured himself a large brandy from a decanter on the table.

"Did you see anyone in the corridor when you came up?" he demanded. They shook their heads. "Must have sneaked up on me when I was asleep. Damn cunning individual. I haven't seen a Crossbow of Exquisite Sensitivity in years. Blackpitt!" he shouted.

"Yes, Master Brunholm," the announcer said sweetly, "you called?"

"Get McGuinness up here at once," he said, "and inform Master Devoy that there's been another assassination attempt."

"Another one?" Blackpitt said. "How exciting!" Blackpitt loved gossip.

"Probably too late," Brunholm said. "I can't imagine this character leaving any clues behind."

They waited while Brunholm went off up the corridor and returned several minutes later fully dressed.

"Look!" Dixie said from the window. Danny went over and looked down. They were much higher up than he'd imagined, but Wilsons could deceive you like that. At the front door was a sleek black car, and beside it stood Devoy and another man.

"Wait," Danny said, digging in the pockets of his coat and producing a battered pair of binoculars. He focused on the man beside Devoy. He was wearing a suit and a black overcoat, his hair swept back. If you saw him in the street you wouldn't look twice, but Danny recognized the sallow skin and dark deep-set eyes.

"Toxique's dad," he said. "We have to keep Smyck away from him!"

"Why would that be?" a quiet voice said behind them. They turned to see the detective McGuinness.

"Detective," Brunholm said, "I am glad to see you, though if you were doing your job I wouldn't have been put through this ordeal."

"Ordeal?" McGuinness said.

"A Crossbow of Exquisite Sensitivity! In my bedroom!"

"Wait here," McGuinness said, striding off down the corridor. A few minutes later he was back with the crossbow in his hands.

"How did you do that?" Danny asked. McGuinness looked bleakly at the device.

"Its secrets are not easily uncovered. Many a good man has died learning all there is to know about the Crossbow of Exquisite Sensitivity."

He placed the device on a low coffee table. Danny stepped forward to look at it. The crossbow was beautifully made of silver metal with intricate springs and other mechanisms. When he touched it, he could almost feel its coiled power.

"Who made it?" Danny asked.

"It is very old," McGuinness said. "It was made by the Cherbs, who were great craftsmen."

"That's enough of that foul object," Brunholm broke in. "Have you seen what it did to my bedroom? I can't think where I will find silk wallpaper to match what it ruined, not to mention my chair."

Here he turned and gave Dixie a dirty look. McGuinness moved to Dixie's side.

"You're hurt," he said. Blood was oozing from beneath her blond hair, just above the ear.

"It's nothing," Dixie said. "That thing nearly got me with the second-last arrow. It was almost like it could hear me thinking!"

McGuinness parted Dixie's hair and examined the wound.

"Inside pocket, just above the left breast," he said to Danny without looking around. Danny fished in the pockets of his coat and brought out a battered tin with *Field Dressings* written on it in felt-tip pen. He opened it and handed it to McGuinness, who took out a tube of foul-smelling paste and smeared a little on Dixie's wound.

"Arrow was probably poisoned," Brunholm said. "Cherb weapons usually are."

"There was no poison used when that arrow was made," McGuinness said, finishing off with a plaster. "There now, but I wouldn't recommend any schoolwork for the rest of the day, and it would be better if Danny here kept her company, just in case of any adverse reaction." McGuinness didn't exactly wink at Danny, but there was the hint of a twinkle in his eye.

"Of course, of course," Brunholm said irritably, waving his hand at them before pouring himself another large brandy. "I couldn't possibly teach them anything today."

"Let's go," Danny whispered, "before he changes his mind." He turned to thank McGuinness, but the detective was already on his hands and knees in the corridor, examining the floor through a large magnifying glass.

"This way," Danny said quickly to Dixie. "I want to show you something."

He led his friend toward the front of the building. He wanted to show Dixie the room that he and Les had found when they had first come up to the master's quarters, simply as a curiosity, the way you would look at something gruesome in an old castle or museum. But as he stood in front of the nondescript door he felt a sudden reluctance. A sign read DEPARTMENT OF INFORMATION EXTRACTION.

"What is it?" Dixie asked.

"Nothing," Danny said. "We should go back."

"Don't be silly," Dixie said. "Let's have a look."

She took hold of the door handle and pushed. The door swung silently inward. Danny followed her.

"What is . . . all this stuff?" Dixie whispered. There were racks and thumbscrews and devices for making you think you were drowning. There were whips and manacles and strange, cruelly shaped metal devices. And in one corner was an iron maiden, a metal coffin in the shape of a human body, lined with iron spikes.

"It's a torture chamber," Danny said, unable to hide his own horror. For last time he had been here, the equipment had been dusty and covered with sheets. This time, the sheets were gone and the instruments of torture were oiled and gleaming.

"I don't think I like the look of this," Dixie said.

"Neither do I. Who would be preparing torture instruments? And why?"

9

A LOOPHOLE IN THE LAW

The following morning Danny and Dixie were summoned to Miss Duddy's room. Duddy taught Camouflage, Concealment and Deception, and she was breathless with excitement at the idea of preparing them for the Upper World.

"I have consulted widely with my colleagues as to what might be appropriate," she said, "and I have selected some classic disguises for you. Now, Danny, please try this on."

She produced a long blond wig, a caftan, a pair of bell-bottoms and a string of beads.

"I believe this look is known as the 'hippy,'" Duddy said, looking pleased with herself. Danny groaned inwardly.

"You will be almost invisible," Duddy went on. "You'll blend into any crowd."

Duddy handed Dixie a long Afghan coat, a flowery skirt and a headband. Dixie slipped on the coat and did a twirl.

"Vandra isn't here," Duddy said, "but I think I've picked out a look that will make her totally inconspicuous." Danny shook his head as Duddy took out a pink Mohawk wig, a torn T-shirt and a leather motorcycle jacket.

"This is the 'punk' look I believe is common in the Upper World," Duddy said. "I have some makeup to go with it. Her teeth will be part of the look."

Dixie grabbed the pink wig and stuck it on her head.

"Yes . . . ," Duddy said, "I do believe you can mix the two looks."

Danny shook his head. How would they stay undercover in the Upper World?

"These are only samples of the garments I have prepared," Duddy said. "You can look at the others later."

"We'll look at them now," Danny said firmly, picking out jeans and T-shirts for them all.

To be fair to Duddy, Danny thought afterward, she had provided useful aids for their mission. She gave them a selection of voice dyes—sprays that changed your voice to make it unrecognizable. She gave them a small packet of fake warts and boils. Dixie turned up her nose at them, but Duddy looked serious.

"A wart or a boil on your face draws attention away from the other features," she said. "Often a witness can only remember the gross feature."

There were hair dyes and artificial eyebrows and various items of makeup for the girls.

"Now, Danny," Duddy said when they were almost finished, "there is one important thing remaining—or rather two. Your eyes. Everyone will recognize and remember you unless we do something about them."

"I could wear dark glasses," Danny said.

"Not at night," Duddy said. "No, that is not satisfactory. There are semipermanent eyeball inks. They involve first removing the eyeball and rolling it in the ink . . ."

Danny gasped. "Er, maybe not."

"No," Duddy said, "it takes a good deal of time for the inflammation and swelling to go down. No, we'll have to go with a simple membrane."

"You mean like a contact lens," Danny said, relieved.

"I don't know what you're talking about, but if it's anything like a simple colored organic membrane placed over the lens of the eye, then you are right."

Duddy brought them into an empty classroom and sat them down. Her face was serious.

"This is a deadly mission you are embarking on," she said, "and I wish I could go with you to share my skills. But obviously I can't. So you must remember the important principles: Don't draw attention to yourself. Remember that things or people hidden in plain view are often the last to be discovered. Think stealth. Think concealment. The greatest of spies did not need disguises.

117

They knew how to direct attention away from themselves. The great Steff Pilkington could move undiscovered among a group of his closest colleagues, avoiding their attention by studying how they reacted to others. Keep it simple, keep it safe is my motto. Good luck!" Duddy shot to her feet, saluted smartly, then turned away, took a large handkerchief from her pocket and blew her nose loudly.

Dixie and Danny looked at each other. Dixie made a face but Danny was touched.

"Steady on, Miss," Dixie said. "We won't be setting out for a while."

"You never know," Duddy murmured. "Things happen quickly in the spy business."

Things did indeed happen quickly in the spy business. Ten miles away, on the road leading to Wilsons, a small black car took a bend at top speed, the rear end sliding out before the driver regained control. Behind it came a black jeep, swaying as it rounded the same corner, its powerful engine roaring as it gained on the smaller car.

The jeep was full of men, roughnecks and renegades from the nearby port of Tarnstone. They'd been sent to intercept the driver of the car at the docks as she disembarked from a ship from Grist, the great fortress of the Cherbs. She had given them the slip there, but they were gaining on her. She was taking risks with the small underpowered car and had almost crashed several times. But she had news that would not wait. She knew she must get through.

As the jeep neared behind her, she cursed her luck. For many years she had posed as a man and used the identity of John Cheryl, a trader, to get in and out of Grist. That identity had been compromised, but she had decided to use it one last time. Unfortunately, one of the agents of the Ring had recognized her on the ship. It had been a close thing to get out of Tarnstone, and now . . . Would she reach Wilsons?

Behind her the front of the jeep loomed over the rear of the small car. The jeep engine roared. It was going to ram! The woman spun the steering wheel to the left. The front of the jeep dealt a blow to the rear of her car and she fought to stay on the road. A piece of bodywork fell off and clattered on the pavement. At the same time there was a bang and she heard a thud as a bullet embedded itself somewhere in the car. Frantically she scanned the way ahead for help. There was nothing . . . except a small figure making its way nonchalantly along the side of the road. She recognized Vicky the siren, who was gazing with interest at the pursuit. Cheryl Orr leaned out the open window as she drew level.

"Vicky," she shouted, "anything you want if you get rid of them!"

"Anything?" Vicky shouted back.

"Anything!"

Bullets churned up the pavement beside her as a machine gun chattered. Steam poured from the car engine. Then another sound crept in, a voice almost unbearably sweet and sad, speaking, it seemed, of a heart broken by terrible sorrow yet capable of infinite love. Cheryl shredded some tissue and rammed it in her ears. She knew a siren's song when she heard it, its endlessly seductive tones, and she had already lifted her foot from the accelerator, the song drawing her back toward Vicky.

The jeep slowed before coming to rest with both front wheels in a ditch. The men got out, moving as if in a dream, smiles on their ugly faces as they turned toward the song of the little siren who stood in the middle of the road. She was beckoning to them with her hands, but her eyes were on Cheryl, reminding her that a promise made to a siren was not easily broken.

Cheryl shrugged. There would be time to deal with Vicky later. Right now she had to get her intelligence to Wilsons.

Two hours later she stood in Devoy's study, watching the master digest what she had told him.

"You are absolutely sure," Devoy said, "it's not some information that has been fed to you to further their own purposes?"

"I have been spying on the enemy for many years," Cheryl said stiffly. "I am aware of their ruses." She did not have to say that she had put her life on the line many times; Devoy acknowledged this with a graceful nod. There was the sound of feet on the stairs outside and Brunholm burst in.

"I have to presume you have heard of the disgraceful attempt on my life . . . ," he burst out before seeing Cheryl.

"Ah yes, the Crossbow of Exquisite Sensitivity," Devoy said. "I am glad to see you hale and hearty, Marcus."

"We really need to devise a strategy to protect key staff members from attack," he said, flinging himself down in an armchair, adding churlishly, "What's she doing here?"

"She has traveled in great peril from the fortress of Grist," Devoy said, "to bring us some alarming news."

"What?" Brunholm said, eyes narrowing.

"I'm afraid the Ring of Five has happened on the loophole in the treaty."

"They have picked a team of cadets, under-sixteens, to travel to the kingdom of Morne," Cheryl said. "Ostensibly to study, but of course their real aim is to steal and break the Treaty Stone."

"According to Cheryl," Devoy said, "the team has already departed. There isn't a moment to lose."

"Do we know who these agents are?" Brunholm asked.

"No," Cheryl said wearily, "I barely escaped with the information that I got."

"And grateful for that they are, aren't you, gentlemen?" A quiet voice spoke in the doorway. It was the detective McGuinness. He strode forward and took hold of Cheryl's arm, for the detective and the spy were husband and wife.

"She will come with me now," McGuinness said, pulling her to himself. "She's exhausted."

"And has earned whatever poor reward we can give her," Devoy said. "The information she has brought is priceless, and we are indeed grateful." Devoy bowed graciously as McGuinness and Cheryl withdrew. But the moment the door had closed behind them, Brunholm whirled round in a fury.

"How did they know that under-sixteens were exempt from the death sentence?"

"Longford is clever, cleverer and more ruthless than I," Devoy said. "There is a logic to it. In the bitterest of times there was always a door left open for education, that the young might learn from the mistakes of the past and make a better future."

"He seems to know everything that goes on in Wilsons," Brunholm snarled.

"He is a spy," Devoy said, "that's his job. In the meantime we must send our team straightaway. Tonight, if possible."

"They're not ready!" Brunholm cried. "Besides, the physick is still recovering."

"Then Danny and the girl must go," Devoy said. "Longford's team has a head start. Have you sent messages to Morne to expect our team?"

"Yes, of course," Brunholm said, "but what about Fairman—can he take them across?"

"Certainly," Devoy said. "Do you not think I know about your smuggling runs, and how you pay Fairman to do your dirty work? At this very moment he is waiting at the back of the building ready to embark on some mission that I am not supposed to know about!"

Brunholm looked abashed. Fairman's taxi was the only vehicle allowed to cross the border according to the terms of the treaty. Brunholm had his spies in the Upper

World, and he often used the taxi to carry messages for him.

"Now that we have the transport," Devoy said, "we should assemble our team."

Danny and Dixie were awakened by Blackpitt. "Cadet Caulfield! Cadet Cole! Library of the third landing in five minutes!"

Danny rolled out of bed and looked over the top of the partition that divided his sleeping quarters from Les's. The young Messenger was still asleep. Danny pulled on trousers, a sweater and his battered overcoat, then guiltily crept toward the door. He knew his friend would be wounded when he found that Danny had not woken him to tell him about the midnight call. Danny groaned inwardly. Would the impulse to betray never leave him?

He needn't have worried. Les had merely pretended to be asleep while Danny had crept out. He slid out of bed, shoving his pillows under his blankets in case Exspectre or one of the others was to look in his bed. Only one event would have led Devoy to summon Danny and Dixie in the middle of the night. The mission was on.

Thirty minutes later a very sleepy Danny and an over-excited Dixie were standing in the library of the third landing while Devoy briefed them on Cheryl's information.

Danny shivered. For some reason it was less frightening to take on adults than it was to take on people his own age.

"Can you tell us anything about the enemy team?" he asked Devoy.

"Nothing," Devoy said, "except that if they were chosen by Longford, they will be resourceful and dangerous."

"That's nice to know," Dixie said.

"Hurry," Brunholm broke in. "Fairman tells me that he brought students across the border from Grist twenty-four hours ago. A girl and a boy."

A flustered-looking Duddy burst into the room. She was wearing pink flannel pajamas and fluffy slippers.

"This is most unusual," she said, "most unusual!"

"You must work on Danny's eyes at once," Devoy said.

"But my lovely disguises!" Duddy cried.

"No time." Devoy's voice was like a pistol shot. "The fate of Wilsons hangs in the balance."

The detective McGuinness made a meal for Cheryl and waited until she had gone to bed before he left. She had told him what she had learned, and he knew that there would be activity until late at night in Wilsons. He crossed the gardens quietly and found a favorite vantage point in the shrubbery from which he could watch the building.

It was cold, but he hadn't long to wait before a figure

crept stealthily across the lawn. McGuinness reached into his pocket for a long-barreled revolver and set out in pursuit.

Five minutes later he found himself behind the school, outside a disused kitchen annex. There were half-collapsed wooden huts with old crates and scaffolding piled around them. Hidden in the debris stood a black taxi, the engine rumbling. The stealthy form made straight for the taxi and McGuinness set a course to head it off. There was a flash of tools; then the trunk of the cab opened silently. McGuinness, who had approached silently, put the gun to the side of the figure's head.

"Move a muscle and you won't see tomorrow," he said. A frightened face turned toward him. It was Les.

"Do you have any idea what Fairman would have done to you, if and when he found a stowaway?" McGuinness said. They were sitting on two old oil drums at a safe distance from the taxi.

"I want to go on the mission," Les said sulkily. "I pretended I don't care, but I do."

"Stop that," McGuinness said sharply. "You're not a child, and the fate of Wilsons, if not the Two Worlds, hangs in the balance."

"But I could help!" Les said.

"You can help more in Wilsons," McGuinness said. "Do you know that your friend Toxique is in danger? His father thinks that it was he who tried to kill the

Messenger Daisy and failed. Who will help clear him if you do not? And Vandra—would you leave her alone at Wilsons in a time of deadly peril? You are needed, Les. Let the others go to the Upper World. There will be enough danger here."

A TRAP SPRUNG

The membrane to disguise the color of Danny's eye was surprisingly comfortable, and now he had two brown eyes. When Duddy said it was made of "fish intestine marinated in cuttlefish ink," Dixie had made a face and mimed throwing up in the corner.

"There is only one thing that you have to remember," Duddy had said. "You absolutely must not cry. The concentrated salt in the tears will dissolve the membrane."

"Don't forget," Devoy said now. "You are exchange students. I wish we had more information on the kingdom of Morne to give you, but all I can say is that it was known as a place of intrigue and danger, although there are dire warnings in the treaty that students should be looked after. There is some protection in that."

Danny and Dixie were given an hour to put their bags

together. They raced back to the Roosts. All the other pupils were asleep. After Danny grabbed his toothbrush he went to Les's cubicle to find the bed empty, pillows under the blankets.

That's odd, he thought.

"Perhaps he's gone to the apothecary to see Vandra," Dixie said when Danny met her outside.

"We've just got time to get there," he said. "I want to see her before we go." They raced off.

Les knew that Danny and Dixie would not leave for their mission without seeing Vandra, so when he left McGuinness he made his way to the apothecary. It was dark and spooky as he mounted the stairs. In the anteroom he could see the dim shapes of organs and other anatomical specimens preserved in jars. Above his head the vast skeleton of a Messenger, hung from wires as though in flight, cast a sinister shadow on the tiled floor. Les moved quietly, lost in thought, considering the detective's advice. Ever since he'd heard that the others were to be sent on a mission, Les had plotted and planned and listened at doors, knowing that Fairman was the only way they could cross the border and figuring out how he would climb into the trunk and appear triumphantly when they had arrived in the Upper World. That wasn't going to happen now, he thought bitterly. He would never get the chance to see the Upper World.

He was so lost in thought that he forgot to turn on the light when he got to the ward where Vandra was sleeping.

The Messenger was light-footed and made little noise as he crossed the floor. At the last minute he saw the figure crouched over Vandra, knife in hand. Les threw himself aside as a knife flashed in the darkness. He hit the flagstone floor hard and felt the air being forced from his lungs. He was winded, helpless, his lungs on fire as his attacker fled into the night.

As he gradually got his breath and attempted to sit up, he caught a fleeting hint of a scent, an expensive aftershave perhaps, hanging in the air. He forced himself to his feet and stumbled over to Vandra's bed. She was still sleeping peacefully. He bent to pick up the pillow that the attacker had dropped. It had a strong medicinal smell, and the minute he bent to it his head began to swim. He staggered backward, into the arms of the apothecary, Mr. Jamshid. The small man, wearing heavy glasses and a white coat stained with nameless matter, caught Les with one hand and the pillow with the other. A frown wrinkled his large domed forehead and he flung the pillow with great force across the room and into the embers of the fire. The fire blazed, huge flames and great gouts of black and dirty green smoke billowing up the chimney.

"Psychochloroform," the small man spat. "Deadly in twenty seconds. The victim never wakes up. Give me one reason why I should not slit your throat here and now!"

"It . . . it . . . wasn't me," Les gasped. "Someone was holding it over Vandra's face!"

"Is that so?" Jamshid said. "It's a long time since I dissected the corpse of a Messenger. . . ."

129

"I'm sure!" Danny's voice rang out. "Les would never hurt Vandra."

"If you insist," Jamshid said coldly, releasing Les.

Dixie appeared between Jamshid and Les, pressed close to the apothecary, at eye level with the larger stains on his coat.

"Interesting," she said, studying something green and globular adhering to his lapel.

"What happened?" Danny demanded. Les quickly explained what he'd seen.

"Death is stalking this place," Jamshid said darkly. As if to underline his words, a raven fluttered across the light and disappeared into the shadows of the roof space.

"Whoever did this must know Wilsons like the back of their hand," Danny said. "They're able to get about without being seen."

"Why Vandra?" Les said.

"Well, I don't know about you, but if I was planning to poison one or more people in Wilsons," Danny said, "I'd make sure the only physick in the place who could cure them was out of the way."

Danny realized that his voice had taken on an edge and the others were looking at him strangely. There was a harsh, almost eager tone, as though he relished the wickedness of the plan.

"We—we have to stop him, I mean," he stammered. Dixie looked at Danny with one eyebrow raised.

"I'm sorry, Les," he said. "I tried to leave without you noticing. I should have told you we were going on the mission—it's been brought forward."

"That's all right," Les said. "I was going to sneak along with you, only McGuinness caught me. He reminded me that Toxique and Vandra need to be looked after, and he's right."

Dixie hugged him. Les grinned at Danny.

"You take care of him, Dixie," Les said. "He thinks he's the most cunning of the lot, but I know different."

Les looked suspiciously like he was going to give Danny a hug, but to Danny's relief, Blackpitt interrupted.

"Caulfield, Cole. At once!"

Danny looked down at Vandra. She looked so young and vulnerable. Without really knowing what he was doing, he took the gold ring out of his pocket, the "S" and "G" ring that the Unquiet had given him, and slipped it onto her finger.

"Look after her," he whispered, not knowing whether he spoke to the Unquiet or some other being. With a last glance at her face, he turned to Dixie.

"Let's go," he said.

Les and Jamshid stood looking after them.

"Hope they make it," Les said.

"You think they won't?" the apothecary said anxiously. "I couldn't bear it if Caulfield was killed somewhere else. He's a very promising specimen—I very much looked forward to dissecting his corpse." Jamshid turned to face Les. "Don't look at me like that, young Messenger. They say he is the Fifth. Is it not likely in these turbulent times that many people will wish him dead? All I want is the chance to use my knives on him in the interests of science, if he should be assassinated. . . ."

Les gave him a disgusted look and hurried from the room. Things were bad enough already without all this talk of assassination. He would spend the night in the summerhouse, his refuge when he didn't want to talk to anyone. He went outside and turned left at the shrubbery.

At least everyone else is asleep, he thought as he followed the path toward the summerhouse, yawning as he went.

But not everyone was tucked up in bed. The door of the boys' Roosts opened without a sound and a figure in a trench coat slipped in, closing the door behind him. The fire in the stove had almost gone out and the room was dark, but the tall man moved catlike down the center of the room. He stopped at the cubicle where Les slept and drew a gun equipped with a bulbous silencer from his shoulder holster. He aimed and squeezed the trigger three times, each shot sounding like a muffled cough. Three small holes appeared in the blanket at chest height. Then the Unknown Spy slipped quietly from the room. He might have forgotten his own name, but he had forgotten none of his skills. His wife's murder had been avenged.

Danny and Dixie waited with Devoy. The taxi drove out from behind the pile of debris.

"I sent you out once before," Devoy said, "withholding much of what I knew about what you were facing.

This is different. No one now lives who knows much of the kingdom of Morne. We do know that the kingdom is always hidden by extreme weather, so look for great storms, floods and other natural phenomena. Protect the Treaty Stone if you can, steal it if you must, but do not let it be broken!"

The taxi rattled to a stop. Devoy opened the back door. Danny and Dixie threw their bags in and climbed in after.

"I have told Fairman to bring you to your house," Devoy said to Danny. "At least you know the territory there. After that you're on your own."

Danny was torn. The people he had known as his parents had cheated him, yet one part of him longed to see them, while another part longed for revenge.

"Go with care," Devoy cried, "go like shadows in the night, go like spies."

Dirty smoke billowing from the exhaust, the cab trundled off into the night, merging with the darkness.

Many miles away in the fortress of Grist, deep in the Lower World, Ambrose Longford reached for a decanter and poured another glass of honey-colored dessert wine for Nurse Flanagan. The remains of a meal sat on the table in front of them. Longford lit a cigar from the candelabra on the table.

"Is the trap set?" Nurse Flanagan inquired languidly.

"I believe so."

"Conal was a fool, sending Seraphim to attack the boy's house," Nurse Flanagan said. "Everything could have been lost."

"Perhaps," Longford said, "but it keeps the Cherbs in line—this failure has shown them that brute force is not the way."

"No," Nurse Flanagan said, raising her glass, "your way is always best, Ambrose—subtle and devious."

"A compliment indeed," Longford said, raising his own glass in return.

"We shall have the boy this time," Nurse Flanagan said, "and the treaty will be broken."

"Even though I say so myself," Longford said, puffing on his cigar, "it is an excellent idea."

11

MACARI'S ORIGINAL! REALLY NOURISHING AND EXCELLENT!

The taxi hurtled through the night, swaying from side to side. Dixie tried to engage Fairman in conversation but gave up after ten minutes of nothing but grunts from the cabdriver.

"Where are we?" Dixie peered through the glass into the darkness beyond.

"I think they're called the Darklands," Danny said. He knew the journey would be long and uncomfortable, so he wedged himself into a corner and tried to doze. In a few hours he'd be back home. Dangerous as Wilsons was becoming, he began to long for its shadowy halls.

"I like adventures," Dixie said, "do you like adventures? I think they're the best thing in the whole world."

"Put a sock in it, Dixie," Danny said. "I know you're excited, but there's a limit."

On and on the journey went, the back of the ancient cab getting colder as the night wore on. Danny was warm in his trench coat, but he could see his breath in the air, and Dixie's lips were turning blue. He took the coat off and spread it over both of them.

"That's cozy," Dixie said. "Do I get a story?"

"I don't have any good stories," Danny said shortly. Suddenly Dixie sat bolt upright.

"You are going to Morne as a student of the Lower World, aren't you?"

"Yes."

"But they forgot to tell me what I'm supposed to be a student of!"

"You'll think of something," Danny said. Dixie stared out the window, frowning.

"I know," she said. "I'll be a student of the Upper World. Tell me about it!"

So Danny told her about everything he could think of, including cars and planes, cell phones and televisions. Dixie's eyes grew wider and wider, her expression more and more childlike. As he told her about tanks and war-planes and atom bombs, her hand crept out from under the coat and took his.

"Do people in your world really do such terrible things?" she asked. "Please don't tell me any more."

In a moment she was asleep. It took Danny a lot longer, but in the end he too was lulled by the endless motion of the cab.

* * *

They were awakened with a jolt and thrown forward so that they slid off the seat and onto the floor.

"What . . . ?" Danny cried as his head slipped into the foul-smelling space under the seats, Dixie on top of him. Daylight and cold air flooded in as the door was opened. With a groan Danny straightened and crawled from the cab, Dixie tumbling out behind him. He raised his head and found himself staring at the front of his house, or at least something that resembled his house. The front was scorched, the brickwork hacked as if by tearing claws. Slates had been blasted from the roof. The snow was still deep.

There was a thud as their bags hit the ground. It was the first time Dixie had seen the dark caverns that were Fairman's eyes, and she flinched. Fairman bared his great yellow teeth.

"You're here," he growled. He clambered back into the cab and sped off, the car soon becoming a tiny spot in the distance.

"Doesn't look like there's anyone here," Dixie said, and Danny felt a chill.

"Look," Dixie said, reaching up and taking down a huge feather stuck in a crack of the wall. She smelled it and shivered. "Seraphim?" she said.

"Conal," Danny replied.

Cautiously they stepped through the wreckage and into the main body of the house. Leaves blew along the corridors, and signs of the Seraphim's attack were

137

everywhere, for they had smashed things wantonly as they went.

Danny and Dixie had just reached the front hallway when a familiar voice rang out.

"Stop right there or you're dead."

"It's me," Danny said. "It's me, Danny!" He almost added "Mum" to the sentence, and felt sadness wash over him. He was shaken out of his sorrow by a loud crack. A splinter of wood flew from the doorframe beside him and scored his cheek.

"Hit the deck!" Dixie yelled. "She means it."

Danny dived for cover as another shot whistled over his head.

"It's me, Danny!" he shouted again.

"It's enough that he's disappeared without being taunted about it," Agent Pearl cried. Danny lifted his head and saw his mother in the door of the downstairs bedroom. Her face was gaunt; the cool poised woman he remembered was gone.

"It's me!" Danny insisted. She did not lower her gun. Danny raised his head.

"Danny, don't!" Dixie warned. But he slowly stood up, his eyes on the barrel of the gun.

"It looks like Danny," the woman said to herself, "but the eyes . . ."

"It's a trick," he said, "look." He bowed his head and let the membrane fall into his hand.

"Danny . . . ," the woman breathed. She dropped the gun and ran forward, and for a moment it was as if they were truly mother and son.

* * *

Fifteen minutes later they were sitting on a scorched sofa in front of a fire they had made from broken-up dining room chairs. Dixie had found a saucepan and was busy boiling water for tea over the fire while Agent Pearl told them what had happened since Danny had left. Dixie and Danny glanced at each other when they heard about the attack by the Seraphim and how they'd been repulsed by the ravens. Agent Stone's wound had gotten worse. For days he had hovered between life and death while Pearl tended to him. When he slept, she guarded the house, dreading the return of the Seraphim.

Now, she said, he was weak but recovering.

"He sleeps for most of the day, but he'll be so glad to see you, Danny."

Danny looked away. Part of him wanted to put his arms around her; part of him wanted to wound her, to repay betrayal with betrayal.

"But there are other things to talk about," Pearl said. Danny glanced sharply at her. "We have had no communication from the outside world. We used to be asked regularly for written reports on you, Danny, but we have heard nothing recently. The radio speaks of a big freeze. The schools and airports are closed. They are even saying that the sea is turning to ice in places. We have to do something."

"It's a pity you have to wait to hear from your handlers so that you know what to do with me."

"I didn't mean that," Pearl said, "I meant that there

139

could be even more danger here for you, for all of us. I wish I had more information so I could protect you."

Dixie's eyes flickered from Danny to Agent Pearl, her face serious for once.

"You should listen, Danny," she said. Danny's eyes flashed.

"The mass of cold air seems to be centered in the mountains about twenty miles north of here," Pearl said.

"Then that's where we need to be," Danny said. "That will be where Morne is located."

"Is that where the Fifth needs to be?" another voice added. Danny stood up and spun around. Agent Stone stood in the doorway. His shoulder was heavily bandaged and his face was the color of parchment, but his voice was strong.

"What do you know of the Fifth, and the . . ." Danny stopped.

"The Lower World? Only a little—what I could find in old books and manuscripts. Most of the writers couldn't accept that such a world existed in tandem with ours. Sometimes it seemed like a dream, even to me."

Stone shuffled farther into the room, grimacing. "Then I saw them! Those wonderful Seraphim! So much more dramatic than they ever looked in the old paintings."

"They don't smell too wonderful close up," Dixie said.

"Allow me to introduce you, Dixie," Danny said sarcastically. "This is the man who pretended to be my father."

"I don't blame you for being bitter, Danny," Stone said, moving into the circle of the fire, "but the truth is we did come to think of you as our own."

"When you were here," Danny said.

"Your fa—Agent Stone spent all his time in old libraries and research centers trying to find out who or what you are," Pearl said.

"And Pearl spent weary days and nights protecting you, seeking to learn about those who gave us the mission of looking after you, and why. Do not judge things you don't know about, Danny."

Danny wanted to reply, but a small cold voice told him not to. *There will be time to show them what you know and don't know.*

"Anyway, Danny," Stone went on after a moment, "I had started to disbelieve the whole idea of the Lower World, when I saw the Seraphim and knew my theory was correct. There *is* a Ring of Five and there *is* a Fifth!"

Danny looked at him. How much more did this man know about him?

Suddenly Pearl held up her hand for silence. They all listened. In the distance was the faint hum of an engine. Pearl went to the window and peered out.

"I spoke too soon about not having contact with our handlers," she said. "They're coming for us."

"Are you sure?"

"There's no other reason for cars to be on this road."

"Whatever happens," Stone said heavily, "they mustn't find Danny."

Danny went to the window and looked out. Two jeeps were speeding down the snowy road. Both carried hard-faced men with guns.

"I'll hold them off," Pearl said. "There's a Land Rover in the garage. Can either of you drive?"

"I can," Dixie said to Danny's surprise, "but we're not leaving you behind."

"Don't be stupid," Pearl said. "What can you do against them?"

In answer Dixie disappeared and reappeared at the other side of the room. Pearl blinked, but Stone muttered to himself.

"The Quality of Indeterminate Location. Staggering."

"It won't stop a bullet," Pearl said. "Get going."

Danny hesitated. There was so much more he wanted to know, but Dixie was pulling at his sleeve. "The treaty is more important."

Danny watched Pearl take up a firing position by the window, Stone struggling painfully to join her. Abandon them and they'll die, he thought.

Exactly! The word came from another part of his brain.

"Okay," he said to Dixie, "come on." And without a glance back he ran out the door. Dixie hesitated, then followed. Pearl was looking at her.

"One day he'll understand," Pearl said sadly. "Look after him."

* * *

142

As Dixie and Danny ran for the garage, they heard gunfire behind them.

"Come on!" Danny said, "leave them to it. It's what they deserve!"

"They're giving you a chance to get away. Be grateful," Dixie said, panting as she struggled to open the garage door.

"They're giving me a chance to put myself in even more danger," Danny snarled. "I don't have to thank them for that!" He looked as if the harsh Cherb part of his nature had taken over.

They wrenched open the doors of the Land Rover as a line of bullets stitched up the snow beside them.

"Quick!" Dixie scrambled into the driver's seat and looked blankly at the controls. "It looks different!"

Danny leaned over and turned the key. The engine caught as wood splinters cascaded from the walls of the shed, torn by bullets. The engine roared to life.

"We can't get out the front . . . ," Danny said, but that wasn't to be a problem. Dixie pulled at the gear lever and stomped on the gas pedal and the Land Rover zoomed backward. With a great rending noise the back of the garage collapsed and the vehicle shot out into the snow. Dixie pulled at the gear lever again. With a gout of black smoke from the exhaust, the Land Rover leapt forward. More bullets struck the garage and flames started to lick at it. Dixie gunned the engine and the tires dug into the ice on the road. Lurching at first, then building up speed, the vehicle pulled away from the house.

Looking back, Danny could see orange muzzle flashes until black smoke from the burning garage obscured the battle.

Dixie knew how to point the Land Rover in the right direction and put her feet on the pedals, but she didn't know anything else. She gripped the wheel determinedly, oblivious to signs, and Danny was glad there was no other traffic on the road. They ate up the miles. Danny forced himself to think about what might be waiting ahead.

"Stupid," Dixie said.

"What?"

"Not you. Me. We don't know where we're going but I have the Globe, the GIPEP, in my bag. Take it out!"

Danny took the glass globe from her bag. Instantly two tiny figures appeared on it, moving side by side as they were.

"I wonder . . . ," Danny said.

"Wonder? Of course you do. We all wonder what's going on," Dixie said.

"That isn't what I meant," Danny said. He held the Globe up and spoke into it.

"The kingdom of Morne!" he said. For a moment nothing happened; then the Globe darkened as though a tiny storm was blowing through it. When it cleared Danny could see the two figures again, and in front of them a tiny castle. Morne!

"Up there," Danny said, pointing into the distance, where the peaks of a mountain range were obscured by sullen snow cloud. "That must be it!"

A few minutes later they met their first car, crawling

through the snow. Dixie waved vigorously at its driver—so vigorously that the Land Rover brushed against a lamppost.

"Keep your eyes on the road, Dixie," Danny said.

"I am," she said happily, bumping over a sidewalk and narrowly missing a mailbox. They were in the suburbs of a small town now, and the next hour was a nightmare as Dixie drove through red lights and veered onto sidewalks. When she spotted a playground, she drove straight through it, waving happily at the small band of bemused children who had braved the weather. Danny was convinced that he and Dixie would have been arrested if it wasn't for the fact that the police had more to do than worry about terrible driving. Blizzards and fallen power lines had resulted in an evacuation of the area at the foot of the mountains, and housing had to be found for all the people. The police were busy dealing with the shelters that had sprung up in the town center. Danny struggled to stop Dixie being distracted by flashing shop signs and phone boxes—all normal things to him, but things Dixie had never seen before. Nor did she see the police barrier at the edge of town warning of the dangers of the snowy roads ahead. The front bumper of the Land Rover caught the barrier and crashed straight over it.

"Now the front is as battered as the back," Dixie said with a dizzy grin. As they passed a sign saying NEWCASTLE 10, she gunned the Land Rover toward the evacuated town.

* * *

Newcastle lay between the sea and the mountains. It looked like a seaside resort that had fallen onto hard times. There were closed amusement parks on the boardwalk, and a frozen pond with half-sunk boats stuck in the ice. The sea had started to freeze, and chunks of ice washed back and forth in the sullen waves. There were small cafes and pizza restaurants, but they were all closed, some of them derelict. The Land Rover came to a halt, jammed against a telephone box, and they got out.

"This looks like a fun sort of a place," Dixie said. Danny said nothing. The Globe in his hand was pointing unwaveringly toward the cruel-looking snowy mountains. It was nearly dark, but could they afford to wait another night? The Treaty Stone might already be lying in pieces, the forces of the Ring streaming across the border to the Upper World. Dixie followed Danny's eyes.

"If you're thinking of tackling the mountain," she said, "I'm not doing it on an empty stomach."

Danny realized that they hadn't eaten all day. His stomach was beginning to rumble.

"Look," Dixie said. At the end of the street, a neon sign winked on and off: MACARI'S ORIGINAL! REALLY NOURISHING AND EXCELLENT!

"Someone wasn't evacuated," Danny said.

The smell of frying fish and chips reached their nostrils as they approached. Dixie was so hungry that she disappeared and reappeared right outside the door of the restaurant.

"Don't do that, Dixie," Danny said. When he got to

her she had her nose pressed up against the menu in the window.

"Starving . . . ," she said, vanishing and reappearing just inside the door. Danny groaned inwardly. If, as Pearl had said, the Ring had agents in the Upper World, then Dixie might as well have been carrying a sign to say who she and Danny were. He pushed the door open.

It was an ordinary chip shop. There was a counter with a fryer behind it, a jukebox in the corner and a few wooden tables and chairs. The aroma of frying fish filled the air. Yet Dixie wasn't paying any attention to the smell. She was staring, awestruck, in the direction of the counter.

"What's wrong?" Danny whispered, glancing nervously at the entrance to the kitchen, where he could see a man slicing potatoes.

"That . . . that!" Dixie breathed, and nodded to a television on the wall behind the counter. "What is it?"

"That? A television. Don't you remember? I told you about it. It's showing the news."

"There are people inside. . . . No . . . don't be silly, Dixie. . . . Are they real or are they moving paintings? Look. A river!"

"They're real people, Dixie. You just point a camera at them and put it on film, then the TV people send a signal through the air. . . ."

Dixie looked as if she only half believed him. Danny smiled inwardly. It *did* sound a bit unlikely when you thought about it. Dixie's mouth made a perfect O as she gazed at an aerial shot of a snow-clogged motorway.

Danny delved into his pocket and came out with a fistful of notes. Better buy some food quick, he thought, and get out of here before Dixie disappears and reappears in the fish fryer. He could see the snow-covered mountains through a side window. They would have to go on foot, he thought; the snow was too deep for the Land Rover.

There was a cough. Danny looked around to see the proprietor standing at the counter. He was a small swarthy man with a neat mustache. One eyebrow was raised, and he had a half smile on his face, as if there was something amusing in the sight of two hungry strangers.

"Er, could we have two fish suppers, please?" Danny asked.

"Certainly, certainly." The man had a foreign accent— Italian, perhaps, Danny thought. Two pieces of cod were slipped into the hot oil.

"Look, Danny," Dixie said breathlessly. "It's here!"

Danny followed her eyes to the television set. The screen was indeed showing an aerial view of the town and the mountains beyond. The news announcer was relating how, after weeks of cold weather, an evacuation plan had to be carried out for towns at the foot of the mountains as food and fuel ran short.

That's odd, Danny thought again. Why would a chip shop be open if the population has been evacuated? He turned back to the counter to question the owner and found himself staring at a large and extremely deadly-looking crossbow in the hands of a now-unsmiling shop owner.

"So," the man said softly, "what are the boy and the disappearing lady doing in the evacuated town?"

"Whoops," Dixie said.

"We came back," Danny said, with as much confidence as he could muster. "We left Dixie's auntie behind in the rush. We were afraid that she would be frozen. She has no food." He was amazed how the lie slipped off his tongue, even with an arrow pointed at his heart.

"She's not very well," Dixie added, with an expression of wide-eyed innocence. "She's kind of forgetful and she's very fond of cats—"

"And we have to find her," Danny cut in, stopping Dixie's flow of information about her imaginary aunt.

"I see," the man said. "And where does this aunt live?"

"Up there," Dixie said, pointing toward the mountains, "right up near the top."

The man smiled, but the smile did not touch his eyes.

"A lonely place for an old lady, no?"

"She's very independent," Dixie said. The man slipped out from behind the counter, keeping the crossbow fixed on Danny. He locked the door and turned the sign so that it read CLOSED.

"Now it is time to learn the truth," he said grimly, beckoning them into the back room with the crossbow. Unlike the warm front part of the shop, there was nothing cozy about the back. The walls were damp cold stone and the floor was earth; it felt and looked like a dungeon. A dark passage led off from the back.

"Now," the man went on, glowering, "we have places

for to put snoopers and sneaks like you two. And there are ways to get truth from you as well. Many good ways." He seized Dixie's wrists and secured them to a set of manacles on the wall. He did the same with Danny.

"Try to disappear now!" He opened a rough wooden cupboard and removed two long steel implements, each with a small horseshoe at the end.

"We haven't done anything to you," Danny said. "Let us go!"

"Like hell I let you go," the small man said. "I find truth."

Danny watched as the man took the steel implements into the front of the shop, where the fish was still sizzling in the hot oil of the fryer. He thrust the rods into the fire beneath the oil.

"What's he doing?" Dixie whispered.

"I think I know," Danny said, "and I don't like it." He twisted in his manacles. There was a gun in one of his inside pockets if he could reach it, but the fetters held firm.

"I should be able to disappear out of these," Dixie said, "but the metal is stopping me. I don't understand how. Who is he, anyway, and what does he want? Is he part of the Ring or something?"

The man took the rods out of the fire and examined them. The ends were glowing a dull orange. He thrust them in again.

"Danny, he isn't going to . . . brand us with those things, is he?" There was a note of terror in her voice. She was a free spirit, not made to be tied. Danny too could feel

150

cold fear in his heart. He made himself clear his mind. There had to be a way out. He called to the man.

"You don't have to torture us—we'll tell you the truth!"

"Sorry," the man said, coming back in and looking genuinely remorseful. "You see, torturers never believe the first thing they're told. Our victims always hold something back, even if they don't mean to, so I'll have to give you a little tickle with the hot irons at some point anyway. You might as well save it for then." He headed out to the front again.

Dixie gulped. Use you brain, Danny told himself; use your cunning.

"Dixie," he said quickly, "did you notice anything funny about this place, something just not right when we were coming in?"

She shook her head. In the front of the shop, the swarthy man checked the irons. They were almost white-hot. He spat on one, and the spit sizzled and evaporated before the irons were thrust back into the heat.

"Have to think . . . ," Danny muttered. There had been something that didn't quite fit. He closed his eyes and tried to recall how the front of the chip shop had looked. The peeling paint, the grease-stained menu in the window. The neon sign . . .

"What did the sign say?" he demanded. "The chip shop sign?"

"I don't remember," Dixie moaned. "Do something, Danny!"

Macari took the irons from the fire and looked them

over. They were now white-hot. He touched one carefully to the hairs on his forearm. The smell of burning hair filled the shop. Dixie had her eyes shut tight and was shaking like a leaf. Danny scanned the shop desperately. No weapon within reach. He looked over the approaching Macari's shoulder toward the street, hoping against hope that he could call out to a passerby. But all he could see was the neon sign blinking on and off. MACARI'S ORIGINAL! REALLY NOURISHING AND EXCELLENT! It was an odd thing for a sign to say. It didn't even make a lot of sense. Really Nourishing and Excellent . . .

"Morne!" Danny shouted. "It's Morne!"

"What are you talking about?" Dixie cried.

"It's Morne!" Danny said. "Macari's Original Really Nourishing and Excellent. 'M-O-R-N-E.' Morne!"

"Have you gone completely daft?" Dixie said, but Macari had paused, the two brands still in his hand.

"What do you know about Morne?" he demanded.

"We're students," Danny said, "sent from the Lower World. Under the terms of the treaty!"

"Are you sure?" Macari peered at them suspiciously. The smell of hot metal from the branding irons reached Danny's nostrils.

"Absolutely sure!" Danny said.

"Certain," Dixie added.

"I'll have to check the book," Macari grumbled. He shoved the irons back into the fire and took a well-thumbed book from under the counter.

"Who sent you?" he demanded.

"Er, Master Devoy," Danny replied, hoping he'd chosen to say the right thing.

"Devoy . . . Devoy . . ." Macari flipped through the book. "Ah. Here. 'Two souls for instruction.' Your names?"

"Danny Caulfield."

"Dixie Cole."

"Of course, of course. I'll have to have a word with the court about this. What a way to treat visiting students!"

Macari hurried to unlock their shackles, closing the door to the front room with his foot as he did so, so that they could no longer see the branding irons.

"Once the others came through, I thought that was the end of the students."

Others? Dixie and Danny glanced at each other as they rubbed at the painful welts left by the shackles.

"What is this place?" Danny asked.

"The gateway to Morne," Macari said. "Welcome, young students!"

His eyes were twinkling now, but Danny was cautious.

"The kingdom travels to various locations," Macari said, folding his hands and reciting as if from a guidebook, "hidden by the weather—sometimes a sandstorm in the sun-baked desert, sometimes a typhoon in the storm-tossed ocean. The kingdom is always on the move, always watchful, for it is the guardian of the peace between the Two Worlds."

"But we thought the kingdom was in the mountains," Dixie said.

"It is. The passage behind you leads to it. We always have a disguised entrance to Morne. Makes things much easier. We just close up the chip shop when the kingdom is elsewhere. But enough talking, my young friends! You must be tired and hungry after your journey. Eat, and then let me take you to Morne!"

Macari swiftly filled two paper bags with fish and chips, then gave a great bow, sweeping out his right hand to show that Danny and Dixie should go first into the passage. With an edgy glance at each other and a nervy disappearance by Dixie from one side of the tunnel to the other, they set out for the kingdom of Morne.

ASSASSINS

The college was in an uproar the following morning. After the Unknown Spy had, as he thought, killed Les, he wandered through the shrubberies until he met McGuinness. He handed his gun to McGuinness and said mildly, "I believe I have killed someone. Perhaps you would take me into custody."

McGuinness had escorted the Unknown Spy to the Roosts and seen immediately that he hadn't killed anyone, merely ruined a good pillow. But not before both Roosts were wide awake and rife with rumor and speculation. The Unknown Spy had repeated his belief that Les had killed his wife, but Smyck immediately took Danny's disappearance during the night as a sign of guilt.

"Maybe Caulfield tried to kill you."

"Don't be daft," Les said.

155

"Well, why'd he run away, then?" demanded Orelia Detestes, a particularly nosey cadet with bright brown darting eyes. Les always said that if you added whiskers, she would make a particularly obnoxious rat.

Les was too shaken to eat breakfast and instead went to see Vandra before class. She was sleeping, and Les did not wake her. He looked out the window. The long black car that had brought Toxique's father was still parked at the front of the building. When Les arrived late for geography class he saw that Toxique was missing. Les assumed his friend had been called to see his father, but when the class ended he found Valant waiting outside.

"Master Devoy wishes to know if you have seen young Toxique," he said.

"No," Les said. "Isn't he with his father?" Valant shook his head.

When classes finished for lunch, Les slipped away—but not before Exspectre stopped him.

"You seem to be losing your friends," the pale boy said. "A bit careless of you."

"At least I've got some friends to lose," Les said, but Exspectre's comment hit home. It was a bit strange with Vandra ill, Danny and Dixie gone to Morne and now Toxique not in class. At least I know where to find him, Les thought as he made his way through the shrubberies, careful not to catch his wings on a branch.

His instinct was accurate. Toxique was sitting in the old summerhouse, moodily feeding crumbs to a column of black ants.

"No poison in that bread, then, Toxique?" Les said.

156

"No," Toxique said, "that's the problem. A real Toxique would be working out all sorts of new ways to poison ants. I just don't feel the need."

"Valant was looking for you."

"My father put him up to it, I suppose," Toxique said
despairingly, "but I can't face him. For a start, I didn't try
to kill the Messenger with the poison dart, but I can't
admit that I haven't even tried to assassinate anyone—
and if I say that I did do it, that's even worse!"

"Then we've got to prove that you didn't fire the
dart," Les said firmly. "After that we'll worry about your
assassination record."

"What about my father?"

"Maybe he's not that mad at you," Les said.

"How do I find out without facing him?" Toxique
said, dread in his voice.

"How about we try a little spying?"

Toxique stood up. Les slapped him on the back.
"That's better," he said.

"You're about to get bitten by the ant you just sat on,"
Toxique said absentmindedly.

"Ouch! That hurt," Les said, rubbing the bite.
"Come on. We'll show your father there's more to a Toxique than assassinating people."

Les guessed that Toxique's father would be in the
room that Devoy favored—the library of the third landing. They were forbidden to enter it upon pain of an
Eighth Regulation offense, but Les had a plan. He dived
under the summerhouse and came back up with a worn-
looking leather attaché case.

"Where'd that come from?" Toxique said.

"Oh, you know," Les said vaguely. He was quite proud of his abilities as a thief, but not everyone shared his view.

The two boys ran back toward Wilsons. They scrambled up to the Roosts, where Les rooted in his bedside locker. He produced the Beetles of Transmission and put one into the leather case. The boys then went to the main building, where Toxique waited outside in the hall while Les brought the case in to Valant.

"Yes?" Valant inquired archly.

"In all the excitement, Mr. Devoy left his briefcase downstairs. He asked that it be brought up to the library of the third landing."

Les made as if to dart through the door beside Valant's desk, but Valant stepped in front of him.

"No you don't," Valant said. "I'll take care of that." He grabbed the case from Les.

"But Mr. Valant, it's urgent," Les said.

"All the better if I take it, then," Valant said firmly. "You know you're not permitted in the library of the third landing without one of the instructors."

Les ran down the steps outside.

"Success!" he said. "Valant's going to bring the case up."

Les and Toxique found a quiet corner of the shrubbery and waited, listening to the second beetle. At first they could only hear Valant's feet and the creak of the bag. They held the big beetle belly-up and waited. They heard a knock and then Devoy's voice.

"Come in."

"One of your cases was left downstairs," Valant said. Les held his breath. Would Devoy be suspicious? He could almost feel the master's eyes on the bag.

"I don't recognize it," Devoy said. "It might belong to Brunholm. Just put it down, please, Mr. Valant."

"Would you and Mr. Toxique like some tea?" Valant asked.

"That would be very pleasant, thank you," Devoy said. The door closed as Valant left.

"Where were we?" Devoy said.

"My son," a cold silky voice said.

"Of course," Devoy said. "Well, as you know, there is nothing to connect your son to the attack on the Messenger."

"The attacker used Toxique darts," Toxique Senior said. "That is proof enough for me, and the fact that the Messenger survived appalls me."

"I have to say I am glad one of the persons in my care survived," Devoy said.

"You know as well as I, Devoy, that assassination is a necessary and honorable branch of spying. And assassins have to be trained. The boy must be blooded. And if he is not capable of fulfilling the role he has been born to . . ."

"I must confess," Devoy said, "that I find your creed a harsh one, Mr. Toxique."

"The Toxiques deal in matters of life and death, Mr. Devoy," the voice responded. "There is no room for sentiment."

Les glanced at Toxique. His friend's face was pale at

the best of times, but now he looked as if all the blood had been drained from his body. They heard a knock on the library door and someone entering.

"I have never had the advantage of a son," Devoy said, "but my assumption was that such matters between father and son went beyond the cut-and-dried."

"Not for the Toxiques," the other man said. "Different rules apply." A sound escaped Toxique. Les watched in alarm as his friend leapt to his feet and raced off through the shrubbery toward the front door!

"Toxique!" Les yelled, running through the bushes after him. Les, hampered by his wings, wasn't a fast runner, so by the time he had cleared the shrubbery, Toxique had disappeared through the front door. Panting, Les ran up the steps and into the hallway, where a dazed cadet was clambering to his feet.

"Which way did he go?" Les gasped. The cadet pointed to the stairs.

As Les scrambled up the first flight, a raven cawed mockingly from the shadows of the roofbeams. Far ahead he could hear running feet. Les raced across the Gallery of Whispers, the great domed room where, if you asked a question at one end, you would receive an answer at the other, but only after your question had traveled round the gallery in whispers. The answer was frequently strange and hard to decipher. Questions flitted through Les's head as he ran. Would he catch up with Toxique before he reached his father? Which of his father's words had sparked this uncontrollable rage?

Suddenly he was on the third landing and saw

Toxique launch himself at the library doors. They crashed open. An unearthly sound escaped the young assassin as he threw himself into the room. There was a mighty crash, then silence.

Les slowed as he reached the library, not knowing what carnage might await inside. Toxique was on the floor at his father's feet. The man stared down at his son with fury. Devoy looked on, expressionless as usual, while Valant gazed in horror at the broken china strewn across the floor.

"The tea," Toxique gasped, "it's poisoned!"

His father bent down to pick up a shard of the cup that had been dashed from his lips. He smelled it carefully.

"No odor of any sort," he said.

"There wouldn't be, surely," Devoy said. "If someone was trying to poison a poisoner, they would hardly make it easily detectable."

Toxique Senior took a small case from his inside pocket, opened it and scrutinized the array of brushes and powders inside.

"What would such a poisoner use?" he said, looking down at Toxique. "Answer me, boy."

"If it was me," Toxique said, "I would use Tasmin arachnoid."

"Colorless and odorless," his father said softly. "We shall see."

He dipped a brush in one of the powders and dabbed the damp surface of the teacup. After a moment the surface turned cobalt blue.

"Tasmin arachnoid it is," the man said. He looked down at Toxique, but his expression did not soften.

"It appears that your son's Gift of Anticipation has saved both of our lives," Devoy said. If Toxique Senior was grateful, he did not show it.

"At least it lured him from whatever hole he was hiding in," he said, his eyes fixed on his son's. Les stepped forward, his face burning. How could this man speak to Toxique like that after what he'd just done? But Devoy held up his hand to silence Les. Toxique Senior got to his feet.

"It is worth reminding you," Devoy said, "that our only physick is out of action following the dart attack. There would have been nothing to save us, Mr. Toxique."

"I have to question those in charge of this institution who permit poisoners and murderers to roam the corridors openly," Toxique said, his voice like ice. "And as for my son, he knows what his duty is, and if he is proved to have failed, then he knows the price he must pay."

He gathered his cloak around him and swept out of the room.

"That's a bit much," Les said indignantly, stooping to give Toxique a hand as he got shakily to his feet.

"People like Mr. Toxique set very high standards for themselves," Devoy said, "and they expect the same of others, whether they have the capability or not. There is a weight of family history on his shoulders. He may come round in time. As for me, young Toxique, I am indeed grateful and will remain eternally in your debt."

"I just felt it as we were"—Les kicked Toxique hard on the ankle before he mentioned the beetles—"walking through the shrubbery."

162

"You boys are late for class," Devoy said. "You had better go. And Mr. Knutt?"

"Yes?"

"Please take your briefcase with you. I'm sure the beetle feels a little confined."

Red-faced, Les grabbed the briefcase and headed for the door, followed by Toxique. Devoy turned to Valant as the door closed behind them.

"It's a good thing they were listening," Devoy said. "Otherwise I might well be dead. We must find whoever is responsible before someone else is killed."

Outside the door, Les turned to Toxique.

"How did he know we were listening?" he said.

"Maybe it's something to do with the fact that you've got the other beetle in your hand," Toxique said. Les looked down at the beetle still gripped tightly in his right hand, its legs waving feebly in the air.

"Bit of a giveaway," he admitted with a smile. "How are you feeling?"

Toxique gave a shrug. "He won't accept me until I carry out an assassination. He told me once that my granddad did the same to him when he was young."

"We won't worry about that for now," Les said. "We've got a killer to catch."

"Knutt and Toxique," Blackpitt announced, "when you are finished with rescuing visitors from deadly toxins, please get yourself to Inks class, where no doubt latecomers will be suitably punished."

THE KINGDOM

The passage wound upward into the mountains for what felt like miles. Danny's calves ached with the climb. Flickering torches hung on the walls at intervals, but between them it was dark, and he had slipped and fallen several times. He ran over his new identity in his head. He was there to study the history of the Lower World. They had decided that Dixie would pretend to be a student of the treaty. That way she could ask to see the Treaty Stone.

If the other team hasn't broken it already, Danny thought.

Suddenly he felt a strange sensation in his head, as if, for a moment, his thoughts were not quite his own. He brushed it off and continued doggedly, but the feeling persisted. Not that someone was trying to get into his head, but that they were thinking about him, and in doing so had connected with him in some way.

He remembered the time he had joined the Ring of Five, how he could feel and hear the thoughts of other members of the Ring in his head. This was a little like that, only very far away. As if someone was trying desperately to find out what was happening wherever Danny was. Longford. It was him! The very second he thought of the name the sensation vanished, as if Longford had sensed Danny's awareness and removed himself. And yet in his eagerness he had left something of himself behind in Danny's mind—more than he had intended. A part of his thinking, like a lingering scent. Danny stopped dead.

"What?" Dixie grabbed his arm. If Longford's thought was a scent, then there would be a foul undertone to it. Danny shook his head to show that he was all right, but fear swept over him. For he knew, from the fragment that Longford had left behind, that a trap had been prepared for him in the kingdom of Morne. He searched his mind for Longford's thought, but it was gone.

"Do your worst, Longford," he murmured to himself, but the brave words were lost in the cold damp tunnel as he resumed his climb.

After another half hour earth and stone underfoot became paving, and the rough stone walls gave way to smooth limestone with paintings and tapestries hung every few yards. More passages ran off on either side. From some, rich scents drifted; from others came snatches of voices or music. Ahead of Dixie, Danny and Macari stood two young men elegantly dressed in embroidered doublets and hose. They were absorbed in whispered conversation, and when they saw the small party approaching they gathered up their cloaks, pulled the hoods over their heads and hurried off in opposite directions.

The corridors widened, their ceilings lost in the dark. Small groups of people stood in opulent rooms off the corridor, many turning their faces away as the trio approached. The women wore silk dresses, the men velvet tunics and hose. Both men and women had powdered wigs.

"What's going on?" Dixie said. "Why is everybody standing around acting secretive? Has something happened?"

Macari turned with a grin.

"No, nothing's happened. Morne is always like this, full of scheming and gossiping and trying to catch the eye of the vizier and the court. No one trusts anyone else. They're always trying to do each other down. Treacherous as sin, the whole lot of them, and the more charming they are, the worse they get."

Danny remembered the hot irons in Macari's hand and thought, I don't trust you either.

"Now," Macari went on, "orders are that you're to be presented to the vizier and the court. It's an honor accorded to all visitors—not that there are many."

"Who's the vizier?" Danny asked.

"The vizier is the Supreme Authority, Lord of Lords, Master of All Domains Pertaining To and Congruent

With the Realm and Kingdom of Morne, Lord High Protector and Beloved—"

"He's got a lot of names," Dixie said.

"Seven hundred," Macari told them. "Takes a good two hours every Saturday to get through them before the Royal Bath, which is followed by the Royal Nap and then the Royal Tea. . . ."

"We get the picture," Danny said hastily. Macari came to a halt in front of a set of enormous doors covered in gold leaf. Two spear-carrying soldiers in golden armor glared at them. From a small kiosk beside the doors a rotund man in a scarlet robe emerged. He was holding a clipboard.

"Let me see," he said, turning a lively if careworn face toward them. "This can't be the delegation from the lower tower or the petitioners from the Southward Gallery, or the keyholders guild of the Keepers of Secrets."

"We're students," Danny said, "from the Lower World."

"This is Noinrum Camroc," Macari said, "Master of Ceremonies and Etiquettes, Songbird of the North, Holder of the Divine Flute—"

"Does everybody have such long names?" Dixie asked.

"We'll dispense with titles since they're from the somewhat . . . er . . . lax Lower World," Camroc said. "We'll just have time for the formalities before the evening ceremonies begin."

He turned to the golden doors and rapped sharply three times with the golden flute he carried on a chain at his waist. The doors were flung open on a high-ceilinged room dimly lit by great candelabra. Danny saw tapestries, banners, the glint of gold. There were many people in the room, all sumptuously dressed. The people were gathered in knots in various parts of the room, scheming and conspiring, the men glancing around before leaning forward to whisper in a companion's ear, the women hiding their mouths behind fans as they exchanged gossip.

All eyes turned toward the door as Camroc led Danny and Dixie in, and whispered comments followed in their wake: "What are they wearing?" "Is that the best the Upper World has to offer?" "They could at least wash themselves properly before meeting the vizier."

"Why do they hate us?" Dixie said.

"They're jealous," Camroc said. "Some of them could wait years for the opportunity of being presented to the vizier, and here you are, just walking in off the street, so to speak, and being brought straight to him."

Danny felt his mind coldly roam over the assembled throng. Without even thinking about it he was weighing up the alliances, the intrigues, the treacheries. The part of him that wanted to spy on others, to betray, was drawn to the faithless crowd. He took a deep breath and tried to shut out the whispers.

They drew near to a great dais. The shadows grew darker. Candles flickered in the gloom; groups of men and women parted, then closed behind them. Suddenly, without ceremony, they found themselves in front of not the gorgeous throne that Danny had expected, but a wooden chair with arms carved in the shape of ravens' heads. Nor was the man sitting on the chair what Danny had expected, a proud ruler in fine robes. The vizier was an ordinary-looking man with gray-flecked brown hair and shrewd eyes, simply dressed in plain black hose and tunic.

"Welcome, young scholars," he said quietly. "It is many years since we have had students from the Lower World, so it is doubly gratifying to have two parties at the same time."

Danny had the uncomfortable feeling that the man knew exactly why both parties were here, and he had to force himself to meet the vizier's steady gaze.

"You and your fellow scholars have picked very serious subjects," the vizier went on, "and I have thought long and hard about how to make your studies a little more interesting for you. I decided that a little competition might add to your pleasure."

There was a murmur of approval from the courtiers.

"The winners will be given access to Morne forever as our guests. Now," the vizier said, "it is time for the newcomers to meet their rivals."

Danny looked up. He had not seen the two figures standing in the gloom behind the vizier's chair.

"Step forward," the vizier commanded. The smaller of the two was a Cherb; his features—the pixielike ears and dark hair, one blue eye and one brown—were unmistakably those of the deadly enemies of Wilsons. The Cherb boy looked at Danny with a mixture of malice and amusement. The taller figure was a girl. Her black hair hung down her back. He face was long and fine-boned and her eyes were a cold, piercing blue, but her smile was shy and a little uncertain. She turned to the vizier. Her voice was low and husky.

"May I ask a question, my lord vizier?"

"Of course."

"You mentioned the reward for the winners of the competition. But you did not mention what will happen to the losers."

"The losers?" The vizier smiled. "A good question. I don't think a competition is any good unless there is a good prize. Equally, I think there must be some real jeopardy for the losers. So the unsuccessful candidate or candidates will stay here to serve in the shadows."

"What does that mean?" Danny said as Dixie gulped beside him.

"As the living have servants, so do the dead." The man's tone was light, but his eyes were dark and burning.

"That seems fair," the girl said calmly. "And what is the nature of the test?"

"It is simple. You merely have to find out what the mountains say." They all looked at him blankly. What did the question mean? How could the mountains say anything?

There was another murmur of approval from the bystanders and some applause.

"They're not clapping because it's an easy task," Dixie said sourly. The black-haired girl stepped forward.

"My name is Lily," she said, putting out her hand to Danny.

"Danny," he said. Her grip was firm and her look

170

direct. He felt, strangely, that she was not necessarily the enemy just because she had been sent by the Ring.

"Come, Lily," the Cherb boy growled, "they'll be bait for the dead by time we finish."

"You can rest tonight and begin in the morning," the vizier said smoothly. "You may use fair means or foul; you may use guile or be plainspoken. The choice is yours. There is nowhere in the kingdom closed to you, but you may find that people defend their territory jealously."

Macari brought them to a comfortable room with two beds off a main corridor. As in the rest of the building, the furniture was ornate and there were silken hangings on the walls. Dixie threw herself down on one bed while Danny explored the room.

"Look!" he exclaimed, pulling back the curtains to show two great French doors that opened onto a balcony. They stepped out and looked at the snow-covered mountainsides, the great peaks rearing above them, the lower slopes lying under the moonlight far below. They stood there for several minutes, lost in the cold beauty of the landscape.

The kingdom of Morne was all about them—a series of linked castles and keeps and towers, spreading up the mountain as far as they could see. Dixie shivered.

"I don't trust one brick of this place. I wish I was back in Wilsons."

Danny knew what she meant. Wilsons could be

strange and tricky, but it was homey, and you had the feeling that, for most of the time, anyway, people were on your side.

"We need to find the Treaty Stone and get out of here," Danny said.

"There's the challenge as well," Dixie said. "Forgot that already? I don't fancy ending up as a servant of the dead."

She disappeared in a way that managed to be moody, and a minute later Danny heard water running in the bathroom. When she reappeared abruptly a few minutes later she was wearing a silk nightdress that shimmered as she moved.

"There's a pair of gold pj's in there for you as well," she said with a tired grin. She clambered into bed and within seconds was asleep.

Danny's mind was racing, however, and sleep felt a long way off. He stayed out on the balcony. The cold air seared his lungs. The kingdom before him was beautiful, there was no arguing, but it was treacherous.

He saw a flicker of movement at the far end of the valley and narrowed his eyes. A small black shape was just visible against the mountain, moving swiftly toward him. A raven! The bird flew fast and high without deviating until it reached the first turret of Morne; then it dipped and turned right so that it was flying along the façade. It passed right in front of him, then slowed, coming to a rest on a balcony about a hundred meters away. It cocked its head to one side and peered down.

It's trying to show me something, Danny thought. He

followed the direction of the raven's head. From the balcony below the bird, a small figure dressed in black jumped lightly onto the parapet, then leapt to the next balcony down. It was the Cherb boy. The raven looked back up at Danny. He realized it wanted him to follow. With a quick glance at the sleeping Dixie, Danny pulled his trench coat tightly around him and slipped over the parapet, swinging his legs inward so that he landed on the next balcony down. As he did so, the dark figure reached the ground.

It was easier than it looked to climb down the front of the building using the balconies. People were still awake in some of the rooms, and once, Danny had to crouch, not breathing, while on the adjoining balcony an unseen couple spoke together in whispers.

"We are surrounded by snakes on every side," one voice said.

"Then we have no hope—what is to become of us?" A woman's voice, full of despair. Danny waited until the voices moved back inside, then resumed his downward progress.

When he reached the ground, he could see footprints in the snow leading along the front of the building. He looked around. The windows of the castle were dark and empty. Pulling the collar of his coat tight around his neck, he set off. The snow was crisp and firm and the tracks were easy to follow, moving purposefully. The two Ring students were a day ahead of Danny and Dixie and could well have found the Treaty Stone by now. Perhaps the Cherb's mission was now to shatter it.

Danny felt alive out here, all his senses honed. To be out alone in the dark, on the trail of an opponent who did not know he was there, touched the devious part of his being. Knowing that he should have wakened Dixie added an extra forbidden pleasure—that of deceiving a friend in a small way.

The footprints turned away from the building and toward a small stand of snow-covered pine trees in the shadow of a crag. Danny slowed. It was dangerous to follow an opponent into a wooded area, where an ambush was possible. A gust of wind sent ice crystals scudding across the surface of the snow. He looked up. Dark clouds had started to gather around the mountain peaks, moving with alarming speed. He hesitated. He should either go back or seek the shelter and danger of the pines. He brushed a snowflake from his lapel and moved cautiously in under the trees.

Danny crept forward, glancing up from the footprints to the dark canopy. A night creature stirred and he jumped. It was a small stand of trees, but the darkness was almost total. The wind stirred the branches. Danny came to the far end of the wood. The footprints emerged from the trees and doubled back toward Morne. A flurry of snow blew into his face, and as he stepped from the trees a blast of frozen air hit him. Much of Morne was already hidden in the fallen snow. The Cherb had led, and Danny had followed like a fool. He staggered as the wind struck him. He'd been tricked, and now he was alone in a snow-storm.

Danny put his head down and began to follow the tracks. As far as he could tell they were pointed back toward the walls of the kingdom, but he couldn't be sure. The prints were filling with snow, and before he had gone a hundred yards, they had faded completely. Danny trudged on against the driving snow. He hadn't been that far from the walls of Morne. If he found them, he could work his way back to his room. And yet no matter how far he walked, he did not reach the walls. It was getting harder and harder to see. The sound of the wind had in-creased to a shriek and the snow blew horizontally. Ice formed on his eyelashes and in his hair. He stepped into a hole hidden by the snow and sprawled on his front. The excitement of the chase was gone. His limbs felt tired and heavy, and he had to force himself to get to his feet and go on.

Snow clung to his shoes and made it hard for him to lift his feet. His coat kept the snow out, but it didn't pro-tect his face or his frozen feet, and he found himself think-ing about stories of frostbitten explorers losing ears and fingers. He cursed himself for falling for the Cherb's trap and for not waking Dixie. He stumbled on a rock and fell. The snow cushioned his fall. He felt a great weariness steal over him and he closed his eyes. A memory of being at home in bed crept into his mind. It was time for school, and his mother was calling, but the bed was warm and deep and he only wanted to snatch another few minutes. . . .

"Danny! Danny! Wake up!" Someone was shaking his shoulder.

"Just another minute," he murmured. As if in a dream, he felt two small hands grip his. He was pulled into a sitting position, then forced to stand.

"Help me, Danny!" The voice came from far away. His arm was draped over slender shoulders. He took one step forward, then another. All he wanted to do was to lie down, but the voice urged and cajoled him until the howling of the wind died away, the snow ceased and he fell to the ground.

Danny opened his eyes to see flickering shapes dancing on a stone roof. He turned his head. A fire blazed in a small grate and a familiar figure moved in the shadows around it.

"Dixie," he said.

"Wait a moment. I have a hot drink for you." A girl's voice, but it wasn't Dixie. "I don't think I could have carried you much farther."

It was Lily, the girl chosen by the Ring to destroy the Treaty Stone.

FAMILY

Danny stared at Lily, then at the proffered cup.

"Don't be silly," she said. "If I wanted to bump you off, all I had to do was leave you out in the snow. I wouldn't have to poison you." He took the drink. It was hot soup.

"Where are we?"

"Must be a shepherd's hut," she said. "Someone left a few tins of soup and stuff in it."

Danny sat up and sipped the scalding liquid, feeling life flow back into his frozen limbs. His brain was starting to unfreeze as well. Why would one of his enemies lead him into a trap and the other rescue him from it?

Lily had turned to the fire.

"I know what you're thinking," she said, "and I would probably think the same. Why did she help me, after I'd been led into danger?"

"Why did you?" Danny asked, his voice sounding harsher than he'd intended.

"I know you have no reason to trust me," Lily said, her voice very low, "but until you do, I can't tell you."

The room went silent, save for the crackle of the fire and the roar of the wind outside.

"I don't have to trust you," Danny said carefully, "but I do need to thank you."

Lily turned and gave him a sad smile.

"That's a start," she said. "We'll wait here until the storm's over, and then we'll make our way back to Morne."

"What are you studying?" Danny said, trying to make his voice sound casual.

"Upper and Lower World relations," she said. "What about you?"

"Early Lower World history. What do you think of Morne?"

"It's a strange place. I think the vizier rules it by setting people against each other. They're so busy squabbling that they don't have time to challenge him."

"You're probably right."

They were talking cautiously, as though playing a chess game, Danny thought, trying not to give too much away. They were on opposing missions. This was what Danny the Spy enjoyed: playing mind games with a cunning opponent.

"How long are you staying?" Danny asked.

"Oh, as long as it takes," Lily said airily, "but I don't agree with the vizier."

"No?"

"I think people pulling together is the only way to achieve anything."

What was she playing at? Was she was saying they should work together—the Ring of Five and Wilsons on the same side? It didn't seem possible. She has to be up to something, Danny thought. But what if she's not? Should she be trusted?

His head starting to hurt, Danny drank the last of the soup.

"I think we should both try to get some sleep—" He was interrupted by a noise that sounded like some ancient being groaning with sadness and regret, with a terrible longing that echoed through the ages.

Almost against their wills, Danny and Lily got to their feet, went to the rough wooden door and opened it. The snow had stopped, and the moon stared down again at drifts piled in weird shapes. The storm was retreating, huge clouds streaming back through the high mountain passes, and as they did, by some trick caused by the speed of the storm or the shape of the rocks, a great voice seemed to speak from the peaks. Danny held his breath, awestruck, as the voice rumbled over the crags.

"AAAA-LONE," the voice keened, and Danny felt his blood turn to ice. "AAAA-LONE!" The sorrow of millennia echoed down the valley. Again and again the voice boomed out; then, as the last shard of cloud raced through the last pass, there was silence. Danny realized he had been holding his breath. He looked down. Lost in the terrible grief of the mountain, Lily had taken his hand

and was holding it tightly. When the sound faded, she became aware of what she had done and quickly released Danny's hand, moving off through the snow.

"We'd better get back," she said over her shoulder.

"Wait," Danny said, running after her. "What did you mean earlier when you said you can't tell me why you helped me until I trust you?"

"I meant exactly what I said."

"You realize," Danny said, "that we both know what the mountain said?"

"Yes."

"And that if we don't both answer the question at the same time then the other team ends up serving the dead?"

"I realize that too."

"Well," Danny said slowly, "that means that either one of us goes straight to the vizier and condemns the others, or we trust each other and deliver the answer together."

"And?"

"I'll trust you, Lily," he said. "I won't go to the vizier if you won't." He stopped in the snow and held out his right hand. After a long moment of hesitation, Lily shook it.

"Right," she said. "Follow me."

She took them along the wall of Morne to a small gate. There was a heavy iron padlock on it, but she took a clip from her hair and with impressive speed and dexterity picked the lock.

The gate opened onto a large room filled with a jumble of old furniture and faded oil paintings, sleighs with one runner and broken beach umbrellas. Moonlight streamed in through a high barred window.

"It's just a storeroom," Lily said, "but you can get back into our rooms from it." She hesitated.

"What is it?"

"You trusted me. It's time for me to trust you."

"Trust me with what?"

"With this." She turned away from him and bent over. He couldn't see what she was doing, but her hands were at her eyes. She turned around.

"Let me move into the light." She stepped into the shaft of moonlight and turned her face to it. At first all Danny saw was the paleness of her skin, the raven hair streaming back. Then he saw her eyes. He blinked and looked again. One was blue, the other brown.

"Yes, Danny. Just like you."

"How . . . ?" he said. "I thought I was the only one. . . ."

"That's what everyone thinks, Danny," she said, "but you're not. You were never alone. They tried to hide it from you, but you have a sister."

"You?"

"Yes, Danny," she said, turning toward him and pushing her head back so that he could see the shape of her face, and the strange brown and blue eyes. "I'm your sister."

The next hour passed in a blur. Danny had gotten used to being alone and had worked at building up a hard skin to protect himself. Now he felt more vulnerable than ever.

He couldn't think of the right questions to ask. It seemed that Lily knew little more about their parentage than he did but, like Danny, had been brought up by adoptive Cherb parents who had made their home in the shadows of the fortress of Grist.

"I was always hidden from the Ring of Five," Lily said. "I was never allowed out without contact lenses, so they never knew about my eyes. But I was smart, like you, Danny. I studied hard, spent nights in the library reading about the Fifth. The Ring had gone through all the books and torn out the pages about the Fifth, but they didn't check the baptismal records. Twelve years ago, a pair of twins was registered, the color of their eyes noted as one brown and one blue. Our first names were there—Danny and Lily—but the second names had been crossed out, as had the names of the parents. I found out about this a year ago and I've been looking for you ever since.

"I got into spy school in Grist. I lied, cheated and betrayed my way to the top. When it looked as if someone else would get this mission, I made sure she fell down the stairs and broke her ankle. I knew Wilsons would send you, if you were still alive. I knew it!"

Danny looked at her, dumbfounded. He had a sister and a family!

"Do you know who . . . who our parents are . . . *where* they are?"

"No," Lily said. "I didn't get that far. But I have a few leads in Grist. The answers are there, I'm sure of it."

"And do you know why they think that I . . . or we . . . are so special?"

"I know that to be complete, the Ring must have someone of mixed Cherb and human blood, and I know they want you—there was great excitement when you joined them the last time. But there is something more going on that I don't understand. We need more time."

"We?"

"You must come back with me, Danny. In disguise, as you are now. Together we can find our parents." She lowered her voice. "I know you have a mission here—to find the Treaty Stone, the same mission I have."

"We both have missions," Danny agreed, "but they are not the same. Mine is to save the Stone. Yours is to—"

"Destroy it," Lily said eagerly. "I thought about that. I must not fail, or else . . ."

"Or else what?"

Lily made a contemptuous noise. "Rufus Ness said he'd kill both of us—me and the Cherb—if we fail, but that's not what matters."

"Of course it matters."

"Shhh . . . someone's coming . . . ," Lily warned.

They ducked behind a pile of packing cases. The door opened and a servant came in, a big man with a thatch of blond hair. He was carrying a box of broken crockery. He set it down heavily just inside the door and straightened; then something caught his eye. He saw the fresh snow on the floor, and wet footprints leading from the door. Scratching his head, he moved forward slowly as he looked from the now-locked door to the footprints. He didn't seem very bright, and Danny thought it would be best to stay hidden in the hope that he would go away.

183

Instead, Lily sprang out from behind the cases with a heavy brass candlestick in her hand. She struck the man behind the ear and he fell with a sickening thud. Suddenly there was a knife in her hand. She grabbed the man's hair and pulled his head back so that his throat was exposed. Her knife hand swept back, but Danny grabbed her wrist.

"What are you doing?" he cried.

"We'll slit his throat and leave him in the snow," she said matter-of-factly. "They won't find him until we're gone."

"You can't!" Danny said. "He hasn't done anything to us."

"Course he has," Lily said. "He could ruin everything."

"Wait," Danny said, rummaging in the cases behind them. He brought out a dusty bottle of whiskey. He unscrewed the top and splashed whiskey over the man's clothes, then poured the rest into a drain.

"There, they'll think he was drunk and fell," Danny declared.

"Not bad," Lily said, "but my way was permanent."

How could she be so quick to kill a man just like that? Danny wondered.

"Look!" Lily pointed. The first light of dawn was showing in the window above their heads.

"We'd better get back to bed," she said. She led Danny up a winding stone staircase that opened onto the bedroom corridor. She kissed him gently on the cheek.

"I've dreamed of having a family all of my life," she

said. "But we mustn't let anyone know." She pointed out a window to a tall tower with a shining silver roof.

"I'll meet you there tomorrow. We'll be able to talk more then."

One more kiss and she was gone. Danny quietly opened the door to his room. Dixie lay in bed, breathing softly. He threw off his clothes, put on the gold pajamas and got into the other bed. A sister! He could still feel the dry touch of her lips on his cheek, and a warmth he had never felt before flooded his heart. At the same time he remembered how she had pulled back the servant's head to expose his throat. That gave him a certain warm feeling as well—warm like spilled blood. His other self stirred, and he knew that this was the side of Lily that Danny the Spy liked.

Could he trust her? Was she really his sister? Every fiber of his being wanted to believe her.

He decided to say nothing to Dixie. He told himself it was to protect her, but part of him thrilled at the deception.

15

THE UNEXPECTED

Les and Toxique had gone back to Vandra's bedside after class, and the three friends spent the evening trying to figure out who the killer of the Unknown Spy's wife might be, until Blackpitt cut into their thoughts.

"Cadets Knutt and Toxique, you are forty-five minutes late for bedtime. Tell Master Brunholm that you have incurred a Third Regulation offense! Now go to bed!"

Les and Toxique looked at each other. Les had a few choice words that he wanted to apply to Blackpitt, but Blackpitt seemed to hear everything. A Third Regulation offense was harsh for being late for bed, and if Blackpitt was in a bad mood, he could easily up the punishment.

"Come on, Toxique," Les said. "Vandra's almost asleep anyway."

The two boys made their way out of the apothecary, under the skeleton of the Messenger and through the silent college.

"Blackpitt," Les said. "Blackpitt, wake up!" There was no reply.

"What are you doing?" Toxique demanded.

"Trying to see if Blackpitt is awake," Les whispered.

"Why?"

"Well, the only person this mystery assassin has managed to actually bump off is the wife of the Unknown Spy. We should have a look at his room while he's safely under lock and key."

Toxique moaned. "Blood and murder. We're in enough trouble already," he said.

"Then a little more won't hurt," Les said firmly.

"McGuinness will already have searched it," Toxique said.

"Stow it, Toxique," Les said. "Come on!"

There was no sign of Valant in the entrance hall. They crept down the corridor toward the Unknown Spy's room. But they were to be disappointed. The door was locked, and nothing Les could do with his lockpicks could open it.

"We'd better get to bed," Toxique said, looking relieved.

"Not yet," Les said. "Hear that?" The faint sound of music reached their ears from the ballroom. Les slipped down the corridor, Toxique following reluctantly. They peered through the crack between the ballroom doors.

Les stifled an exclamation of surprise. Besides the Messengers, who were fond of dancing, all the staff were there: Exshaw, Valant, Brunholm, Duddy, Spitfire . . . all of them. McGuinness stood on the stage with a saxophone in his hand. His wife stood beside him with a double bass. And at the back of the stage, looking every inch a cool jazzman in a black polo, Devoy sat at a drum kit. As Les and Toxique watched, McGuinness counted into a dance number, and Duddy and Brunholm took to the floor.

"If I hadn't seen it with my own two eyes . . . ," Les muttered.

"McGuinness isn't bad on that thing," Toxique said, "and Devoy's technique is impeccable."

"Didn't know you liked jazz," Les said.

"It's good for calming yourself after a . . . you know, a killing. All the Toxiques are well known in the great jazz clubs."

"Well, it gives us the perfect chance," Les said.

"To do what?"

"To go to the teachers' quarters and have a chat with the Unknown Spy."

For the second time that night, Toxique groaned.

Fifteen minutes later Les and Toxique found themselves on the masters' corridor, Les looking out for new traps set since the attack on Brunholm. Brunholm had added security outside his room, none of it very subtle. There was the tried-and-tested piano wire stretched at neck height, and an enormous bear trap. There were classic tricks such as the hair wetted and placed between door and frame so that it would fall off if someone entered. Brunholm had also covered the door in notices: KEEP OUT! BEWARE OF THE DOG! and WARNING: ARMED RESPONSE!

"Fat lot of good that'll do," Les whispered. "Any tricky stuff? What does your gift tell you?"

"Nothing," Toxique said, "but it doesn't always work, you know. A lot of the time I can't foretell stuff."

"We'll press on," Les said. "I think we're safe enough."

The barred window of the little cell in Devoy's study was dark. Les peered in. As he did so, the dim light in the room picked out the Unknown Spy's pale face, his eyes fixed on Les. As the face got closer, Les knew that the man must be walking toward him, but he had the impression of a haunted face floating through the air. The face came to a halt at the bars.

"Who are you?" the Unknown Spy asked.

"My name is Les Knutt," Les said, "and this is Toxique. We're trying to find out what . . . what happened to your wife." The man's eyes narrowed.

"Er, condolences on your loss," Les said hastily, wondering if he had been too blunt.

"I didn't kill you, then?" the Unknown Spy asked.

"No," Toxique said, "it was a pillow you shot."

"A pillow. Can't believe I fell for that old one," he said. "Do bear in mind I haven't finished with you yet, won't you?" Something about the mild way he said this chilled Les even more than bloodthirsty threats would have.

"Wait a minute!" Les said. "I had nothing to do with—"

Toxique had pushed in front of him. "If Les Knutt killed your wife," he said, "then why? There had to be a reason. Can you think of anything?"

The Unknown Spy stared at them, or rather through them, searching his ruined memory.

"Is there anything that she knew that no one else knew?" Toxique said. "Or something she was an expert at?"

"She was awfully smart, you know," the Unknown Spy said brightly. "She invented lots of spying techniques. She had started to remember things too. She was writing them down."

"Could that be what the attacker was looking for?" Toxique asked.

"Possibly. What was her finest technique?" Les asked.

"There was one . . . ," the Unknown Spy said. "It was named after her, but I can't remember her name." A single tear trickled down his cheek.

"What was it called?" Toxique urged softly. "Tell me what it was called."

"What was it again? Oh yes, the Sibling Strategy." The two boys looked at each other in confusion. "It was called that at the start, before her name was put on it."

"What was it?" Toxique asked eagerly. "What did it do?"

"I don't know," the Unknown Spy said mournfully. "I can't remember."

The next day Vandra was well enough to leave the infirmary. Les and Toxique told her what the Unknown Spy had said about his wife.

"Doesn't really get us any further," Toxique said gloomily.

"I have an idea," Vandra said. "Why don't we tell McGuinness?" The other two looked at her. "It's not like telling Brunholm," she said. "McGuinness is pretty straight. It might mean something to him. It can't hurt, anyway."

"We should be in class," Toxique said.

"You can say you were helping me back to the Roosts. I can barely climb up there on my own anyhow."

It was true. The powerful poison had not yet worked its way entirely out of Vandra's system. She was finding it hard to walk in a straight line, and one of the friends kept intervening to prevent her from veering into the shrubbery. But they never had a chance to use their excuse. As they passed under one of the decorative arches in the gardens, a speaker coughed to life.

"Out on your rounds again, Knutt and Toxique?" Blackpitt said coldly. "A Fourth Regulation offense this time, I think."

"He used to always give you a chance to make an excuse," Les said despairingly.

* * *

They found McGuinness at the parade ground. The tunnel in the middle of the grounds that had been opened by the Cherbs the previous year when they tried to invade Wilsons was still full of water. Water plants had started to spring up around the edges, and it made a pleasant pond. The detective was sitting on a dusty bench, seemingly dozing in the sun, but when Les, Toxique and Vandra approached him he opened one eye.

"Next time you come to Monday-night jazz club, Knutt and Toxique, I'll expect you to dance or sing, not lurk outside the door."

"How did he see us?" Les whispered furiously.

Toxique looked taken aback. "Slaughter and guts, he must be able to see through walls."

McGuinness opened the other eye.

"This looks very much like a delegation," he said. "What's on your mind?"

The cadets plunged into the story of the visit to the Unknown Spy and the Sibling Strategy. McGuinness's eyes gleamed under his hat.

"Well done, Toxique," he said. "You've gotten more out of him in five minutes than I've managed to get in many weary hours. I'll have to look into this Sibling Strategy."

A faint flush spread over Toxique's waxen features. On anyone else it would have been a blush of pleasure.

"I'm not sure where the information gets us at the moment," McGuinness went on. "However, the art of investigation is the art of making links, of joining one piece of information to the next."

"But we haven't got any other pieces," Les said.

"There's always something," McGuinness said, "even if you don't know you have it yet. Just look and listen."

"But what do we look or listen for?" Vandra said.

"I can't tell you that since I haven't found it yet myself," McGuinness said, "but I'll tell you one of my rules: always watch for anything different, for unexplained change, something familiar that doesn't seem quite right all of a sudden. Now, it's time you were resting, Vandra, and time you two were back in class."

McGuinness closed his eyes again and tipped his hat forward so that they could no longer see his face. The three friends looked at each other and started to make their way back to the main building.

"It's hard to notice what's different about this place when things are odd most of the time anyway," Vandra said.

"I know," Les said gloomily. Just as they passed back under the garden archway, Blackpitt's speaker burst into life.

"Make that a Fifth Regulation offense, Knutt and Toxique." There was a note of malicious delight in his voice. Les rolled his eyes to heaven.

"As if things aren't bad enough," he said, then brightened. "Maybe the assassin will bump us off. That way we won't have to take a Fifth Regulation punishment."

"Don't be daft, Les," Vandra said. "Don't joke about things like that. What's wrong with you?"

"McGuinness told us to look out for something different, didn't he—something familiar that has changed? Well, something familiar *has* changed, and McGuinness was right—it's been staring us in the face all the time!"

16

THE RING OF FIVE ROOM

The first thing Danny saw the following morning was Dixie's face an inch from his own.

"Wake up, for goodness' sake! I've been shouting at you for ten minutes."

Danny shook his head, groggy with lack of sleep. The night's events came flooding back. A sister!

"Come on, Danny," Dixie said. "We've got to find out what the mountain says, whatever that means, and find the Treaty Stone. *And* stop the other two from doing any harm to it. And I'm starving and I want some breakfast."

Fifteen minutes later, as they walked along the corridor, they were aware of people stopping and whispering. Once they heard a scornful laugh. Dixie disappeared and reappeared right beside a couple who were whispering and pointing, sending them scuttling down a side corridor.

After walking through several hallways, each more gorgeous than the last, they found a dining hall, where wigged and powdered servants carried silver salvers from kitchen to table, whipping off the lids to reveal bacon and sausages and eggs and fried mushrooms and toast. For a few minutes Danny and Dixie forgot their quest as they ate greedily, asking for seconds and more, their cups of sweet milky tea being replenished from enormous teapots.

Once Danny had taken the edge off his appetite, he saw something likely to spoil it altogether. The servants were clearing a small table for two, one that looked as if it had been abandoned a while ago. He questioned one of the servants, who confirmed that Lily and the Cherb had long left. Sister or not, Danny thought, he didn't trust Lily. And he certainly didn't trust the Cherb. He bolted the last of his food.

"Come on," he said to Dixie.

They practically ran out of the dining room. For the first few hours they prowled the endless corridors of Morne. They found themselves in throne rooms, galleries, anterooms and bedchambers. Every hallway looked the same, and there was no sign of a vault or a guarded room where something as important as the Treaty Stone might be kept. They stumbled upon one room so full of bright gold and shining jewels that they had to shield their eyes, and a crypt lined with somber tombs, so deep and dark that their hearts quailed. Everywhere they went there were knots of courtiers, and Danny had no doubt that reports of his and Dixie's progress—or lack of it—were going back to the vizier. Around midafternoon, tired and hungry, they collapsed on a red velvet divan, no closer to realizing their quest.

"You know," Dixie said, "there's probably an easier way of going about this."

"I'm sure there is," Danny said sarcastically. "We could grow wings like Les and fly over the place and the Treaty Stone would be sitting on the roof so all we would have to do is pick it up and fly away."

"No," Dixie said seriously, "I think my way's a little easier than that."

She stood up and walked over to a passing courtier.

"Excuse me," she said, "would you mind telling me where the Treaty Stone is kept?"

"Certainly," the handsome boy said. "Take the third corridor on the left and keep going until you reach the Hall of Secrets."

"Thank you," Dixie said as Danny looked on open-mouthed.

"Would you like me to take you there?"

His name was Louis and he was twelve years old. He had black curly hair and always seemed to have a smile on his face. Unlike the other inhabitants of Morne, he wasn't secretive and suspicious.

"I'm only half Morne," he said with a smile. "My mother was from the Upper World."

"Can anyone just walk in and see the Stone?" Danny tried to sound casual.

"Yes, of course," Louis said. "The provisions of the treaty have to be seen so that people can read them."

"Could somebody not just walk out with it, then?" Danny said.

"Ah, that's a different matter," Louis said cheerfully.

The corridor they had joined opened onto a wide concourse. For the first time Danny and Dixie saw groups of young people, sitting around on marble benches or walking toward the vast iron doors that stood open at the opposite end.

"Who are all these people?" Dixie asked.

"Students," Louis said. "There are many great wonders displayed in the Crypts."

"The Crypts? Where they keep dead people?" Dixie asked.

"That's right," Louis said, "the Dead are the staff of the museum we call the Hall of Secrets, but don't worry about them. They won't harm you unless you try to steal or damage any of the exhibits."

Danny and Dixie exchanged looks. Having the dead running about the Butts at Wilsons was one thing, in secret and in the dark. But here . . .

The entrance hall of the museum soared above their heads. There were the usual fixtures—statues of important-looking people, paintings of battles. It was the staff who were different. A pale and ghastly-looking woman in a uniform was taking coats at the coat check. The security man at the main entrance was skeletally thin, his skin stretched over his bones like yellow paper, his eyes bulging in their sockets.

"Lovely day, kids," he said cheerfully. "Enjoy yourselves."

In the museum proper they ran into a party being led by a guide. She was a young woman, pale but pretty, with long blond hair.

"The Oligarchic period of Morne history under Vizier Kolum was known for its bloodthirsty pogroms. On your left you can see the golden goblet from which he drank the blood of his victims, claiming that it would make him immortal."

The guide was walking backward as she spoke, and she collided with Danny.

"Oh, I'm so terribly sorry," she said, turning around, "that was clumsy of me."

"Don't wor—" Danny started, but then her breath hit him. It smelled of the grave, of earth and decayed flesh and mold. He reeled away, gasping, but she merely smiled apologetically and turned back to the group.

On they went, deeper into the museum. Many exhibits were boring, collections of crumbling stone urns or "Agricultural Implements of the Early Upper Period." But there was a lot more to look at in "Weapons of the Upper–Lower Wars." There were vicious Messenger knives and Cherb flamethrowers. There were torture instruments that reminded Danny of the ones in Wilsons, though here there was a section of devices devoted to Seraphim and Messengers, with feather pluckers and wing stretchers. There were bombs designed to be dropped by Seraphim that sent spinning knives through the air, and cruel-looking blades and small arms described as "Miscellaneous Cherb."

Danny noticed a small black door. A sign over it said THE RING OF FIVE. He tried the handle, but it was locked. Louis took him by the arm. For once, he wasn't smiling.

"We don't go in there," he said, steering Danny away. Danny glanced uneasily back toward the door, feeling the familiar tug, the need to be part of what was secret and malicious.

"Now," Louis said, "here we are. The Treaty Stone Room."

The first part of the room was full of photographs from the war before the negotiation and signing of the treaty. There were aerial shots of the destruction wrought by the conflict—miles of burned-out houses, crowds of desperate refugees. Then there were photos of the treaty-signing ceremony. Serious-looking men and women posed for the camera. In one, Danny saw a much-younger-looking Devoy; in another, an unsmiling Longford bent over a table with a small etching instrument in his hand.

Finally, in an alcove of its own, they saw the Treaty Stone. A spotlight shone on a black stone that was much smaller than Danny had expected. Viewing it through a sheet of heavy bulletproof glass, he could see that its surface was etched with minute gold writing. Red lights blinked here and there throughout the room, doubtless proof of laser beams and pressure sensors—the kinds of devices used to protect famous works of art.

"How are we going to get near that?" Danny asked Dixie in a low voice.

"Do we need to?" Dixie asked. "It looks pretty safe where it is."

Suddenly Danny's heart leapt. On the other side of the room he saw Lily standing with a group of students who were scribbling in notebooks as their teacher rambled on about the treaty and conflict resolution. Lily wasn't writing anything. Her gaze roamed over the security—Danny could tell she was memorizing the positioning of the red lights. Behind the students Lily's young Cherb companion was using a small pair of binoculars, apparently to study the finely etched text on the Stone, but every so often he pointed them at the ceiling.

"It might look safe," Danny said, "but I don't think it is." Dixie followed his eyes. "We don't have the expertise or the gear to get it out of there . . ."

". . . but they do," Dixie said, "by the look of things."

"They're acting that way," Danny agreed.

"Dixie, you're a genius," Dixie said after a pause. "Danny, pat me on the back."

"If you insist," Danny said, "but why are you a genius?"

"I've figured out how to get our hands on the Stone."

"How?"

"We let them steal it, then we steal it from them!"

"You might have something there . . . ," Danny admitted.

"If we can deal with the other thing first," Dixie said.

"What other thing?" Lily looked up and saw Danny.

A smile of pure delight spread over her features. Danny tried to keep his face straight.

"The other thing—you know," Dixie said, "the one that condemns us to serving the dead for the rest of our lives if we don't figure it out, that little thing?"

"Oh, that," Danny said, his eyes still fixed on Lily. "That's okay, I already know the answer to that."

"You already know it?" Dixie said slowly. She was looking at Danny with a serious expression. "What are you saying, Danny? How do you already know?"

"I . . . went for a walk last night. After you went to sleep. I heard the mountain."

"You went for a walk but you never mentioned it?"

"It slipped my mind."

"You found out how to stop us from spending the rest of our lives looking after dead people and forgot to tell me?"

"Er, something like that," Danny said. "But keep your voice down!" Louis stood six feet away, looking at the Stone with admiration.

"What did the mountain say?" Dixie had her hands on her hips. Danny had never seen her look really angry before.

"It s-said . . ." Danny was stuttering. The good part of his mind wanted to protect Dixie, but the spy part of his mind was cold. Let her find out for herself!

Dixie looked long and hard into his eyes. "Never mind," she said softly. "I'll figure it out on my own." Then she linked arms with Louis.

"Come on, Louis, show me some of this kingdom of

yours." She turned on her heel and walked off, half dragging Louis with her. Danny watched miserably as she disappeared into the throng of students. Then he realized that part of him felt glad. Danny the Spy was happy to get out from under Dixie's watching eye. He looked at the Stone, then back to the other side of the room. Dixie was gone. No matter, he thought; he would catch up with her later. In the meantime, there was something he wanted to do.

A few minutes later Danny was standing at the Ring of Five door. He saw one of the security staff sitting at a desk on the far side of the room. He walked over, keeping his gait casual. The guard was an attractive girl with black curly hair, barely out of her teens.

"Yes," she said brightly, "can I help you?"

"It's the Ring of Five room," Danny said. "I'm a student from the Lower World, and the Ring is a really important part of my research. I wonder if I could have a look."

"Oh no, sir," the girl said. "There is a key, but the vizier himself must be asked for permission." As she spoke, Danny watched with horrified fascination as a long pink worm emerged from her nose and dangled over her top lip. "I'm surprised," the girl said confidentially, "that he even allows us to keep the key here." She sniffed and the worm was sucked back up into her head. Danny put one hand on the desk and the other to his temple.

"Are you okay?" the girl asked.

"Yes, just feeling a bit faint." Danny wasn't really feeling all that faint, but it wasn't hard to pretend after watching that worm.

"I'll get you a glass of water," the girl said sympathetically. As she left the desk, Danny saw two bullet holes in her back, surrounded by dried gunpowder and blood. What had happened to her? Was it considered impolite to ask?

Still feigning faintness in case anyone was watching, he slumped into the chair behind the desk, fumbling in his coat for his lockpicks. One-handed, he started to go through the desk. The drawers that were open he didn't bother with. In the three that were locked he found weapons and some syringes and tablets. He had no idea what the dead girl used them for, though he shuddered at some of the images that went through his mind. But there was no sign of the key. He felt underneath the desk. The dead girl would be back at any moment. Then his hand touched a small metal clasp. He fumbled with it. There was a click and a little velvet box fell into his hand. It had to be the key.

As Danny slipped the box into his pocket, the dead guard returned with a glass of water.

"Thanks," he said gratefully, gulping it down.

"That's okay," she said a little wistfully. "Wouldn't mind a glass of water myself, but, you know . . ."

"Yes, of course," Danny said, not really knowing at all. If she took a drink, would the water leak out the holes in her back?

"Never mind." She smiled kindly. "Must look on the bright side, isn't that right?"

Danny thanked her profusely and walked away. He hoped she wouldn't get into trouble for the missing key, though a mocking voice in the back of his mind reminded him that she was already dead, so what could the vizier do to her anyway?

The door was only slightly off the main part of the museum, yet Danny felt a long way from the visiting parties. It was as if the door was instinctively being given a wide berth. When he was sure that no one was watching, he opened the little velvet box. Inside was an ornate metal key. He had been right. Just as he was about to fit it into the lock he became aware of someone behind him. He wheeled around. Lily. Her smile was catlike.

"I wanted to get this door open too," she said, "so I reckoned you would be here. I wouldn't have gotten the key so fast, though. Go on. Open it."

17

THE DIARY OF MATT SCALPLE

The key turned easily. They found themselves in a small ill-lit room dominated by a portrait of Ambrose Longford. There were photographs of Rufus Ness, Nurse Flanagan and Conal, and glass cases displaying robes that had once been worn by the Ring, according to a faded placard.

"Why the big secret about this room?" Lily said. "There's nothing here."

"No," Danny said, disappointed. "I thought there might be something to tell us who our parents were."

"What's this?" Lily was peering at an old notebook in a small case. The case was locked, but it only took a few seconds for her to open it. She blew the dust off the cover.

"'The Diary of Matt Scalple,'" she read. "But it's all burned and the pages are stuck together—it's hard to read."

"Let me see." Danny flipped the pages. It appeared to be an account of events leading up to a battle between the Ring of Five and the defenders of Wilsons Island. At first things went well for Wilsons; Cherb attacks were repulsed. But then it became clear that a great terror was abroad. Matt Scalple referred to rumors of villages being destroyed, of armies devastated. Then came the final page, torn and burned.

They've found out what it is . . . the terror. . . . It's coming now. . . . Nothing can stand in his way . . . the power of the Fifth . . .

The page was torn and dirtied with what appeared to be bloodstains. After that there was nothing.

"The Power of the Fifth?" Lily said, gazing at Danny with something like wonder.

"I don't have any power," Danny said.

"Are you sure about that?" Lily said excitedly. "We'd make them all sit up if you did! Think about it, Danny. What we could do, if the Fifth has powers . . . We could take over anything—both worlds, if you wanted!"

"I don't want to take over anything," Danny said, "and I'm telling you I don't have any power."

"That's the difference between us," Lily said a little mournfully. "I want to take over things. I think we're black and white, good and evil, Danny. I think the good comes out on top in you most of the time, and the bad in me. Most of the time."

Danny wandered around the badly lit room. He didn't want to leave it. For the first time in his life he had real family, and although he and Lily didn't have any clues to who their parents might be, he knew the truth must be close. The members of the Ring looked down on him and he could feel the tug again, as if they were telling him that they were his real family.

Lily sat on a low seat by the wall.

"You know what my mission is," she said wearily. "To break the Stone, or Rufus Ness will kill me. Will you help me, Danny?"

"I have to bring the Stone back, protect it. . . . The treaty . . ."

"You're right, Danny," Lily said. "Wilsons is more important."

"You're the only family I've got," Danny said desperately.

"I know."

"If the Stone is broken . . ."

"If the Stone is broken," Lily said suddenly, sitting up, "it doesn't mean war. Not if you take your proper place at the head of the Ring of Five. You can stop them from attacking Wilsons and trying to invade the Upper World."

"Do you think so?" Danny asked. "Do you really think so?"

"Yes!" Lily said. "We can do this!"

"I'm not sure I want to go back to the Ring," Danny said, uncertainty flooding through him.

"Well, there is another way," Lily said slowly.

"What?"

"If you are the Fifth, then I can also be the Fifth. I

could join the Ring in your place. With you at Wilsons and me in the Ring . . ."

Danny turned it over feverishly in his mind. It could work. After all, even if they protected the treaty this time, the Ring would keep coming after the Stone—and eventually they would succeed. If Danny could control events . . .

"You get it," Lily said, watching him carefully. "It could work."

"I have to think," Danny said.

"Just don't take too long," Lily said. "It's my neck on the line, after all. And talking about necks on lines, we'd better get out of here before they miss their key."

"There's one thing I don't have to think about," Danny said. "You *are* my sister, Lily. I know it in my heart."

They left the room, closing and locking the door behind them. Danny slipped the key into his pocket. As they were walking away, he glanced back at the black door.

"I still don't see why it should be locked," Danny said. His eye passed over a little brass plaque, almost invisible under generations of dirt, in the shadows to the left of the door.

If he had read the plaque, he would have known why the room was kept locked. Underneath the grime, the inscription read: *This a rare example of a Room of Malign Intentions. In this room foolish or evil thoughts are intensified, while good and wise choices are pushed to the background. It was thought that this was a fitting place for a display on the Ring of Five. The room was locked by order of the vizier after a series of attempts to overthrow him, inspired by visits to the room.*

When Danny got to his and Dixie's room he found that Dixie's gear was gone. He went out to the corridor, where he ran into Louis.

"Where's Dixie?" Danny demanded.

"She thought it would be better to have a room of her own," Louis said. "It's just down the corridor. But I think she's gone to the library to work."

Danny eyed the boy suspiciously. Was he as wholesome as he looked?

He spent the rest of the day searching for Dixie without success. There were libraries on the north side of the kingdom, and he went through all of the cavernous disused rooms, many of which held moldy books stuck together with damp. Evidently it had been a long time since there were outside students in the libraries of Morne.

No one bothered Danny, although people still whispered behind his back and he had the feeling that reports were going back to the vizier.

That evening as he walked back toward his room, he caught sight of Dixie in the distance.

"Dixie!" he called. She was intent on a book, but when she heard his voice she looked up and disappeared. When he got to the spot where he had seen her, the open book was lying on the ground, but there was no sign of her, no matter how much he called her name. He picked up the

210

book. It was an old leather-bound tome, and the title, embossed on the cover in faded gold letters, was *On Treachery*. Danny had the uncomfortable feeling that Dixie had meant for him to find it.

The next few days passed without incident. Dixie was obviously disappearing every time she saw him, and her room was always locked. Danny didn't know what to do with himself. He went to the storeroom both nights, but there was no sign of Lily. He saw her during the day, but she was always with the Cherb, who glared at him if he got too close.

On the third day he met the chancellor, Camroc, in a corridor. Camroc was bustling along but stopped when he saw Danny.

"Are you still here?" he said in surprise.

"Yes, well, I'm, er, still studying," Danny said, "and I've still got to tell the vizier what the mountain says."

"Of course," Camroc said. "I'm getting so forgetful. That'll be during the Leaving Ceremony in two days."

"The Leaving Ceremony?" Danny asked, puzzled.

"Yes," Camroc said, "there will of course be music and the singing of the old songs." Camroc looked off into the distance and hummed a few bars, and for the first time Danny realized that there was a strong smell of red wine from Camroc.

"What is the Leaving Ceremony?" Danny asked. Camroc looked at him in surprise.

"It's when the kingdom of Morne moves to a new

location. The rain forest, I think, this time. Canoeing on the Amazon to look forward to, boy!" Camroc burst into song, a strange, harsh noise in an unknown tongue, not without a certain wild beauty. Danny stared at him. He had two days to make up his mind: would he steal the Treaty Stone and bring it to Wilsons, or join forces with Lily?

Many miles away Agent Stone rubbed his tired eyes, put down the book he had been studying and sighed.

"What is it?" Pearl asked.

"It should be one of the great discoveries," he said, "the existence of a whole new world, separated from ours by space and time. The old legends begin to make sense, the stories of the gods and the underworld—so why am I so worried all the time?"

"Maybe because the fate of both worlds now rests on the shoulders of a small boy," Pearl said, "and that boy is . . ."

"Our son?" Stone said.

"Don't say that," Pearl said. "It isn't true."

"Perhaps not in a strict sense," Stone said, "but he has no one else."

"He might have been better off without us. With us around he didn't have to look far to find the meaning of betrayal. We cheated him from the start."

"Then we must make up for that," Stone said.

"If we can," Pearl said, sitting down and staring into the ashes of the fire. "If we can."

THE IRON MAIDEN

Try as they might, Vandra and Toxique could not get Les to tell them what familiar thing he thought had changed in Wilsons.

"I have to be sure first," he said. "What if I'm wrong? It would be terrible if I was wrong. I have to talk to some-one on the staff."

"Who would you talk to?" Toxique asked.

Vandra snorted. "Not Brunholm, anyway. And Duddy's not much use."

"What about Valant? Or Spitfire?"

"No," Les said with a frown, "I'll have to go right to the top."

"To Devoy?" Vandra said.

"To Devoy," Les said grimly, then, as if to himself, "but what if they're all in on it?"

* * *

It was no surprise to Vandra and Toxique when Les got out of bed that night and sneaked out of the boys' Roosts. They had concealed themselves on the roof of the girls' Roosts to watch for him. Les was so lost in thought as he passed them that they could have dropped something on his head and he wouldn't have noticed. Once he had descended the stairs they jumped down and followed him. He made a beeline for the main building. Vandra and Toxique had learned much about tracking in Wilsons, but they didn't need any of their skills, Les was so wrapped up in his mission.

They followed him through the front door, past Valant's empty desk and into the gloomy corridors that led to the heart of the building. They soon lost sight of him in the shifting shadows, and when they came to a fork they argued about which branch to take until a raven flew over their heads and into the left-hand branch.

"I think that settles it," Vandra said, and they followed the raven. On they went, passing one of the interior courtyards where the Messengers exercised, the lighting getting dimmer and dimmer, until they were almost in darkness.

"I don't like this," Toxique said, his voice rising. "I think someone's going to attack!"

The lights went out altogether. Toxique shrieked as a wiry arm wrapped around his neck. Vandra fell heavily against the wall but recovered quickly enough to grab a torch from her pocket. When she turned it on, she saw Les choking Toxique.

"Les!" she shouted. "It's us!" Slowly he released Toxique.

"Sorry. I thought it was . . . Never mind. You'd better come with me now. But stay outside when I'm talking to Devoy."

They jumped at a clanging noise from nearby.

"What's that?" Toxique whispered, a hysterical edge to his voice. They heard the sound again.

"Take it easy, Toxique," Vandra said, but there was something sinister about the noise.

"It's this way," Les said. He set out determinedly. With a glance at each other, Vandra and Toxique followed.

The noise was coming from the other side of the teachers' common room. They crept through it. The Unknown Spy watched them silently from his barred window. They could almost feel his eyes on them as they tiptoed past, approaching the front of the house. Toxique looked terrified.

"The noise . . . ," he said. "It's coming from that room—you know the one."

"The torture chamber," Vandra said grimly.

"There could be work ahead for you tonight, physick," Toxique said.

"I'm in no condition to help anyone."

Reluctantly they moved along the corridor toward the torture chamber. The noise came again, a horrible melancholy boom. Vandra glanced at Toxique, hoping he wouldn't cry out. But he merely rolled his eyes.

"I know what it is," he said. "I know what we're going to see."

The three friends got to the room. Vandra and Les lay down and inched forward so that they were looking beneath the door. They had a clear view, and their hearts sank when they saw what was going on. A man stood with his back to them. He was oiling the hinges of the iron maiden—the steel coffin with the spiked lid. As they watched he moved the lid back and forth, then slammed it shut as if to test the hinges. They heard the boom again as the iron maiden closed. The man turned and they saw him in profile. It was Devoy.

They wanted to leave, but a horrified fascination rooted them to the spot. They watched Devoy polish the thumbscrews, check the tensions on the rack and dust the teethpullers and bonecrushers. The expression on his face did not change—it never did—but there was something demonic about the calm way he moved from instrument to instrument.

It was Vandra who broke the spell, drawing Toxique and Les back from the doorway. In silence they walked back through the common room and the unpeopled corridors of Wilsons; they did not speak until they were out in the open air.

"If it was Brunholm," Les said at last, "it wouldn't have been so bad. You would have expected it. But Devoy?"

"Yes," Vandra said, "and who is he planning to torture? All that stuff is ready to go."

Toxique said nothing but made a snuffling noise. Vandra put her hand on his arm.

"I don't know about you," Les said, "but I don't really feel like bed."

"Me neither," Vandra said. "What about the summerhouse?"

"Okay," Les said, "I've got some tea there, and some muffins we can toast."

The friends made their way to the gardens and on through the forest to the summerhouse. The night was calm, cold and quiet, and they moved without making much noise. A careless observer would have thought that everyone was safely in bed at Wilsons, but nighttime at Wilsons was sometimes busier than the day, and at least one pair of eyes was watching them.

Vicky the siren was in a bad mood. For weeks now she had been aware of another presence in the building—someone who was using her secret routes for getting around without being seen. Whoever it was didn't seem to care very much about covering up after himself. Manhole covers were left askew, secret entrances to hidden passages weren't properly replaced after use, and food and tools and all sorts of trash were strewn about. For all that she was vicious, amoral and untrustworthy, the Maid of the North Shore was also extremely tidy. She might have tolerated sharing her secret world with someone who kept it looking shipshape, but she wasn't going to put up with a mess.

She had tried laying traps for the intruder, but he was

cunning, and the traps had been contemptuously thrown aside. There was nothing for it but to use the siren songs that in years gone by had lured innumerable ships onto the rocks and sent scores of sailors to a watery grave.

Vicky had gotten rusty, so she had just spent a week in the woods refining her technique. She had charmed the birds from the trees at first. She had tempted spring flowers into opening, then left them to blacken and die in the frost. She had charmed blind moles from the ground, and by the end of the week she was able to lure foxes and weasels and all animals that were cunning and wary. She was ready.

She had picked a spot where her voice would travel along part of the network of secret passages but would not penetrate the walls to lure other inhabitants of the school. She cleared her throat and tried a few practice notes, then began.

The sweet music drifted through the tunnels and passageways, gathering in force until it seemed that the very stones of the passages would weep, and the creeping crawling creatures of the night stopped their business and dreamed. Vicky gave herself up to her treacherous song until it seemed that nothing, neither man nor beast could resist it. . . .

"Oi!"

Vicky blinked and her song faltered. Had she heard a noise?

"Oi, you!" The siren's song came to an abrupt halt. Was she hearing correctly?

"Me?"

"Yes, you. Would you shut up with that bloody singing? I'm trying to get some sleep here."

Vicky couldn't tell where the gruff voice was coming from. The speaker was evidently able to use the twisting tunnels to disguise his location.

"What do you mean 'bloody singing'?" Vicky said crossly. "That's a classic siren song."

"Just sounds like noise to me," the voice said, "and it's keeping me awake."

"I'll have you know that this voice has lured ships onto rocks for decades . . . longer!" Vicky said.

"Must have been tone-deaf sailors, then," the voice grumbled. "It doesn't do anything for me, so put a sock in it."

Vicky's mouth hung open. Never in a long career had she been told to put a sock in it. She put her hand in her pocket and produced a slender razor-sharp knife.

"Maybe if you told me where you are I could sing you a lullaby," she said in as sweet a voice as she could manage.

"Stick your lullaby," the voice said. "I'd rather have the ravens sing me to sleep."

Vicky crouched to listen. The owner of the voice was either very smart or very lucky, for such were the echoes that she still could not tell the direction from which his words came.

"Now push off," the voice said. Almost crying with vexation, Vicky retreated. She had never been so insulted. And, as if to add insult to injury, extremely loud snoring immediately began to echo from the passageway behind her.

219

Despite the cold, the summerhouse always felt welcome, as if its old planks retained the warmth of distant summers. Les busied himself making hot milky tea while Vandra toasted the muffins. Toxique lit some old candle stubs.

"There's nothing we can do about Devoy at the minute," Vandra said firmly, "and if Les still won't tell us what or who he suspects—"

"In case I'm wrong," Les said, looking torn.

"—then we'll have to go with what we have. Which is what the Unknown Spy told us. That one possible reason for his wife's murder was that she was the inventor of the Sibling Strategy. But what was the strategy? And why was she murdered for it?"

"To tell you the truth," Les said, sounding a little ashamed, "I don't even know what a sibling is."

"A sibling is a brother or a sister!" A cloaked figure carrying a revolver stepped into the circle of candlelight. Toxique stifled a scream. Les cursed out loud and Vandra jumped to her feet. The figure threw its cloak back. It was Cheryl.

"Phew," said Les. "I thought you were a Cherb."

"If I had been, you would all be dead," Cheryl said. "I could hear and see you for miles."

"So much for the Gift of Anticipation," Les muttered to Toxique.

"Don't look at me," Toxique said. "I told you it doesn't work all the time."

"Just keep better watch the next time," Cheryl said.

"Your carelessness will cost you, though!" They looked at her nervously. "A cup of tea and a muffin," she continued with a laugh. "Now, what's all this about the Sibling Strategy?"

"We just want to know what it is," Vandra said.

"It's simple enough, though it requires a lot of skill and experience," Cheryl said. "All you do is use a close relative against the subject. There are variations, of course. There's the Double Sibling Strategy, the Older and Younger variations, the Fake Sibling Variation. McGuinness has been researching it. It appears that the Unknown Spy's wife developed it after she was betrayed by her younger brother. His betrayal haunted her all her life."

"But what would she use the strategy for?"

"That's what I don't know," Cheryl admitted, her words garbled by the muffin she was eating. Melted butter ran down her chin. Vandra turned the "S" and "G" ring on her finger, feeling that something in this conversation was vital to Danny. But what? At least the ring made her feel connected to him. She reminded herself that he had given it to her and to no one else. She flushed. Toxique asked her if she was feeling warm, but she turned away from him with a half smile and did not answer.

WHAT THE MOUNTAIN SAID

The following day Lily came to Danny's room early.

"I didn't mean to wake you," she said, "but I haven't been sleeping all that well. We need to decide what to do, Danny."

"Where's the Cherb?" Danny said, peering up and down the corridor.

"He's doing the final preparations for stealing the Treaty Stone," Lily said. "We have the day together. Whatever you decide, Danny, we'll always have this day."

As he and Lily left the room, Danny saw Dixie disappearing at the end of the corridor. Why can't she understand that I've found my sister? Danny thought, the influence of the Room of Malign Intentions distorting his thoughts.

But for that day there was nothing to do but to walk in

the gorgeous halls and corridors of Morne, ignoring the courtiers muttering in corners. Danny and Lily climbed towers that neared the soaring granite peaks of the mountain. It was beautiful and silent. They had brought a picnic from one of the dining halls, and as they ate, Danny told Lily of his upbringing by two secret agents who had pretended to be his parents. Lily said her childhood had been hard. There had been no pretense that the couple who reared her were her real parents. She'd been abandoned, they said, usually adding that they weren't surprised since she was lazy and no-good, despite the fact that she worked from dawn to dusk, cleaning the cheap boardinghouse that they kept.

"Think about it, Danny. When we rule the Two Worlds we'll be able to find our real parents!"

It was dusk before they returned from the high peaks, walking slowly. They parted outside Danny's door. When Lily reached the end of the corridor, she turned and gave him a long steady look.

Danny went into his room and sat on the bed. He had made up his mind. He could not let his sister be at the mercy of the Ring. If he had been able to think about it properly, he could have found another way out. He could have taken Lily back to Wilsons with him. He could even have joined the Ring again and protected her that way. But the influence of the Room of Malign Intentions still hung over him, clouding his judgment, an influence that was still there when Dixie appeared right in front of him.

223

"I wish you'd stop doing that," he said sourly.

" 'Hello, Dixie' would have been nicer," she said. She looked tired. There were dark shadows under her eyes.

"Danny, we need to do something about getting the Treaty Stone. If it's broken . . ."

"If it's broken, then so what? Devoy isn't right about everything, you know."

"I can't believe you've gone over to . . . to the Ring, just like that!"

"I haven't gone over to the Ring!"

"Well, what's going on, then? Who is that girl? Why are you hanging round with her?"

Danny wanted to scream at Dixie to stop being so stupid, that Lily was his sister. But the Room of Malign Intentions stopped him, and somewhere in the fog of his mind prowled Danny the Spy.

"Just leave her out of it," he mumbled.

"I can't," Dixie said. "I don't trust her. . . ."

"That's enough," Danny snapped. "I do."

"Danny, we're friends," Dixie said. "Tomorrow at the Leaving Ceremony we have to stand up and tell the vizier what the mountain says, and after that we have to get out of here with the Treaty Stone. We're a team."

But a voice in Danny's head said, *She's wrong. You and Lily are a team.* He felt a wave of cunning sweep over him, warm and sickly.

"It's all right, Dixie," he heard himself say. "We'll get the Stone. I'm really just following your plan, getting close to the girl so that I can get the Stone off her once the Cherb has stolen it."

"What about getting it out of Morne?"

"I've found a side door. Can't you trust me?"

"Are you sure?" Dixie looked at him closely.

"Of course," he lied. "Sorry. I should have told you what I was doing. You get used to not trusting people."

"You can say that again," Dixie said, looking a bit more cheerful. "This Louis character, I don't think I trust him as far as I could throw him. None of the people here."

"I'm getting a bit tired," Danny said, faking a yawn.

"Okay, I'm off, then," Dixie said. "By the way, do you definitely have the answer? What the mountains say?"

"Yes, I'm sorry. I should have told you sooner." Danny hesitated. "They say . . . 'storm.'"

Dixie smiled at him. "I knew you wouldn't leave me as a slave for the dead. Night!"

One minute Dixie was there; the next she was gone. Danny stared miserably at the spot where she had been standing. Why had he told her the wrong answer? And why had he not told the truth about Lily?

He went to the window and looked out onto the snowy mountains. He could tell Dixie the real answer tomorrow. He could pretend it was a joke. He wouldn't let his friend end up in the hands of the dead. He lay down on the bed and fell into an uneasy sleep.

The following day, though, it wasn't easy to get close to Dixie. She always seemed to be in the distance, and when he approached her, the boy Louis appeared and tried to engage him in conversation on some pretext or other. The

Leaving Ceremony would begin that afternoon, and Danny became increasingly desperate. The people of Morne, in even greater finery than usual, flocked into the hallways around the vizier's court. Camroc walked through the crowd, looking around with great satisfaction, humming snatches of obscure songs. Danny found himself face to face with Macari, in bright blue silk and a hat with a peacock's feather in it. Macari winked at him.

"Glad I didn't have to leave my mark on you," he laughed. Danny wasn't sure whether being branded with a white-hot iron was funny, but he grinned mirthlessly back.

A hand plucked his sleeve and drew him aside. Lily. Her face was taut with anxiety.

"The Cherb will steal the Treaty Stone during the festivities," she whispered. "We can get out by the storeroom. Danny, I . . . I need to know . . ."

"I'm coming with you," he found himself saying. "We've been let down enough."

"What about your friend?"

"Don't worry about her, she's taken care of." Danny barely recognized his own voice. It reminded him of the time he had taken voice dye and acquired a gruff tone.

More and more people crowded into the hall. The great doors to the court opened and the people surged forward. Danny was separated from Lily. At the edge of the throng he could see the Cherb boy slipping away. Macari grabbed Danny's arm.

"Your presence is required, my friend." Across the

room Danny saw Lily being escorted by Camroc, and Dixie, whose arm was being held—presumably to stop her disappearing—being escorted by a not-so-friendly-looking Louis.

The crowd parted as Danny, Dixie and Lily were led toward the dais where the vizier sat, his gaze resting on each of them in turn. The room fell silent.

"Where is our little Cherb friend?" he said quietly. Camroc paled and looked around wildly. "Never mind," the vizier said, his voice cold, "we'll deal with that lapse later. He would have been little use to the dead anyway, being treacherous and untrustworthy. No. We will deal with the others only."

He motioned to Camroc, who handed them each a quill and parchment.

"Each of you will write down what the mountains say and hand your answer to Camroc," the vizier said.

Now is the time! Danny thought. Tell Dixie!

"You are not to speak, on pain of death," the vizier said smoothly, as though reading his mind. Dixie smiled confidently at Danny. He stared at her, frozen.

"Write down the answer," the vizier said. Dixie bent over and rested the parchment on her knees. Danny watched his friend as if she was signing her own death warrant. "Write!" the vizier commanded. Lily bent to her parchment. Danny watched his own hand moving as though it was being controlled by someone else.

"Turn and show what you have written to the subjects of Morne." Lily turned first. She held up her parchment, a single word on it: *Alone.* Dixie looked confused, then looked at Danny. Of course Danny had given her the right word! She held up her parchment. A great sigh ran through the crowd. Louis shook his head slowly and smiled. Treacherous! Danny thought, then realized with shame, and a vile sense of accomplishment, that his was by far the greatest treachery. He held up his own parchment. *Alone.*

"Take the girl," the vizier said quietly. Two of the dead appeared and grabbed Dixie's arms before she could disappear. With a cry and a look of disbelief, she was pulled off into the crowd. Danny stared after her, stunned. Her parchment landed faceup on the ground. *Storm*, it read.

There was a long silence in the room; then, with a thin sneer, Louis began to clap. The applause spread in ripples until the whole room was clapping. Then the vizier held up his hand. The clapping stopped. Camroc coughed, cleared his throat and emitted a long ululating wail.

It was the signal for the festivities to begin. Jugglers and fire-breathers poured into the hall. The ceiling flowered with brightly colored trapeze artists. Great tables groaning with food appeared in alcoves around the hall. Danny watched, bewildered. The room exploded in flames and firecrackers and music. He prowled the perimeter, looking for his sister, but she was nowhere to be seen. Dixie's frightened face kept coming into his mind, but somehow he was able to thrust it away.

Finally a frantic Lily grabbed him.

"Where have you been? I've been looking for you everywhere. Nala is about to make his move, but the minute he gets his hands on the Stone we'd better be ready to go!"

Nala? Danny hadn't even thought of the Cherb as having a name.

They slipped out of the hall and raced through the empty corridors toward the museum. The dead blond girl wasn't at her desk.

"That was a good move, throwing your pal to the dead," Lily said. "They'll be distracted with her for a while."

A shudder ran through Danny. They ran on into the museum. Lily stopped in front of the Treaty Stone. Danny gasped. Nala had woven a cage of strong golden thread around the case. The thread shone in the spotlights aimed at the kingdom's treasure.

"It's made of Thread of Independent Motion," Lily said. "You tell it where to go and it'll go there. The best thing is that it's very strong. You can climb on it. Go, Nala!"

The Cherb leapt up from his hiding place and grabbed one of the golden threads. Hauling himself arm over arm, he climbed. Danny could see that the thread had been positioned to avoid the many beams and security fixtures around the Stone, and he could only marvel at the complexity with which it had been strung up. The Morne people had complete confidence in their security, but they hadn't reckoned on Nala. With breathtaking nimbleness the little figure swung in and around the security beams.

Danny held his breath as the Cherb got closer and closer to the Stone. Once, the boy slipped, only just holding on to avoid the pressure sensors on the floor below him.

After half an hour Nala reached the Stone. Danny felt a hint of admiration for the little Cherb, his bravery and skill. He watched as Nala went behind the Stone. He took an ordinary stone of the same size and shape as the Treaty Stone from a side pocket. With one swift movement he removed the Treaty Stone and dropped the plain one in its place.

"Weight sensors," Lily said, her eyes not leaving the Cherb. "Hurry, Nala." He began the long climb back, doing everything in reverse. Nala appeared to be at the limit of his strength, sweat running from his face, his limbs beginning to falter, but still Lily urged him on.

It was bound to happen. Nala lunged for the final golden thread, but his hand slipped and he tumbled to the floor. Alarms started to sound, loud and mournful. There was a great rumbling at the entrance to the Treaty Stone Room and a massive gate started to slide across the entrance.

"Hurry!" Lily shouted. Nala limped toward them, holding the Stone. Lily grabbed it and began to run toward the entrance. The gate was already halfway across, and gathering speed. Danny took the Stone from Lily. It was surprisingly light. They had almost reached the gate when they heard a cry behind them. Nala was limping heavily. He stretched out his arms for help, but Lily pushed Danny ahead. They stumbled through the shrinking gap and the gates closed with a clang behind them.

Nala gripped the bars. He said nothing, but his eyes were fixed not on Lily but on Danny.

"Leave him," Lily said. "He's played his part." Danny followed her, but he felt the Cherb's eyes drilling into his back.

They heard running feet and shouting, but Lily had planned her route well. They ducked down side corridors and unused maintenance tunnels. Within minutes they were in the little storeroom. Lily opened the door. She pushed Danny through. They stood in the snow, the evening shadows lengthening. There were free of Morne. They had stolen the Treaty Stone. And Dixie was a prisoner, betrayed and abandoned.

20

A DISCOVERY

For some days Les had noticed that the mood of the other pupils wasn't good. There was continuous grumbling at mealtimes and in the Roosts.

"Everybody seems to be on some sort of punishment detail," Vandra pointed out. Les nodded. He had spent all his spare time that week scraping ancient raven droppings from one of the disused buildings in Ravensdale as part the punishment for his Fourth Regulation offense. Everywhere pupils were engaged in difficult and sometimes dangerous cleaning jobs, or studying long into the night. There had been several fistfights among the boys, and cliques had formed in the girls' Roosts.

"Who's handing out all these punishments?" Toxique asked. Les looked tight-lipped. Vandra watched him.

"Hang on a second," she said. "I know what you're thinking."

"What?" Les said defensively.

"It's Blackpitt, isn't it? He's the one who's handing out all the punishments. He's the familiar thing that's changed!"

"I didn't want to say," Les said miserably. "Blackpitt was always dead good to me. I can't understand what's happened to him. He's been got at somehow, blackmailed or something."

"We have to find him and make him talk," Vandra said.

"How do we do that? None of us has ever seen him."

"I suppose," Toxique said, "we find a wire and follow it."

It proved harder than that. There were miles of ducts, and the wires were well concealed. When they did find one, it was difficult to separate it from other wires. All they could really discover was that all the wire led up toward the roof.

"I'm not sure I want to tangle with that roof man again," Les said, remembering Danny's run-in with the guardian of the roofs.

"I don't think we have a choice," Vandra said.

"But how do we get there?" Toxique asked.

Help came from an unexpected quarter. Vandra and Toxique went back to the Roosts to think, but Les, on his way to Ravensdale, ran straight into Vicky the siren as she leapt from a ledge above his head.

"Sorry, Vicky," Les said. The siren glared at him.

"Just be more careful next time," she said.

"You don't look very happy."

"Things aren't the same around here," she said darkly, "not at all the same."

"What's up?" Les fell into step beside her.

"There's a sneak about," she said. "I keep looking for him, but he stays out of my way."

"A sneak? Listen," Les said carefully, "you're only one person. A few more sets of eyes might make it easier. I wouldn't mind helping you. The roof would probably be the best place to look, don't you think?"

"Would you look?" Vicky said suspiciously. "I wouldn't be able to pay you."

"That's perfectly all right," Les said. "Glad to be of service. The only thing is how to get to the roof."

"That's no problem," Vicky said airily. "I'll show you."

Soon Les, Vandra and Toxique found themselves climbing up through an extremely dirty and wet drainage pipe with Vicky dancing in front of them, seemingly able to negotiate the dirtiest and tightest spaces while remaining spotless. When they got out of the pipe they had to crawl through a ventilation duct, then up a series of back stairs and decrepit ladders with missing rungs. Looking back, Les could see the pale, determined faces of Toxique and

Vandra, who climbed grimly through the dark behind him.

After what seemed like hours Vicky threw open a rusty iron door and they emerged. There was a strong cold wind blowing across the peaks and valleys of the Wilsons roof, and Les gulped great lungfuls while trying to rub the cobwebs and dust off his face and out of his eyes.

"We'll spread out in a line," he said, "and try to find Blackp—I mean, the intruder."

They crisscrossed the vast roof for an hour but didn't see anyone, although they stumbled across all sorts of rusting and abandoned equipment—pumps, compressors and old spy tools such as broken telescopes and satellite dishes. It wasn't until they reached the edge that they found something suspicious—a little nest that had been concealed with camouflage netting. Inside were a pair of binoculars and a microphone with a large dish around it.

"It's a directional mike," Vandra said. "You can listen to far-off conversations with it."

"And whoever was here had a perfect view of everyone who was coming and going from Wilsons."

"Something's going on."

They hunted until dusk. The wind had turned colder and they were tired. Les slipped on a broken slate and cut his leg. As he sat with his trouser leg rolled up, Toxique came over.

"There's nothing here," Les said.

"You probably right," Toxique said, "but with Danny and Dixie gone, we've got to do something. I wonder how they're getting on?"

They were about to give up when Les spotted something. The evening light had cast strong shadows across the rooftops, so that the wet slates showed different tones.

"Look." Les pointed. Leading up to an old wooden door was a trail that had been invisible earlier on. They followed the path to the door. It looked as if it hadn't been opened for years, but Toxique rubbed his finger around the battered lock and sniffed.

"Oil," he said. "Somebody's been keeping it lubricated." All four went for lockpicks and hairpins, but Vicky was first. In a flash she had a long hairpin in her hand and the lock was picked. The others followed cautiously.

The room was a prison cell. The windows had been barred. There was a bare wooden bunk in one corner. On the floor was a tin mug half-full of brackish water, and beside it a tin plate with a few crusts. On the bunk lay a figure dressed in a dirty paisley dressing gown with what had once been a silk handkerchief in the pocket but was now a pathetic rag. A few scraps of hair clung to the skull; a pathetic attempt had been made to smooth them. Underneath the dressing gown were badly stained trousers. The person's uneven breathing was only just audible.

"I do believe we've found Mr. Blackpitt," Vandra said.

Blackpitt was unconscious. Vandra examined him.

"There's nothing I can do for him here," she said. "He's severely malnourished. Whoever's been keeping him here hasn't bothered to feed him."

"What's this got to do with my intruder?" Vicky

demanded. Vandra rounded on her crossly, but Les intervened.

"Could be everything," Les said. "The person who's giving you a hard time could be the person who's keeping Blackpitt here."

"We need to get him to the apothecary," Vandra said.

"I need him to talk," Vicky said.

"In that case you'd better help us," Vandra said. Vicky sprang to the bed and scooped up the unconscious Blackpitt as if he weighed nothing at all. She was out of the door like a shot. The others ran to catch up as Vicky leapt lightly across the rooftops.

Even Vicky couldn't carry Blackpitt down the way they had come, though his emaciated body weighed very little. Instead, she led them to a little hut on the roof, which opened to reveal a rickety-looking lift. The cage was broken and the flywheel rusted. Vicky jumped on board. The others followed, Les looking nervously at Toxique.

"You getting any feelings about this?" Les whispered.

"Nothing," Toxique said, "but that doesn't mean the cable isn't going to snap."

"Thanks, Toxique," Les said, and immediately grabbed the side of the cage as the ground was snatched away from under his feet. With a cacophony of shrieks and groans the ancient lift plummeted into the building. Sparks and flakes of rust flew from the cable. Toxique's mouth was moving but Les couldn't hear him. Even the normally calm Vandra was clinging to the side of the cage. Vicky looked unperturbed and punched a button with her fist. The lift came to a halt as if it had hit a brick floor. Toxique groaned and fell over. Les felt as if all his internal organs had been hurled downward and squashed into his feet. The door screeched open and Vicky skipped out, still holding the unconscious Blackpitt.

Les staggered to the door. They were outside the apothecary entrance. Vicky pushed in and dumped Blackpitt on an examining table in front of a surprised Jamshid.

"Fix him," she said.

An hour later Blackpitt was in bed, sleeping peacefully. Vandra had ingested a glucose solution that Jamshid had prepared and injected it into Blackpitt's veins. He had whimpered a little and held up one frail hand, murmuring "No!" before falling back on the bed. There were bruises and marks of beatings all over his body. Vandra looked furious. Les bit his lip. He knew what he would do to whoever had done this. Jamshid shooed them out of the place.

They made their way out of the apothecary toward the stairs, not willing to chance the lift. As they set foot on the first step a familiar voice sounded from a hidden speaker.

"My three favorite cadets," it snarled, "and with the beautiful if somewhat treacherous siren in tow. Another Fifth Regulation offense this time, I think. Latrine duty for the little Messenger. He'll be picking filth out of his feathers for a month."

They looked at each other. Whoever it was obviously hadn't discovered that Blackpitt had been rescued.

"Toxique," Les whispered. "I've got a plan. Go to the Roosts. Get as many people as you can and line them up as if they're welcoming a visitor coming up the front drive. Quickly."

Toxique looked at him in puzzlement; then realization dawned. He hurried off.

"Come on," Les said to Vandra. "I didn't want to risk having Toxique scream out when we're sneaking up, but I want you to stay in the background, Vandra, when we make our move on whoever it is. Let's go!"

Vicky took them back to the roof in the lift, the way up being no less terrifying than the way down. When the lift arrived, it fell back about six feet, then shot up again, striking the interior of the little hut with a crash.

"Ouch," Les muttered as his head thumped against the wire cage. He and Vandra followed Vicky out of the lift. The wind cut through their clothing like knives. They found the shelter of a chimney and huddled behind it. Only Vicky was unperturbed, as usual. She produced a nail file and started manicuring her nails.

It felt like hours before they heard cheering coming from the direction of the front drive. It wasn't very loud, and in fact sounded more like the grumbling of a large number of people who would rather be in bed. They waited another few minutes, then crept out. The rooftop was slippery from frost, and they had to move slowly; though the wind and the creak of aerials and dishes and battered old surveillance equipment covered the sound of their advance as they moved toward the nest at the front of the building.

As they got close to the edge of the building, Vicky held up her hand. They could just see the outline of someone crouched in the nest. Moonlight glinted from binoculars. Down below there was another forced cheer from the gathered cadets.

Les, Vandra and Vicky approached the nest along the edge of the roof, not daring to look to their left, where the crumbling parapet had given way in places so that there was nothing between them and the sheer drop below. There was a flash of steel in Vicky's hand. Closer and closer they crept. Les stopped Vandra. He didn't want the physick getting caught up in a struggle; she was too important. The figure in the nest was intent on what was going on below and didn't move.

Les and Vicky were almost at the edge of the nest when disaster struck. A small door onto the roof was flung open and Brunholm strode out.

"Hey!" he shouted. "You cadets! What are you doing up here? Get down right now!"

Things happened very fast after that. Brunholm stepped on a patch of ice and, with a howl of anger and pain, flew into the air and landed on his back. The figure in the nest whirled around. Les felt fingers like iron hawsers around his throat as he stared into a pair of red-rimmed eyes, one brown, the other bright blue. It was Rufus Ness, the spymaster of the Cherbs.

Suddenly, Ness gasped and his grip weakened. One

hand went to his shoulder, where bright red blood was spilling onto his tunic.

"So Cherb blood is red after all." Vicky wiped her knife fastidiously with a lace handkerchief. Ness bellowed with rage and charged at her, but Vicky skipped out of the way. Les stood up and swayed, light-headed, dangerously close to the parapet. Down below, the crowd of cadets stared in silence at the combat on the rooftops.

"Don't move!" Brunholm leveled a revolver at Ness. Ness spat on the ground and ran lightly along the parapet. Vandra tried to get out of his way, but she slipped. With a contemptuous grunt, Ness swung an arm at her. She staggered toward the brink and the rotten parapet beneath her feet gave way. There was a gasp from below, and a horrified intake of breath from Les as Vandra, without a sound, fell from view.

It was Toxique who later told them what happened next. He had found his fellow cadets asleep and had bullied and cajoled them out of bed by threatening to slip a mild but potent emetic into one of their meals if they didn't come with him. He had led them to the driveway and ordered them to cheer, then watched as Vandra tumbled through the air, her fall taking an age, seeming almost graceful as the ground rushed toward her. A scream died in his throat. There was nothing to be done. Then, with the speed of an arrow, a small shape flew across the façade of the building. As Vandra turned in the air, she was seized by a pair of frail arms. The watchers held their breath as the little rescuer struggled to maintain altitude, the weight too much for the small body, the ground approaching too fast. At the last second the rescuer found strength from somewhere, slowed, hovered in the air for a second, then fell straight into a patch of gooseberry bushes.

"Now, my dear," the elderly Messenger Daisy had said, picking herself out of the bushes and attempting to remove several thorns from her legs, "one good turn deserves another, don't you think?"

On the roof, Ness had disappeared in the confusion. Brunholm began to fire into the darkness. A ricochet struck the chimney beside Les's head, and he had to wait until Brunholm had emptied the revolver and the hammer was clicking on an empty chamber before he could emerge from cover.

"Where's Vicky?" he asked.

"Gone after that murdering scum," Brunholm growled, pocketing the gun. A skylight in the roof was open and there was fresh blood on the entrance. "Let them go. Neither is any great loss."

An hour later Devoy and Brunholm sat in the library of the third landing while Les, Vandra and Toxique told him what had happened.

"The levels of punishment were severe, I see that now," Devoy said. "My thoughts were with Danny and Dixie, and I wasn't paying attention to what was happening right under my nose. It shakes me to my core to know that Rufus Ness infiltrated Wilsons. He was obviously responsible for the assassination attempts on you, Les—he must have planted the idea of killing Les in the Unknown Spy's head—and the attempt on poor Daisy."

"And me," Brunholm put in. "That crossbow is a Cherb trick, all right."

Devoy had been standing in front of the fire. Now he moved across the room until he was in front of the Mirror of Limited Reflection, which showed his face but none of the room behind him. He was indeed shaken to the core by the fact that Ness had been at large in Wilsons, might even still be there. He looked up at the portrait of Ambrose Longford. It had been an achievement in itself for the Ring to get Ness into Wilsons, but Devoy knew Longford always had a larger scheme up his sleeve.

"What about the Unknown Spy's wife?" he asked.

"Ness, without a doubt," Brunholm said. "It was done to turn the Unknown Spy against Knutt." He looked at Les with dislike. "Though why he would go to so much bother to get rid of a mere Messenger boy . . ."

"Quite," Devoy said, "no offense, of course," he said to the reddening Les, "but it seems unnecessarily complicated. If he wanted to kill Mr. Knutt—and we are all glad that he did not, of course—why did he not just kill him and be done with it?"

"Unless," Vandra began hesitantly, "it was a double bluff. We were meant to think he killed the Unknown Spy's wife as a way of getting the Spy to kill Les, whereas in fact the attempt on Les's life was a cover for getting rid of the Unknown Spy's wife, if you know what I mean . . . ," she concluded lamely.

"Excellent," Devoy said, "you're starting to think like a spy!"

"Yes," Brunholm said, "it makes sense, but why?"

"Why indeed," Devoy said. "How did Ness get into Wilsons? He couldn't have done it on his own. Blackpitt is the announcer now, but in his early years he was an exceptionally efficient and cautious agent. Ness would have needed help to overpower him and to take over his position."

"Excuse me," Toxique said, "but we did find out something. We know that the Unknown Spy's wife was an expert at the Sibling Strategy, but we don't know what that is."

Devoy's expression did not change, although it came closer to changing than it had in many years. His eyes gleamed. Longford always had another motive, a hidden agenda. And these children had stumbled upon it. The Sibling Strategy? How could he have been so blind?

CRYING

The walls of Morne towered above Danny and Lily. Danny sprawled in the snow, panting, then leapt to his feet.

"Run!" he said. "They'll be hunting us!"

"It's all right," Lily said. "They don't leave the walls of Morne. Ever. That little door we came through is for visitors."

"What about Macari?"

"The tunnel to his chip shop is part of the place. He never actually left the kingdom."

"Still," Danny said, "we need to get going. Night's coming on. We have to get to the shelter of the town."

The urgency of his own voice surprised him. It was as if he needed to get away before he became fully aware of what he had done. That moment wasn't far off. Outside the walls of Morne, the influence of the Room of Malign Intentions was wearing off quickly.

There was a loud rumble like distant thunder. The ground around them shook a little. A small piece of masonry fell from the wall above them and landed at Danny's feet.

"What's that?"

"It's the kingdom getting ready to relocate," Lily said. "It's breaking free of the mountains."

There was another loud rumble and this time a tiny maze of cracks ran along what had looked like a seamless join between the castle and the bedrock it stood on.

"It's going, of course," Danny said, "but won't it be back?"

Lily shrugged.

"According to Louis, it won't be back for eighty or ninety years, maybe more."

Danny stared at the castle. The full realization of his betrayal of Dixie came crashing down on him. If he had not put out a hand to steady himself he would have fallen. Nausea gripped his stomach. He had given her to the dead. He would never see his friend again.

"What is it, Danny? Are you okay?"

"I have to go back," he said, his voice thick and strange.

"Are you crazy?" Lily asked. "It'll take you with it. I'll never see you again."

"I have to go."

"Don't," she said despairingly. "Really, Danny! Don't forget. We stole from them!"

"If we go now," he said, "we'll have time to get Dixie out."

"No . . . I can't." Lily's face was white. She clutched the Treaty Stone tightly to her chest.

"Lily, come on. . . ."

"I can't."

Danny moved toward the door as another shudder sent snow cascading from one of the roofs.

"Wait here for me, then."

"Danny. You have to come with me. We're a family. We don't have room for anyone else."

"Dixie is my friend. That's important too."

"Not as important as family. She'll come between us. She doesn't like me." Lily took hold of Danny's sleeve and looked imploringly into his eyes. One large tear ran down her cheek, then another. She held Danny with her gaze, daring him to drag himself away. As her eyes brimmed, their color turned milky, and a single blue tear ran down her cheek. One brown eye emerged, its true color revealed by the salty tears that destroyed the membrane she had said she wore, like Danny, to disguise her half-Cherb nature. One brown eye and one blue, Danny thought, as it should be if she was his sister . . . except that there wasn't one brown and one blue.

As Lily's tears flowed, Danny found himself staring into a pair of liquid brown eyes. She saw the expression on his face. She used her sleeve to wipe her eyes, and it came away blue. She stared at it, then looked up at Danny. Danny stepped back. At first Lily looked shocked; then a smile spread across her face, a smile he had never seen before and did not like.

"Well," she said softly, "it had to be, didn't it, Danny. I really had you fooled."

Her voice was different too; the gentle girlish tone was gone. This was a woman's voice, sure of itself. Danny felt as if an abyss had opened at his feet.

"Lily—" he began.

"Is not my name," the other said, looking him up and down. "So you are the Fifth. You're not very cunning, if you don't mind my saying."

"Who are you?" Danny asked, feeling sick.

"It doesn't matter now. The important thing is that I have the Treaty Stone. I had hoped to string the whole thing out a little more."

"What whole thing?" Danny said.

"You and me, Danny," she said, in Lily's voice once more. "We can do anything we want. We can control the treaty. . . ."

"Stop," Danny said, holding his head.

"Yes, I'll stop." It was the woman's voice, harsher this time. "After all, I have the Stone. I'll be able to hold both worlds for ransom."

"I thought you were working for the Ring," Danny said. She laughed.

"So did they. They inserted me and Nala into Morne. But they are interested in conquest and I am interested in myself. Longford and Ness think it is good enough to keep their agents in poverty and send them into danger time after time. No more! They will have their Stone, but I will set the price!"

Behind Danny the kingdom walls shook again, and more snow was dislodged. From high up the valley came a low rumbling sound. He stared at the girl in despair. She had taken everything, every scrap of trust he had in the world. He did not know what she saw in his eyes, but she took a step back and a gun appeared in her hand. For the first time her voice was uncertain.

"I'm not afraid to use this, you know." Danny said nothing. He kept on staring at her. There was a low buzzing coming from Morne—or was it coming from inside his own head? With all his being he wished that she would disappear, that it would be as if she had never existed.

"I warn you!" The woman's voice rose to a scream. "I'll shoot if I have to." Danny said nothing. All he knew was that he wanted her destroyed. The buzzing noise in his head became a wild roar. He was dimly aware of the trigger being pulled, of a shot flying past his head. Then he was staring into her eyes, and they were filled with terror. He knew he had the power to obliterate her, and that he would. The gun fell from her hand.

As he began to unleash the terrible power that had gathered within him, a small voice spoke, asking if he could live with killing Lily for the rest of his life. At the very last second, a force he could not understand burst from him, and he struggled to control it, tried to contain the lethal impulse. He did not have the strength. There was only one place to focus.

The Treaty Stone in the girl's hands vibrated. She cried out as it began to warm, became hot, then white-hot. She dropped it, and a great cloud of steam rose from the melting snow. There was a loud cracking sound.

Without looking, Danny knew that the Treaty Stone was broken.

They both stared in horror as the snow cleared and the Stone emerged, sitting in a pit in the bedrock where it had melted through, smashed into many pieces.

Danny was numb, stunned by the enormity of what he had done. The Treaty Stone was smashed; the Upper World lay helpless to invasion from the Lower. Countless lives were in danger. And he had done it all because someone had lied about being a member of his family. He felt weak. The surge of power he had felt moments before had drained him. Lily, or whatever her name was, backed away from him, afraid that this time he really would kill her.

The rumbling from the mountain was increasing. More snow fell from the roofs. Danny looked up the mountain and saw a vast plume of white moving toward them, traveling faster than a man could run, picking up speed as it came. He shouted out to Lily, but she couldn't hear him. He beckoned to her, but she shook her head. She would not approach him. He shouted again and again, her betrayal forgotten, a single word.

"Avalanche!"

She turned too late. The avalanche was almost on her. She had time to turn back to Danny, her face a mask of horror; then the snow struck. Danny pressed himself against the wall as fine, powdery snow filled his nose and his mouth. There was a roar as if a hundred express trains were thundering down the mountain, and through it all he heard a distant shriek. The power of the avalanche threatened to suck him away from the wall, and he clung to the door handle behind him for hours, it seemed, his whole world white and cold and full of noise.

The silence, when it came, was almost louder than the avalanche. Danny blinked and rubbed snow from his face. The landscape in front of him was piled high with new snow. There was no sign of Lily. And there was no sign of the fragments of the Treaty Stone. For a long time Danny sat by the door, waves of remorse and of loss running through him. He had been given a sister and had her taken away. He had betrayed his friend and failed in his mission. Worse, he had destroyed the very thing he had been sent to save. The wall he leaned against shuddered and shuddered again, and once he thought he felt it lift from the bedrock and settle down. He slumped back against it, and as he did so, iron formed in his soul. He had failed at everything, but he would not let Dixie go to a living death. If he could not stop it, he would go with her.

He straightened, his mind hard and cold. No one would get past his defenses again. But he had betrayed a friend, and that was a wrong that had to be righted. He grabbed the door handle and wrenched it open.

Danny ran through the empty storeroom and up the stairs. To his surprise the courtiers of Morne wore working clothes and were busily engaged in packing away exquisite objects and fastening paintings to the wall with wire. Furniture was being secured and the pillars checked. Danny ducked into a side room and found a pair of overalls and a cap. He put on the overalls and pulled the cap down over his eyes, put his overcoat on again, then moved stealthily along the corridors. He saw Camroc coming toward him, so he scooped up a piece of statuary and carried it in front of himself to hide his face.

He got to the museum, and for the first time in Morne, he had a stroke of luck. The dead girl he had stolen the key from was standing by her desk. It had been turned upside down and ransacked. She was crying as she went frantically through a pile of paper and files.

"What's up, love?" he said, making his voice deeper.

"Nothing's up," she said, "only lost the most important key in the place. They're threatening to send me to the Crypts forever!"

"What would you do to get it back?"

"Anything," she said, crying bitterly. Danny leaned close to her so that she could see his face. He lowered his voice.

"I can get it for you. Key for a key." She looked at him, then recognized him.

"You! You took the key!"

"Shh," Danny said. "Will you do it?

"Depends," she said. "What key do you want?"

"The girl," he said, "the one the vizier sent as a servant to the dead. I want the key to her cell."

"Her . . . I don't know. . . ."

"What are the Crypts like, anyway?" Danny asked. "I have no problem if you want to spend ten or twenty years there for losing the key." Something hard in his voice caught the girl's attention. "Well?" he said.

"Okay," she said in a small voice. "I hear she's not much good as a servant anyway."

The entire building gave a lurch, which almost threw Danny off his feet.

"Quickly," he said. The girl followed him. A raven flew overhead. If it had any opinion on how the slight boy had so cowed one of the dead, it did not say so.

They opened a small metal door and began to descend a spiral staircase. Down they went, the air getting colder, an odd musty odor in the air. There were lanterns to start with; then the only light was supplied by an unpleasant green mold on the walls that gave off a sickly glow. A mold, Danny thought, that you might find on the inside of a coffin. They were in the realm of the dead now, and everything in the darkness spoke of it. There were rustlings and slitherings and foul odors and sickly-sweet-smelling flowers growing in niches in the wall. How could he have let Dixie be brought here?

At last, when he had despaired of ever reaching his destination, he heard a distant voice singing in quavering, reedy tones.

> *"You all smell foul.*
> *You're a bunch of old ghouls.*

You want me to serve—
I'll stick your dead head in the toilet
And push it round the curve. . . ."

Dixie! Danny hurried forward, pushing the dead girl
in front of him, then snatching his hand back as it
touched the damp suppurating bullet wound in her
back.

The passage opened into a row of old cells with iron
doors. Dank water ran down the walls.

"Hello?" A voice came from one of the cells. "Is anybody there? Can a dead person be anybody? I'll rephrase:
Is nobody there?"

"Unlock the door," Danny said.

"The key . . . ," the girl said.

"Unlock it!"

The girl took an iron key from a hook in the wall.
Danny could feel the building shudder.

"Hurry!" The cell door was flung open. Danny
stepped forward. Dixie was sitting on a low bed. She was
filthy, and her hair hung lankly about a wan face. She
peered up at Danny.

"Not another trick, is it?"

"No, Dixie," he said, "it's not another trick. We're
going home."

He grabbed her by the arm. It was cold and clammy,
as if contact with dead flesh had contaminated it.

"The key!" the dead girl demanded.

"When we get out!" He dragged Dixie down the corridor. As he did so, something made him glance through

254

the spyhole in one of the other cells. Nala sat inside on a bench. Danny began to walk on but stopped. He couldn't leave Nala to the mercy of the dead, even if he was a Cherb and an enemy. He seized the key from beside the door and unlocked it. Nala looked up.

"Come on," Danny said. Nala stood up. His expression didn't change, but he rose and followed.

The climb up was a nightmare. The building swayed from side to side with grinding and rending noises as it began to tear itself loose from the mountains. They were flung from one side of the stairs to the other so much that Danny thought the dead girl was losing lumps of flesh here and there. When they got to the top, he threw her the key to the Ring of Five room. She took it without speaking and ran. Danny looked around. The floors were tilting. Morne folk were hastily lashing themselves to the nearest solid object with belts and bellpulls. Dixie faded a little, as if she was trying to disappear, then reappeared, looking even more exhausted. Danny lifted her in his arms and raced toward the storeroom, Nala keeping pace.

As they reached the storeroom the whole building shot upward four or five feet. Dust flew from the floor and the walls.

"The door, Nala!" Danny yelled. The Cherb threw the little door open and held it as Danny charged toward it and dived through, Dixie in his arms. He hadn't realized that the kingdom had already lifted off. They were fifteen feet from the ground. Danny tumbled down, losing hold of Dixie. He landed in a snowbank, Dixie beside him. Nala fell but landed lightly on his feet. They gazed upward in awe as the massive bulk of the kingdom of Morne rose above their heads and hovered there, gigantic chunks of masonry and slates and huge slabs of ice and snow falling from it. It filled the entire sky for what seemed like an eternity; then it started to whirl faster and faster, growing smaller and smaller until it took on the dimensions of a dollhouse and finally disappeared, leaving them alone in the frozen landscape.

FLIGHT

Danny stood up. Nala regarded him warily, but Danny ignored him. He was more concerned about Dixie. She was shivering already, and when she tried to stand her legs gave way beneath her. A flurry of snow blew down from the high peaks. Danny shivered.

"We can't stay here. There could be another avalanche. Can you walk, Dixie?"

She shook her head. Danny tried to help her to her feet but it was all he could do to get her upright. He looked around helplessly. They would die on the frozen mountain, either from avalanche or from cold.

"I'll carry her." It was the first time Danny had heard Nala speak. Without waiting for a reply he stepped forward and threw Dixie over his shoulder, then set off down the mountain, moving quickly on the soft snow. Danny, caught by surprise, took off after him.

As the night grew darker and colder, Danny walked in Nala's footsteps. On and on they went, but the mountains were high and they still had not gotten to the lower reaches. The wind rose and the moon disappeared behind swirling cloud. Nala was tireless, but Danny didn't know how much farther he could go.

It began to snow. A few flakes at first, then heavier, until, in a few minutes, they were walking in a full-blown blizzard. Danny kept losing sight of Nala and after ten minutes had lost him completely. A Cherb, he thought. And you trusted him! He forced himself onward, though all he wanted to do was lie down in the snow and go to sleep. Ice had formed on his eyelashes and in his hair, and he could barely see, so when a red glow appeared ahead, he had to rub his eyes several times to make sure it was real.

He made his way toward the glow and saw that it was a fire, lit in the partial shelter of a huge boulder. Nala had laid Dixie beside it and he was busy digging in the snow for furze branches he was feeding into the blaze.

Danny slumped gratefully beside the fire. Nala jerked his head at Dixie.

"The girl needs shelter," he said. "The fire isn't enough." He fed more branches into the fire, then sat down a little way off, looking out into the blizzard. Danny's eyes went to Dixie, who was already half covered in snow. He tried to think, but the day's traumas had drained him. He realized that he was still wearing his coat. At least he could cover Dixie, he thought, starting to take it off. Then he remembered how when he'd first met McGuinness, the detective had laid the coat on the ground and shown him what it could do. . . .

Danny threw the coat on the ground and started pulling at the buttons. Strong metal rods appeared. He quickly worked out how to bend each rod and stick the ends in the ground, putting the rod through belt loops and epaulettes. Within five minutes the coat had formed a tent—a surprisingly roomy one. Danny looked at it in astonishment. He coaxed Dixie up and got her inside. Nala was still staring out into the storm.

"Come in," Danny said. "Get out of the blizzard." Nala looked at him as if surprised to be asked, then got to his feet.

Inside the tent it was warm. (How did that work? Danny thought.) The wind howled against the stretched coat, but it held firm. The pockets were on the inside, and Danny was able to fish out the torch and a few bars of chocolate. They sat in silence, a silence that couldn't be described as companionable, considering that one of the company was a Cherb and that loss and betrayal haunted them. But despite that, first Dixie fell asleep, then Danny, and finally even Nala slept.

Danny woke to sun streaming through the tent flap. He looked out to see Nala staring down the valley. Dixie was still asleep. He crawled out. The blizzard had ended, but the tent was half buried and there were mounds and hills of soft snow everywhere.

"Not good," Nala said. "Too deep."

"I have to get back," Danny said. He had to warn Wilsons that the Treaty Stone was broken. The Ring might already be moving against them! Dixie stirred and stuck her head out of the tent.

"Morning," she said. "Have they stopped serving breakfast?" She grinned at Danny and he knew that things would be all right. He would have to explain himself to her, but the glint in her eyes told him that she would forgive him. Dixie's loyalty pushed all thoughts of cunning and treachery from his mind. He would get back to Wilsons and warn them. But how?

He leaned back against the exposed side of the tent. It was frozen taut as a drum, and his hand slid off it so that he fell in the snow. Dixie laughed, but Danny got up and stared at the tent.

"Get up!" he said.

"What?"

"Get out of the tent, Dixie!"

Working frantically, Danny pulled the ends of the steel rods from the ground. He was glad to see that when Dixie got in his way she was able to disappear and reappear several yards from him.

He lifted the whole tent out of the ground and turned it upside down on the snow. He grinned to himself. It looked like a little cloth boat, with the steel rods forming the ribs and the coat fabric the hull. It was stiff with frost and rocked gently when Danny touched it.

He hauled it out onto the snow and looked down the mountain, picking out a route.

"Hop aboard!" he said.

"What?" Dixie said. Nala eyed him dubiously, then walked forward and lowered himself gingerly into the boat.

"Hurry up, Dixie," Danny said. Dixie disappeared and reappeared beside Nala. Danny pushed them to the edge of a downward slope, then tipped the coat-sled onto the slope. He shoved as hard as he could, and the sled started to pick up speed. Danny had misjudged it. The half-frozen canvas made a perfect surface for sliding over the powdery snow, and the sled's momentum carried it away from him. He stumbled, almost lost his grip and stretched out his hand. Nala looked at him, his strange brown and blue eyes impossible to read. Now would be the moment, Danny realized, for his enemy to shun his despairing hand, to leave him floundering in the snow. Nala looked at Danny for what felt like an eternity, then reached out and grasped his hand. With one effortless pull he hauled Danny on board.

"All is paid," Nala murmured. "You save me. I save you. All is paid." Danny didn't know if that meant that they were now enemies again, but he didn't have time to think about it. As a sled, the upturned tent was almost too successful. They were hurtling down the mountain at a ferocious rate, crashing over hidden rocks, one minute airborne, next minute plowing through a snowdrift.

"Where's the steering wheel?" Dixie yelled, but Danny was too busy clinging to one of the metal ribs to avoid being thrown out of the frail craft and did not answer. Down the mountain they plunged, fine arcs of snow

261

flying from either side, deadly crags everywhere they looked. Danny's hair was flattened to his skull and his hands ached from holding on, but a wild exhilaration was growing in him. He looked at Nala crouched at the front of the sled and saw his teeth bared in a grin. He met Dixie's eyes. She threw back her head.

"Yeeeehawww!" she yelled, and Danny, for the first time in what felt like years, laughed out loud. But almost instantly a jagged rock loomed in front of them. Danny threw his body weight to one side. It was enough, if only just. Nala turned his head to avoid being split open by the rock face. Another rock loomed. Dixie disappeared from one side of the sled and reappeared at the other. Her weight wasn't quite enough to change their direction, but Nala flung himself to the same side and the sled almost capsized as it rounded the rock.

The three careered down the mountain, steering the sled with their body weight, inches from disaster at every turn, yet Danny had never felt so alive, Dixie was whooping, and even Nala showed his teeth in a fierce smile. It was perhaps three miles to the foot of the mountain, and they covered it at an incredible rate. The ground began to level off, but the sled showed no sign of slowing down. Buildings started to appear, some of them just rooftops sticking up from the snow. They narrowly avoided having the bottom of the craft torn out by a road sign. There were more and more buildings as they approached the town, and they had no way of stopping.

"There!" Danny shouted. They steered toward the bed of the river that flowed through Newcastle. Once they hit the ice on the surface of the river, their speed picked up. Bridges flashed by overhead; the buildings of the deserted town were a blur.

"We're going out to sea!" Dixie yelled. Danny's mind worked fast. Sea would be the best way to travel, but they had no way of propelling themselves. He looked down the river. In the distance he could see a riverside restaurant, its collapsed canvas awning lying over the tables and chairs.

"Dixie," he yelled, "could you get that for me?" Dixie's eyes narrowed as she judged the distance; then she was gone. Danny and Nala sped toward the restaurant. They could see Dixie struggling with the awning. She was still struggling as they flew past. Danny gazed back anxiously. The restaurant was almost out of sight when Dixie re-appeared breathlessly on the sled, the canvas draped over her head. Danny snatched a loose fence post as the river suddenly widened and they slewed out of control, turning round and round and hitting the open water with a huge splash. The craft came to rest and bobbed about on the gentle swell. Dixie looked around her in admiration.

"That's some coat," she said. "What did I get the canvas for?"

"A sail," Danny said.

Danny set about rigging up the fence post as a mast. The pockets of the coat yielded up scissors and a needle and thread, and Nala and Dixie started creating a sail. Dixie was useless at sewing, but Nala worked like lightning, and within an hour they had a makeshift sail rigged. Danny found a drifting plank and made a rudder from it.

263

A fresh breeze had sprung up, and soon they were scudding along toward the northeast.

"We're cutting straight across the bay toward my house," Danny said. "It'll save us half a day." And indeed the far coast was getting clearer by the minute. Danny felt his heart sink. Would Stone and Pearl still be alive? One part of him longed to see them, but in a dark cold corner of his mind, a sly voice wished them dead. In the distance he could see church spires now, and the masts of boats in the harbor.

The hours passed. Danny looked in the coat pockets for food, but even the coat had its limits, and they were tired and hungry as they approached the town.

"We'll land on the beach," Danny said. "We'd look a bit odd sailing into the harbor in an overcoat."

They ran aground on the deserted strand close to the pier. Danny undid the buttons, and the steel poles withdrew into the buttonholes. Within a few minutes there was no sign of the little boat. Danny slipped the overcoat on again. It had been cold in the boat, but not as cold as it had felt before Morne had gone, and there were signs of a thaw: water dripping from a tree, the ice in rock pools melting.

"First we need to get something to eat," Danny said. They walked up toward the town. Danny could hear traffic and the sound of music from the amusements on the seafront.

"What are we going to do about him?" Dixie said, pointing to Nala. "Those eyes are a dead giveaway."

"So's disappearing," Danny said, but it was too late.

Dixie had disappeared and reappeared beside a souvenir shop. She picked out a pair of sunglasses from a display and reappeared right beside Danny.

"That's better," she said as she fitted the heart-shaped pink sunglasses to Nala's face.

"Dixie," Danny said despairingly, "you're supposed to pay for . . . Never mind. Let's get some food."

Danny bought pizza and they walked through the town eating it. Danny was silent and moody. He kept seeing Lily's face as she disappeared in the avalanche. The wrenching pain of having had a family and losing it would not leave him alone.

Dixie marveled at everything, pointing to mannequins and television sets in shop windows. She went into ecstasies when an airplane flew high overhead. Beside them Nala stomped along in the pink sunglasses.

If the Ring has any spies here, we're in trouble . . . , Danny thought. Then he looked back at Nala. Could he be working some double cross? Perhaps leading Danny into the hands of the Ring? Sly thoughts filled his brain, threatening to overwhelm him. How could he and Dixie dump Nala? Perhaps Danny could break a window or steal something and throw the blame on the Cherb so that he would be arrested. He remembered how Nala had saved him but pushed the thought to the back of his mind.

It was getting late. The shops were beginning to close. Danny didn't want to be caught out on the deserted streets at night, so he made Nala and Dixie wait in a bus shelter, then went into a phone shop, where he bought a cell phone.

"What is it?" Dixie said when he returned.

"A phone," Danny said.

"What's that?"

Danny looked at her, but she wasn't joking. She still had no idea what a phone was. He explained it to her. She looked at him, half disbelieving.

"When we were walking down the street there were plenty of people talking into phones," he said. "Didn't you see them?"

"I thought they were just talking to themselves," Dixie said, as if it was the most natural thing in the world to be walking around talking to yourself. She looked on in awe as he turned on the power and, taking a deep breath, entered Stone's number. Dixie took several steps back when she heard Stone's voice coming through. The agent sounded tense.

"Did you succeed?"

"No," Danny said flatly, "the Treaty Stone is broken."

"Then the Upper World is open to attack from the Lower. I had no idea your mission was so important," Stone said. "Do you still have the Land Rover?"

"No."

"Then walk to the edge of town. I'll pick you up there."

"What . . . what about Pearl?" Danny asked.

"Alive," Stone said tersely. "We were well trained, Danny. She's alive."

Danny ended the call and put the phone into his pocket. Dixie looked at him curiously.

"Danny," she said, "your eyes—the brown is coming through again. Doesn't that only happen when—"

"Come on," Danny said, cutting her off roughly, "it's starting to get dark."

There were few people around, and by the time they walked to the suburbs, they were on their own, the icy conditions making driving dangerous and keeping the roads empty. Nala was uneasy and kept glancing upward.

"What's he looking for?" Danny whispered to Dixie. "Surely the Seraphim can't be here already?"

"I hope not," Dixie whispered back. They had reached some trees and fields where the houses petered out. Without a word Nala drew them into the shelter of the trees.

"I never asked you," Danny said, forcing himself to address Dixie. "What was it like . . . I mean with the dead?"

Dixie shivered. "I don't want to talk about it," she said. There was an uncomfortable silence. Nala had moved a little distance off and was watching the sky.

"I need to explain," Danny said. He told her about Lily and how she had pretended to be his sister, how he had found out the truth and then watched her being swept away by the snow. Dixie listened in silence.

"So," Danny said at the end, "I know I betrayed you, Dixie, and I know what that means. I just wanted to explain why." There was a long silence. When Dixie broke it there was no trace of the quirky and mercurial girl Danny was used to.

"There's a big struggle going on inside you, Danny. We all know the part of you that would betray us. But there's the other part of you, the one we like, and the one we want to win out in the end. When bad things happen—like me going to . . . going to the dead—I know it's because you're not the same as the rest of us. We've just got ordinary good and bad going on inside us. You've got bigger stuff."

She squeezed his hand, and they sat in the growing darkness under the trees until they heard the sound of a car approaching.

The car pulled over and stopped. They waited until Stone got out before they emerged from the trees. Agent Stone's face was tired and strained, but he managed a grim smile, then a look of surprise when he saw Nala.

"Who's this?" His expression changed when he moved closer and saw Nala's eyes.

"Surely he's a . . ."

"A Cherb," Danny said shortly. "It's a long story."

"We don't have time for long stories if the treaty has gone," Stone said. "You can tell me later. Get into the car."

Dixie got in. Danny opened the car door and waited for Nala, but the Cherb didn't move.

"Jump in," Danny said, but Nala shook his head.

"Your world. My world. Maybe again." Something that might have been described as a smile crossed his strange face. He glanced upward. "Watch out for Seraphim!" he said, then turned and, without a backward glance, bounded off into the woods.

"That's the end of him, then," Dixie said.

"I don't know," Danny said. "I've got a feeling we haven't seen the last of Nala."

Stone turned the car around and started to drive back toward Danny's house.

"What was that about Seraphim?" Dixie asked. "They can't have moved that quickly after the Stone was broken."

"Think again." Stone pushed a laptop toward Danny. "Search for 'Angel Sighting.'"

Danny took the laptop. Dixie gazed in fascination as he opened it and waited for it to boot up.

"Television?" she said in delight.

"No," Danny said, "it's a computer." Dixie gazed at it in rapt attention as it flickered to life. Danny's search turned up several newspaper articles in which people described seeing four or five large winged figures in the air. Air traffic controllers said that unexplained objects on their screens could have been birds, but a policeman was reported to be undergoing psychiatric examination after claiming to have seen a "sinister winged figure" standing outside the prime minister's country residence.

"Seraphim!" Danny said.

"I'm afraid so," Stone said. "Checking things out, letting the few people who are aware of their existence know that the barrier between this world and the next has been breached. I have always suspected that the Ring has spies in the Upper World. I expect those networks will be strengthened now. We will have to fight them. It will be a secret war, a war of spies—to begin with, at any rate."

He turned to Danny.

"They will want their greatest asset at their side. Be careful, Danny."

Danny was barely listening. He stared with unseeing eyes at the winter fields. He could still see Lily's face as she was buried by the wall of snow. Bitterness welled up in him. First Stone and Pearl had masqueraded as his parents; then Lily had pretended to be his sister. His friends at Wilsons were good, it was true, but he yearned for some deeper connection—if not with a family, then maybe with the Ring. He had not forgotten the way his mind had joined with theirs.

They fell silent as they drove through the countryside. Dixie went to sleep on Danny's shoulder, and Stone appeared to be lost in his own thoughts. Danny's mind would not let him rest. What if the Ring did conquer all? Would he not be better off as part of it? At least he would be able to protect his friends, and perhaps put a stop to the worse excesses of the Ring. Apart from anything else, he would be able to use all the power of the Ring to find out who he was.

Before he knew it, they were pulling up to the old house, which had been left scarred and shattered from the Seraphim attack. Dixie woke up and shivered.

"Will Fairman come for us, do you think?"

Danny realized that she was far from home in a foreign world, full of strange things such as cell phones and computers. She was homesick for Wilsons.

"I think so," Danny said, "although he's not the only person allowed to cross the border anymore."

They parked the car around the back and went in. Stone and Pearl had worked hard while Danny had been away. The house was fortified with sandbags in the windows and the doors.

"I've got heat and movement detectors rigged outside," Stone said. "We won't get caught by surprise again."

Inside there was a cheerful fire burning and a smell of baking pie. Pearl came to the kitchen door wearing an apron, flour on her hands. Her face lit up when she saw Danny, and she looked like a picture of a mother from an old book. When Danny turned away, he could feel her hurt.

The pie was put out on the table and they ate hungrily. Danny was exhausted, but Stone said that he needed to talk to him. Pearl took Dixie off, clucking over her tangled hair and dirty face. Stone led Danny into the library. They sat down in front of the fire.

"I've been researching your background for years, Danny, going through old records and libraries, trying to find out who you are. No one paid any attention before, but I accessed a copy of an old manuscript online, and someone was keeping an eye on it. Opening that document brought the pursuit where I got wounded, and probably brought the Seraphim."

"What was in the manuscript?"

"It's to do with being the Fifth, Danny. I don't know how you came to be here in the Upper World, but I think I know why. The Fifth has access to a terrible power. I believe special powers are not unusual in the Lower World?

It comes from the very core of the Fifth's being and lies dormant until powerful emotion causes it to be unleashed, for good or evil—but mostly for evil.

"Certain influential government agencies learned of this and thought they could harness the power of the Fifth to develop a new generation of terrible weapons. That was why you were given into our care, so we could keep you safe until you were old enough to be exploited.

"Of course, we never knew of this terrible plan. We're not sure what happened. It may be that someone is protecting your identity."

"What are you trying to say?" Danny asked.

"I'm saying you can't stay in this world. You are being hunted at this very moment."

"I'm being hunted in the other world as well," Danny said despairingly.

"Yes, but there they will not conduct experiments on you to find out if you have a power and how it works. And there you have many friends. Here you only have two, me and Agent Pearl. I know you're angry that we pretended to be your parents, a charade for which I can only say I am sorry. We thought we were acting for your good."

Danny looked at him and for a moment longed to call this man Father, and to tell him about Lily. But the moment passed.

"Fairman will come for you and Dixie in the morning. I have had no luck in finding out who your parents are. That is another mystery, and it strikes me that both worlds have an interest in suppressing the answer."

They went back into the living room. Dixie had showered and was dressed in a Chinese dressing gown. Pearl was brushing her hair.

Dixie sighed. "I hope everyone at Wilsons is okay."

"We're going back in the morning," Danny said. Dixie clapped her hands.

"Brilliant," she said. "I wish I knew what's happening there."

"The Radio of Last Resort!" Danny said. It was still in his bedroom. He ran upstairs and carried it down to the living room. He switched it on, and they all sat in frozen silence when they heard the message that came through the speaker. Brunholm's voice was being played on a loop, and there was a note of triumph in it that turned the blood cold.

"Attention. Attention. This is Marcus Brunholm. Mr. Devoy has been suspended from his post as master of Wilsons and is now in custody. I, Marcus Brunholm, with the assistance of Rufus Ness, head Cherb, am now in charge of all affairs at Wilsons Academy, pending a full agreement with the Ring of Five in relation to their participation in the running of this institution."

Danny and Dixie looked at each other, stunned. Devoy was in prison. Brunholm, in cahoots with Rufus Ness, had taken over. They were going to hand the school over to the Ring!

A PLACE OF TORTURE

After rescuing Blackpitt, Les, Vandra and Toxique were pleased with their day's work but haunted by the sight of Devoy attending to the torture chamber. They had not thought him capable of contemplating such cruelty.

"But who do we tell?" Les said.

"It's obvious," Toxique said. "McGuinness. He's honest. He'll help us."

"Good idea," Vandra said. "In the meantime, I'm exhausted and it's the middle of the night."

They decided they would meet in the morning after class and seek out the detective. A simple decision, they thought as they went gratefully to bed, but they would have been less comfortable if they had sensed the pair of red-rimmed eyes that watched the Roosts from the rooftops. Ness's bloody shoulder had a rough bandage on it, but otherwise he was unharmed. He had not finished with Wilsons—not by a long shot—and events were about to play into his hands.

The next morning the three cadets woke late and almost missed breakfast. They yawned their way through Spitfire's class—Les earned three strikes with the eraser—and through a double period of maths with Exshaw, which Les thought would earn them at least a Third Regulation offense. But Exshaw merely smirked at them, saying that "punishment, like revenge, is a dish best served cold."

McGuinness could be elusive, but they found him with ease, sitting on one of the summer seats in the garden as if he had been waiting for them. His face darkened as they told him about Devoy and the torture instruments, and he shook his head in disbelief.

"We'll have to go upstairs with this," he said.

"Upstairs?" Vandra said.

"Well, we can't go to Devoy, so we'll have to go to Brunholm."

"We can't go to Brunholm!" Les was appalled.

"Torture is a treasonable offense in Wilsons," McGuinness said sternly. "We have no choice."

Events moved with lightning speed after that.

"I knew he would slip up somewhere along the line," Brunholm had cried and had immediately summoned the other teachers. Some of them, such as Spitfire, refused to accept Brunholm's word, and Les was called in front of them to relate what he had seen, which he did, barely able to look Spitfire in the eye.

"It seems that what you are saying is true, Marcus," Duddy said, "and the news could not come at a worse time. Is the Treaty Stone broken, as we have heard?"

"It must be true," Valant broke in. "The ravens are in an awful state, wheeling around in the sky all day. And they attacked one of the Messengers when they saw him on the roof."

"Devoy must be arrested at once," Brunholm said. "Who will come with me?"

The only person to step forward straightaway was Exshaw. It appeared that he was already heavily armed in preparation. He had tear gas canisters and an expandable baseball bat, as well as a collection of brass knuckles.

"You won't be needing any of that," Valant said gruffly as he stepped forward. "I'll come along to make sure nobody gets hurt."

"And since it's a criminal matter, I'll come along as well," McGuinness said.

Devoy had not accepted the charges against him lightly and had barricaded himself into the library of the third landing. He had asked for a copy of the Wilsons book of rules, and when McGuinness went to fetch it, Exshaw and Brunholm had mounted a sustained assault, despite Valant's protestations. When Devoy refused to come out, Exshaw smashed in a panel on the door and lobbed two tear gas canisters into the room. Devoy opened the door, coughing and with tears streaming down his face; Exshaw had gone for him with the collapsible baseball bat, dealing Devoy two good blows before a scowling Valant wrestled it from him.

The pupils were having tea in Ravensdale, the place a cauldron of gossip with cadets taking sides. Les had almost gotten into a fistfight with Smyck over his role in the Devoy affair, when the lights went up on the platform from which teachers addressed the school. There was a gasp as the pupils saw the bleeding and handcuffed Devoy, his eyes still streaming from the tear gas. Brunholm and Exshaw accompanied him, and Brunholm read out a long list of charges, alleging that Devoy "did knowingly and feloniously create a place of torture in breach of Article Six of the penal code."

Vandra got up. There were tears in her eyes. "I must go help Master Devoy with his wounds."

"Sit down!" Brunholm told her harshly.

There was chaos in Ravensdale. The cadets spilled out into the streets of the ancient village. There were several fights; factions formed and re-formed while the ravens cawed overhead. The cadets only calmed down when McGuinness appeared in their midst, fired a shot over their heads and threatened to arrest them all for violent assembly. Even so, there were scuffles on the way back to the Roosts as rumors spread that the Messengers were backing Devoy and had taken over the top two floors of the main building.

Worse was to come the following morning. A clearly

unwell Blackpitt announced that the Treaty Stone had indeed been shattered, and that peace overtures with the Ring had begun. To that end, Rufus Ness had been accepted as envoy and joint head of Wilsons until a new treaty could be put in place.

Les and Vandra met Toxique on the landing outside the Roosts.

"What are we going to do?" Vandra said. "Rufus Ness joint head? The Stone broken? Something terrible must have happened to Danny and Dixie!"

"Who can we trust?" Toxique said. "Seems all the teachers are on Brunholm's side."

"What about Blackpitt?" Les said. "He owes us one. At least we'll find out a little bit about what's going on around here."

But when they got to the main building, they found another obstacle. While they had been talking, Exshaw had been waiting at the entrance to Ravensdale handing out prefect badges. Smyck had been appointed head prefect, while Exspectre was close surveillance monitor. A mean girl named Frieda had been appointed monitor of junior Messengers, physicks and assassins.

"I think that means us," Les said.

"I think you're right," Vandra said as Frieda appeared and announced in a self-important voice, "I am going to escort you three everywhere, and you must tell me your movements in advance."

The rest of the morning was passed in trying to evade her. Les and Toxique spent half an hour in the boys' toilets discussing how to lose her, but it was Vandra who came up with the solution. When the boys came out of the toilet, she was waiting, Frieda hovering in the background.

"Quick," Vandra whispered. "Les, fall down as if you're poisoned."

Les threw himself to the floor, gurgling and clutching his throat. Frieda darted forward.

"He's been poisoned!" Vandra cried, and threw herself on him. She bent over his throat for a minute, and when she came up her fangs were dripping with a green liquid that smelled so vile the two boys almost gagged. Frieda stared at Vandra, turned green herself, then dashed for the door of the girls' room.

"Hurry!" Vandra said, spraying gobbets of the foul green substance. "Let's go!"

"Entrails and pus, what is that stuff?" Toxique said as they ran.

"Kind of a physick party trick I used to do when I was small," Vandra said, wiping her chin with a handkerchief. "It's a mixture of bile and small intestinal—"

"Stop," Les gasped, "or I really will throw up."

They ran up the stairs to the apothecary. Blackpitt was sitting up in bed. He was thin and ill but he had made an effort with his appearance. He wore a floral dressing gown, and he had slicked his hair over to the side with some kind of oil.

"My dear young friends!" he exclaimed. "I am so grateful for your part in my rescue. That fiend came to me posing as a salesman of colognes and tinctures for the fashion-aware mature gent. Caught me completely unaware."

"No time for that now," Vandra said urgently. "We need to know what's going on and how we get organized."

But Blackpitt merely gave them a resigned look.

"You must understand," he said, "everything has changed now. You may not like Rufus Ness's being part of Wilsons, but there's nothing we can do. With the treaty ended, we must do what we can to come to terms with the Ring and the Cherbs."

"But what about Devoy?" Les said. Blackpitt held out his hands palms-up.

"Again. He has breached the law and he must answer for it."

The cadets looked at each other in despair. They heard footsteps behind them and turned to see Frieda.

"There you are," she said. "That'll be a Fourth Regulation offense. Evading the lawful attentions of a monitor."

Jamshid came in and glanced at Frieda in dislike.

"You have to leave the patient alone," he said, "and the infirmary must be cleared, except for you, Vandra. I might need a physick."

"What's wrong?"

"Trouble among the Messengers. It seems that one of them has been an agent of the Ring all along. He revealed himself and demanded to be made chief Messenger. A fight broke out and several Messengers were badly injured."

Just as he finished speaking, the doors crashed open and two makeshift gurneys were wheeled in by Gabriel and several other Messengers. Each gurney carried a pitiful body, bloodstained wings crumpled under it. Vandra gasped when she recognized Daisy. And gasped again when she saw the figure that walked in after the gurneys—the head Cherb, Rufus Ness.

"Take a good look," Ness growled, "and learn the price of rebellion."

The cadets stared, shocked. Ness turned on his heel and strode out.

"I can't believe that one of our own would do this," Gabriel said despairingly as Jamshid examined the wounded Messengers.

"Don't forget how many of the Messengers became Seraphim," Jamshid said. "It is in all of you, I think." He pointed to Daisy. "Vandra, I'll take this one first; she is in the most danger. You work with the other. I think some toxin has got into his bloodstream."

Vandra turned instantly to the injured Messenger. For a long wearisome afternoon, Les and Toxique waited outside with Frieda, her eyes flickering from one to the other. In the end Vandra emerged exhausted. Her Messenger was out of danger, she said, but Daisy's life hung in the balance.

Blackpitt announced teatime from his infirmary bed and they walked slowly down to Ravensdale. In contrast to the previous evening, the mood among the cadets was somber, and they took their places without much talk, save for smirks from Smyck and his gang. As they ate a poor tea of boiled potatoes and cabbage, the mood worsened.

The platform from where the teachers spoke was illuminated. Four figures stepped out: first Rufus Ness, then

Brunholm, then a tall aristocratic Messenger with a seemingly permanent sneer. Finally, to the cadets' dismay, Exshaw stepped out.

Brunholm was elbowed to the back of the platform. Ness did the talking.

"You are all now subjects and pupils of this newly renamed institution, Longford Academy. I have appointed a provisional ruling council of loyal servants of the Ring who have proved their worth over the years: Messenger Hotspur, Master Brunholm and Master Exshaw."

The cadets stared. They did not know Hotspur, but they couldn't believe that Brunholm and Exshaw had been traitors all along. Brunholm looked a little abashed, but Exshaw could not hide his triumph.

"The Ring will assemble here in the coming days to decide what is to be done with all of you." Brunholm seemed startled. He looked as if he was about to protest, but Ness spoke first.

"The trial of Master Devoy will take place when the Ring assembles. The judges will be the members of the Ring."

The cadets looked at each other. In a matter of a few days, the Ring had taken over. They were under constant surveillance, and their teachers were helpless. Vandra touched the ring Danny had given her.

"Where is he?" she whispered.

A TRIAL

Stone had wakened Danny and Dixie in the predawn darkness. They were exhausted but were partly revived by a breakfast of bacon, eggs and toast, washed down with hot tea. Dixie helped Pearl with the cooking and they chatted softly at the end of the kitchen. Stone looked at Danny with worry in his eyes.

"Keep in touch if you can, Danny," he said. "Send messages through Fairman. The more we learn about the Lower World, the easier it will be to protect this one. I will keep searching and trying to find your real parents. I owe you that."

Danny wanted to believe Stone, but he remembered the day he'd spent walking with Lily in the snow. He'd wanted to trust her too, but she had been laughing at him the whole time. He got to his feet abruptly.

"I'm going outside to wait for Fairman," he said. Stone watched him leave.

"He's had a hard time," Dixie said.

"I know," Stone said, "and we are part of it. I worry about him."

From outside they heard the clatter of a diesel engine.

"Time to go and face the music," Dixie said.

"Face the music?" Pearl said.

"Well, we were supposed to bring back the Treaty Stone."

"I was reluctant to bring it up—what did happen to the Stone?" Pearl asked.

"I don't know," Dixie said simply. "I wasn't there and I didn't ask what exactly had happened."

Dixie hugged Pearl before she and Danny got in the black cab. Danny shook Stone's and Pearl's hands stiffly, and there was an uncomfortable silence.

"If you ever . . . ," Pearl began, but something in Danny's eyes told her not to continue. Pearl and Stone watched in silence as the taxi drove off into the snowy landscape.

"Will we see him again?" Pearl asked. Stone took her hand.

"We will, and we must be ready for that day. I cannot tell if he will come back as an avenger, worse than anything this world has ever seen, or if the other part of him will win out, the good part."

They raised their arms in farewell, but no answering arm was raised from the taxi.

Danny thought that because it was day he would get to see the landscape between the Two Worlds as they drove through it, but a strange dusk fell once they turned off the motorway, and as the cab built up speed and started to shake and judder he could see nothing, though it felt as if the journey to Wilsons was taking longer than the other times he had made it. There were many changes of direction, and at times Fairman appeared to be confused.

"If I get my hands on whoever broke that Treaty Stone," Fairman said, "I'll break his neck. I'll break his neck and then I'll rip his throat out."

At one point Fairman peered upward through the windshield as though something was flying through the sky in front of them.

"Is it the Seraphim?" Dixie asked, but Fairman didn't reply. Danny and Dixie wedged themselves into opposite corners against the incessant bone-jolting shaking of the cab as it sped on through the everlasting dusk.

Finally it grew light and they could see trees on either side of the road. The cab slowed a little and the juddering eased. They were on the outskirts of Tarnstone, the nearest town to Wilsons. Although it was now broad daylight, there was no one on the streets.

"What's going on?" Danny asked.

"They're afraid of attack from above by the Seraphim," Fairman said, turning onto the road that led to Wilsons. "Where do you want to be dropped off?"

"Wilsons," Danny said, "of course."

"Not the best idea," Fairman said. "You might get more of a reception than you bargained for."

"Why?" Danny demanded, but the more they asked, the less Fairman would say.

"I'm supposed to be neutral," he growled. "It's more than my job's worth to tell you any more."

In the end Danny told him to drop them at the wall of the school. They could approach through the grounds and get some idea of what was going on without being seen.

The cab screeched to a halt at the wall. Danny and Dixie were relieved to get out, and Danny was surprised to feel a sense of homecoming when his feet touched the ground. The cab sped off, and he and Dixie were left standing by the side of the road.

"I'm getting worried," Dixie said, shivering. "Let's go."

Dixie was able to disappear over the wall and reappear on the other side. Danny had to clamber over. They found one of the Paths of Infinite Return, which would only lead to its destination if you walked on it backward. This made it difficult to move quickly. It took them twenty minutes to get through the overgrown grounds to a place where they could get a view of the school.

Everything looked fairly normal. It was quiet, but it was still class time. They waited for five minutes, but nothing changed.

"I think we should just walk right in," Dixie said. "There's Brunholm. He doesn't look as if anything's wrong."

Brunholm had come around the corner of the building, deep in conversation with another man. Danny was about to stand up when Dixie grabbed his sleeve.

"Look, Danny—look who he's with! Rufus Ness!"

Their hearts beating faster, they backed into the undergrowth. Ness stopped and turned in their direction. For a second Danny could feel Ness's mind, a virile, cunning presence, searching for his. He closed his mind off. Ness looked almost to be sniffing the air, as if he could smell Danny; then he turned back to Brunholm, who stood like a dog waiting for its master.

Once the men were out of sight, Dixie and Danny made for the summerhouse, their minds racing as they tried to absorb the implications of seeing Ness and Brunholm in cahoots. Had Wilsons been captured by force or overthrown from within?

At the summerhouse they found that they were not the only refugees. Two people had got there ahead of them. A weary Cheryl disguised as a sailor lay on the window seat, while a put-out-looking Vicky tried to ignore her. Between the two women, Danny and Dixie got a tangled story of Cherb forces massing, of Devoy being imprisoned and of the Ring making its way to Wilsons, where it had taken over.

"Brunholm, this Messenger named Hotspur, and Exshaw, the traitors," Vicky spat. "Devoy's in the same cell that I was put in."

Cheryl had been investigating Cherb movements, so Vicky was the only source of information about Wilsons, and Danny questioned her closely. Who had joined with the Ring? When was Devoy being tried, and who were his judges? When were the Ring arriving? And how had the ravens reacted?

"The ravens haven't been seen since Ness declared himself master," Vicky said. Danny sat for a long time, his brow creased.

"When did you say Longford and the others were arriving?" he asked.

"Any time now," Vicky said, and spat into the fireplace in a most unladylike way.

"I understand what's going on," Danny said slowly.

"I'm glad you do," Dixie said. "I haven't got a clue."

Danny got up and opened the door.

"Where are you off to?" Dixie asked. He didn't answer but stepped through the door. Dixie made to go after him, but Cheryl grabbed her arm.

"Don't," she said. "Let him go on his own."

Dixie stood in the doorway, silently watching Danny walk toward Wilsons.

"I'm not sure I like the look of this," she said.

"He has a grim face on him, all right," Vicky said.

Danny crossed the gardens and made his way around the front of Wilsons. His mind was clear. He could see what was happening laid out in front of him like the pieces in a great chess game. He knew what had to be done—and the consequences of getting it wrong, not just for him but for the Two Worlds.

Without breaking stride he ran up the front steps of the school. Valant was standing at the reception desk and looked up in surprise.

"Tell me when the Ring arrive," Danny said. "I want to greet them." Valant looked at him with narrowed eyes. He wasn't used to being told what to do by pupils. But there was something in Danny's tone that brooked no argument.

Danny went to the teachers' common room. Duddy looked up as he burst in.

"You're back!" she said. "What are you doing here? You should be reporting to Mr. Brunholm."

Danny ignored her and went straight to the small cell. He looked through the bars. Devoy was sitting on one bunk. The Unknown Spy was sitting on the other. They were talking quietly.

"Master Devoy?" Danny spoke quietly, but Devoy was instantly on his feet.

"Danny! The Treaty Stone . . ."

"Is broken. An agent of the Ring," Danny said, lying smoothly.

"I knew it was gone, but I didn't know how."

"All is lost," Danny said. "The treaty is no more. I intend to rejoin the Ring."

Devoy held Danny's eyes, then sighed.

"I have thrown the dice and lost. Do what you must. I will go back to my conversation with the Unknown Spy. I do not have long left."

289

He turned away. Danny froze as he heard a familiar civilized voice behind him.

"So, Danny, you are to rejoin the Ring. I knew you would. Congratulations."

It was Ambrose Longford. And behind him stood the other members of the Ring: Nurse Flanagan, in a low-cut red dress; Rufus Ness; the dreadful Conal the Seraphim, like a giant malignant praying mantis. Danny opened his mind to them and felt his unite with theirs, Nurse Flanagan's mind voluptuous and perfumed, Conal's hard and cold with something rancid about it. And then there was Longford, subtle and probing. Danny felt Longford looking for something, and the leader of the Ring smiled.

"The power of the Fifth. You have found it and used it, to no good end, I expect. Congratulations, Danny."

"Who was she?" Danny said bluntly.

"Was, Danny? You mean she is gone? Her real name was Euphonia Haslam. She is one of my best agents. She was meant to lure you back to the Ring."

"It's called the Sibling Strategy," Nurse Flanagan said, almost purring the words. "An agent poses as a long-lost brother or sister in order to gain the subject's confidence. Well used, the ploy can be devastatingly effective."

"My plan was to have her . . . let me say . . . terminated," Longford said, "and to put the blame on Masters Devoy and Brunholm. In reaction to their crime, you would join with us against Wilsons—a brilliant plan, I thought, but now it seems that you have dealt with her yourself. You obviously weren't fooled by the Sibling Strategy. At least she broke the Treaty Stone before she went."

290

"Enough of that," Danny said harshly. "What is the plan now?"

"We need to move swiftly, Danny. Devoy must be put on trial and punished for his crimes. The trial must be open and public, as must the punishment."

"Punishment?"

"Yes." Longford allowed himself a swift smile in the direction of Devoy's cell. "I have too much respect for my old adversary to permit anything sordid. I have engaged the services of the greatest assassin in his field. Mr. Toxique will be arriving here this evening. I believe he will be eager to help. He has been deeply disappointed by the educational services his son has received at Wilsons."

"The Toxiques never fail," Nurse Flanagan said happily.

"But the end is always dignified," Longford said. "So, Danny, you are ready to take your place among us. I can feel the anger seething in you, the sense of betrayal. We know about the people who posed as your parents, of course. If Conal had succeeded, you would have been avenged."

"It was news we very much wanted to give you," Nurse Flanagan said, "but it wasn't to be."

"Now, down to business. Danny, will you join us as one of the five judges to try Devoy?" Danny felt Longford's mind probing his, searching for hesitation.

"Of course," Danny said. "In fact, we should do it before the cadets start to organize resistance. A dead Devoy should knock any rebellion out of them."

"Splendid," Longford said. "And if and when it

comes time for the sentence to be pronounced, regrettable an end as it may be for a man whose career has been as distinguished as that of Master Devoy, we will grant you the privilege of giving the order!"

Danny smiled. Devoy, who had come to the barred window, watched him closely. Longford was smiling too. Brunholm looked apprehensive. Suddenly a raven swooped from the rafters. It flew into Danny's face, plunged its feet into his hair and stooped over his forehead, aiming blow after blow at his eyes. Danny managed to get his hands up, and the sharp beak penetrated the backs of his hands time and again. He wheeled in pain. Longford lifted a walking stick from a hat stand and aimed a careful blow. The raven squawked once and tumbled to the ground, an untidy heap of feathers. Longford kicked the dead bird into the corner. Danny examined his bleeding hands with cold eyes.

"The ravens really don't like you, Danny," Longford said. "Always a good sign in my book. Now, Rufus, perhaps you will escort Master Devoy to the ballroom. It seems as good a place as any for a trial. Might as well bring that babbling idiot the Unknown Spy with you as well. We'll kill two birds with one stone, so to speak!"

As they walked down the stairs, Longford explained how Ness had penetrated the school.

"He had to kill the Unknown Spy's wife, of course. She had started to remember things, so she was liable to spill the beans about the Sibling Strategy. But more importantly, she was also an expert on voice recognition, and Ness knew she was capable of recognizing his voice and unmasking him as the voice of Blackpitt. It was an elegant solution to the problem of Knutt, we thought, to blame him and send the Unknown Spy after him. Unfortunately the poor man's brain is so addled he can't see through a simple trick."

"What about the dart attack on the Messenger?"

"Mostly fun," Longford chuckled, "though it didn't hurt to turn the Toxique family against the school. And the attack on Brunholm was the most fun of all. I wish I had seen that. The real purpose was to make sure that Brunholm was seen as a victim, to deflect suspicion from him. Meanwhile, our fake Blackpitt was busy activating our agents in Wilsons, old and new."

"Like Exshaw?" Danny asked.

"There are three reasons people become traitors, Danny: money, love and anger. Exshaw had been embittered for years because he was passed over for head in favor of Devoy. We went back over the files—I credit myself with that research. Once we knew about his resentment, it was a simple matter to turn him to our side with a promise to make him head when Devoy was rightfully punished for his crimes."

"You're going to make Exshaw head?"

"Of course not, Danny," Longford said, lowering his voice. "He has almost outlived his usefulness. No, Exshaw will not be head. On the other hand, if the trial goes the way we want it to, we think that *you* should be principal of Wilsons."

Danny stopped dead and stared at Longford. Danny Caulfield, head of Wilsons!

Longford walked on. The rest of the Ring walked past him, Nurse Flanagan entering his mind so that he could feel her arch amusement at his surprise. She patted him on the cheek.

"It would be ideal, really," she murmured. Even Conal appeared amused at his surprise. Danny stood with his mouth hanging open, then hurried to follow the others into the ballroom.

All the cadets and Messengers and staff were crowded in. On a dais were five chairs, one for each of the judges. Devoy was already sitting in a single chair facing the dais. Behind him, dressed in black, pale and dreadful, stood Toxique's father. The four members of the Ring waited for Danny. He joined them and they filed onto the platform and sat down. Danny could see his friends' disbelieving faces below. Outside, through the tall ballroom windows, serried ranks of Seraphim perched on the gable walls and rooftops of Wilsons. There would be no disputing the outcome of the trial.

Longford stood up.

"We are here to bear witness to the trial of Master Devoy for the making and keeping of Instruments of Torture.

"In keeping with tradition, Master Devoy will defend himself. He may call any witnesses he chooses. Prosecuting on behalf of the Ring, all rise for Danny Caulfield."

25

PARENTS

There was an audible gasp when Danny was announced as the prosecutor, followed by a scraping of chairs as the room got sullenly to its feet. Danny tried to keep his face still. Not only was he to pronounce sentence, but he was to prosecute!

"Remember, Danny . . . principal of Wilsons," Longford whispered; then, in a louder voice, said, "Who is the accuser?"

"I am, if you please," Exshaw said, rising to his feet.

"State your case!"

"I saw the defendant, Devoy," Exshaw said, not succeeding in keeping a note of triumph out of his voice, "I saw him refurbish and renovate a museum of torture. He made the instruments workable again, tended them with loving care, obviously intending them to be used again, perhaps against cadets of this very school!"

Devoy, as ever, displayed no emotion. Every eye in the ballroom was on him, waiting for the denial, but it did not come. Spitfire half rose to her feet as though to defend him, but she was the only one, and she sank back into her seat.

Danny's eyes flickered restlessly over the crowd. He sat beside Rufus Ness, and more than one person noticed that Danny's alert pose was uncomfortably similar to the reptilian stillness of the Cherb leaders. If the audience had been able to see inside Danny's head, they would have been even more disturbed. Quietly, the other members of the Ring had entered Danny's mind, not speaking to him, but stoking the turmoil and the hurt. "Parents." "Sister." The words were not spoken, but they did not have to be. Visions of himself at the head of the Ring, as master of Wilsons, came unbidden into Danny's head. He heard his own voice without being conscious of opening his mouth.

"Do you deny the accusation, Devoy?" he said.

"I cannot," Devoy said, "and it would make no difference to these proceedings if I did."

"Come, come," Longford said, "we cannot convict the man just like that. There must be someone who will give some explanation."

No one in the room stirred. Pained faces looked at Devoy: Valant. Gabriel. Old colleagues of Devoy's trying to read his expression. They knew how he felt about Wilsons, how his mind ever searched for information that would protect it. Now he had stepped over the line.

Condoning the use of torture would make Wilsons worse than its enemies.

"Corroboration!" Spitfire cried. "He cannot be convicted without another witness to back up this assertion."

"Good idea!" Longford said. "There must be another witness."

Danny scanned the silent throng, his eyes moving from face to face. Dixie looked up at him imploringly. Vandra glared at him. Toxique studied the floor and wrung his hands, not able to look up for fear of meeting his father's gaze. But one cadet refused to meet Danny's eyes. . . .

"Les," Danny said, "come up here, please." At the sound of his friend's name, Toxique emitted a low moan and rolled his eyes. Vandra grasped his hand to comfort him. Les got to his feet and walked forward slowly until he stood alone in front of the dreadful tribunal of the Ring of Five.

"Tell us what you know," Danny said.

Les hesitated.

"Don't lie, Les," Danny said. "If you don't tell the truth I'll just call Toxique up here and get it out of him."

Toxique moaned even louder. Vandra put her arm around him, and his father turned to give him a bleak look.

"Les?" Danny said.

"I . . . I saw Devoy," Les said. "Me and Toxique. He was in . . . the torture room."

"Tell them," Brunholm said. "Don't hold anything back, Knutt."

"What was he doing?" Danny asked.

"He was . . . he was polishing things. He was oiling the iron maiden." There was a shocked silence, as if people had not really believed the accusation until this moment. Longford spoke again.

"You may pass sentence, I think, Danny. No time like the present." Danny turned to Longford and met his gaze. The whole room could sense the malice and cold calculation flowing between the two members of the Ring. In that moment Danny was truly the Fifth, all that Longford had wished him to be. Danny turned back to Devoy, and those near him flinched at the dark power in his face. Toxique Senior flexed his fingers. Danny knew exactly what Devoy had done and why he had done it, but that did not matter now. He held the power of life and death, and Devoy, looking into his eyes, knew how capable he was of exercising it.

Vandra got to her feet. She took Danny's ring from her finger, her eyes accusing, and threw it at his feet. Danny picked it up.

"Master Devoy," he said, "by your own admission and the testimony of others, you have transgressed against the penal code, for which there is only one sentence. . . ."

"Excuse me . . ." A weary, civilized voice spoke out. "Excuse me?"

The Unknown Spy had been sitting forgotten at the foot of the dais throughout the proceedings. Now he was looking up at Danny, a thoughtful expression on his face.

"You're Steff and Grace's boy, aren't you? I wondered what had happened to you after all these years. They covered it up, you know. They didn't want people to know."

Danny stood like a statue, staring at the Unknown Spy.

"Didn't make you out to be a wrong 'un. Grace had her moments, of course, but when she was with Steff she was different. It upset them that no one thought marriage between a man and a Cherb possible or desirable. Steff wouldn't have liked you being involved with this Ring business. Wouldn't have liked it at all. Master and mistress of disguise, those two. Wonder what happened to the pair of 'em."

Turmoil raged in Danny. Time stopped. He could still feel the presence of the Ring in his thoughts, but there was another presence, something that was his own, a person who had parents called Steff and Grace. With a great wrench he freed his mind. A calm descended over him, a calm in which he saw everything with absolute clarity. He turned to Devoy.

"You restored the torture instruments, didn't you?" Devoy nodded, eyes fixed on Danny. "But you didn't do it to torture," Danny went on, "far from it. You did it to save a cadet. You knew that Toxique had not assassinated anyone, as was required by family law. You hoped to save him by pretending that he had developed a talent for torture, a talent that Wilsons was nurturing. You were going to show his father around the chamber and pretend that Toxique was torturing people in it. Then you could say, 'You can be proud of your son now. He has a profession, even though it is not as an assassin.' Isn't that right, Master Devoy?"

Devoy nodded slowly.

"It would have been seen as an honorable profession for a Toxique—not as honorable as an assassin, of course, but it would have sufficed to avert the wrath of his father."

"What is this?" Longford's voice cut across the room like a whiplash. "Is he or is he not involved in the maintenance of a torture room? His reasons for doing so are irrelevant. Danny, instruct Mr. Toxique. Finish this now!"

Danny shook his head. The other members of the Ring were on their feet now, anger on their faces. Dixie, looking bewildered, cried out, "What's going on here?"

"It was all a sham from the start," Danny said, "a scheme of Master Devoy's. Once he had renovated the torture room, he saw the possibility of using it for another purpose. He had himself accused of torture and imprisoned."

"Why?" It was Spitfire's turn to look bewildered.

"Because he knew there were traitors in Wilsons. Information had been escaping. With the Treaty Stone broken it was imperative that these traitors be exposed. Brunholm was in on it, of course. He allowed Ness to replace Blackpitt. He invited the Ring to take over Wilsons, knowing that the traitors would come out into the open. As they have done. Exshaw and Hotspur are the real traitors. The others, like Smyck, are merely foolish."

Danny had never liked Brunholm, but he had to admire the way the man had pretended to be a traitor to Wilsons and carried it off. He nodded to Brunholm, who stood and bowed. Nurse Flanagan eyed him coldly.

"An elegant strategy, Master Devoy," Longford said with a smile, "and it almost came off—*would* have come off, if I had not had the foresight to bring a large force of Seraphim with me." All eyes in the ballroom turned to the Seraphim roosting like vultures outside.

"As I say, you almost succeeded, but unfortunately you lost in the end. You have your traitors, but I still have Wilsons. Any resistance will be of course be met with the sternest reprisal. Danny, I will deal with you later. You have disappointed me twice. You are not the true Fifth. Never mind. You are not the only mongrel that history has thrown up. There will be another. But I cannot have you alive, Danny, trying to disrupt my schemes. You have interfered for the last time. Ness!"

A long knife appeared in the Cherb leader's hand. A flick of his wrist and it flew through the air, aimed straight at Danny's heart. The ballroom was frozen. Danny could see the knife coming toward him as though in slow motion, cleaving the air, and knew that he could not avoid it.

"No!" The Unknown Spy, once more forgotten, flung himself forward. The knife buried itself with a terrible thud in his chest. Danny's hand went into his coat. The Knife of Implacable Intention was at the ready before the Unknown Spy fell, with a low moan, to the floor. Devoy ran to his side. Danny aimed the knife at Longford.

"You know this knife never misses its intended target," he said in a dangerous voice. "Do not make me kill you." He turned slightly. "Les!"

Les ran up from the ballroom. Danny handed him the knife.

"Keep it aimed at Longford. If any of them move, just throw it."

"I know what to do," Les said. "I gave you the knife, remember? Way back when you first came to Wilsons?"

Danny quickly knelt beside the Unknown Spy. Vandra was already there. Her gentle hands probed the wound.

"There is nothing I can do," she said softly after a few seconds. "The knife has penetrated the heart, and I am a healer, not a surgeon."

Danny looked into the man's face. He'd been so close to finding out where his parents might have gone. The Unknown Spy's breathing was shallow and ragged. He beckoned Danny closer.

"Your father . . . your father asked me to look after you if something . . . if something happened to him. Didn't do a very good job, did I? Forgot everything. Didn't realize when I saw your eyes the first time. Talking to Devoy in the cell . . . it all started to come back. . . ."

"You did everything you could and more," Devoy said, kneeling down beside the man.

"Maybe," the Unknown Spy said. "It's getting dark in here."

"The light hasn't changed," Danny started to say, then stopped, realizing that the man was slipping away.

"Please," Danny said, "if you could only tell me . . ."

"I would tell Steff's boy everything if I could. It was terrible what they did to him. He told me he had discovered how to conquer all. 'Pass it on to my boy,' he said, 'if something happens to me. Make sure he knows.'"

"Knows what?" Danny cried. But a fleeting smile flickered on the Unknown Spy's lips, as though he had seen a familiar face just over Danny's shoulder. He turned his head to one side.

"The things we love are always closer than we think," he whispered, and closed his eyes.

"He's gone," Devoy said gently. Danny bowed his head. He had been so close.

"I'm sorry, Danny," Vandra said. Every pair of eyes in the room was turned toward the little group around the Unknown Spy. Rufus Ness saw that Les was distracted. Moving so quickly that his feet barely touched the floor, the Cherb circled behind Les. There was a cry and Les fell to the ground, clutching his arm. Ness picked up the Knife of Implacable Intention.

"Thank you, Rufus," Longford said. "A most touching scene. The Fifth and the master of Wilsons kneeling before the corpse of a ragged old spy who can't remember his own name. Conal, I fear we will have to teach Wilsons a lesson. In your honor, Danny, I will make the theme of our attack the number five. Have the Seraphim slay every fifth pupil and every fifth Messenger—and it wouldn't be fair to leave the staff out, would it, so we shall have to kill every fifth faculty member as well."

Conal lifted a chair and threw it through one of the great windows. Then he launched himself from the edge of the dais and flew with great slow wingbeats through the window. Longford turned to Danny.

"So you are Steff Pilkington's pup, are you? I should have guessed. He was a meddling fool, and he appears to have passed it on. I wonder who your mother was?

Grace . . . Grace . . . let me think . . . of course—I know!"
He started to laugh. His laughter went on and on. From
outside came a great rush of wings as the Seraphim rose
triumphantly into the air. Some of the younger cadets
cried out as the dreadful creatures drew swords. Danny
lifted his eyes from the body of the Unknown Spy, tears
streaming down his face. Longford's mocking laughter
echoed around the room. Dixie saw what was in Danny's
eyes.

"Danny, no!" she cried, but it was too late. There was
a roaring sound as though a terrible wind stirred in the
ballroom; then, with a crash, all the windows blew out.
Ness dropped the knife in his hand. The Seraphim's triumph turned to trepidation, then to outright panic. A gale
laden with broken glass from the shattered windows broke
upon them and blew them like leaves before it. With cries
and shrieks they were driven across the sky, their wings
useless against the wind summoned by Danny. He
watched as they grew small in the sky and then were gone,
the only sign of their presence a few feathers floating
gently to the ground.

Danny turned then to the four members of the Ring,
but they had fled. A car started in the distance and wheels
spun on gravel. The Ring had made good their escape.
The stunned silence in the ballroom stretched on; then,
as if at a signal, everyone began to talk at once.

26

TREACHERY AND LOYALTY

Danny sat alone in the summerhouse. He held the ring given to him by the dead, the intertwined "S" and "G."

"Put it on," a voice said. He looked up to see the detective McGuinness standing in the doorway. "They're in a right state up at Wilsons," he said. "Seraphim feathers everywhere. Hotspur and Exshaw fled with Longford and the rest of the Ring. Brunholm is delighted with his part. As for you, that is a great power you have, Danny. Use it wisely."

"This coat," Danny said softly, touching the battered old trench coat. "It belonged to my dad, Steff Pilkington. Is he dead, then?"

"I believe so, Danny. I would not hold out any hope for your mother and father. But I knew Steff. He was a great spy."

"Not great enough to keep himself alive."

"It is part of the work, Danny. Danger always follows you. And if you are good at what you do it will catch up with you at the end. That is the fate of the great spy, if he does not turn to evil. Your father knew that."

"He abandoned me," Danny said. "And my mother left me."

"I'm not sure you're right about that. I didn't know your mother, but Steff was not a man to abandon anyone. Spying was everything to him, you have to remember that," McGuinness said.

"No I don't. I know I'm right," Danny said, "and right now, at this moment, I feel like walking to Tarnstone and taking a ferry across to join the Ring of Five, if they'll still have me. At least then I'll belong to something."

"You will—belong to them, I mean. You'll be owned, heart and soul. Corrupted by the Ring."

"But I won't be alone."

"You're not alone here. You have friends. One of them needs you now and you're not there."

"How could they need me? What did Longford call me? A mongrel!"

"Even a mongrel still has a bark," McGuinness said, looking at Danny coldly, "if he chooses to use it. Do as you will, Danny. I have work to do."

The detective left without a backward glance. Danny sat alone in the darkened summerhouse, turning the ring over and over in his hands.

*   *   *

Toxique waited in the hallway, his suitcase packed, Valant watching him from behind his desk but not daring to intervene. Toxique's father had been closeted with Devoy for over an hour, and Valant didn't need a Beetle of Transmission to know what was going on. Toxique had failed as an assassin. The treaty might have been shattered, the Ring gathering strength for incursions into the Upper World, but the code of the Toxiques held firm. Valant shook his head. It had always been so. He heard light measured footsteps approaching. His eyes were dull and hopeless.

Mr. Toxique strode into the hallway. He looked down at his son. There was no anger in his gaze, only sorrow.

"Let us be gone from this place," he said. Toxique got to his feet.

"Stop!" a girl cried from the doorway. Dixie stood shoulder to shoulder with Les. The Knife of Implacable Intention was in her hand, pointed toward Mr. Toxique.

"Say the word, Toxique," Dixie said.

"I can't," Toxique said, "he is my father. Put the knife away, Dixie. I have to go home with him."

"Don't," Les said despairingly.

"I must," Toxique said.

"Not until my investigations are complete." A new voice spoke. It was McGuinness.

"What is this?" Toxique's father demanded.

"This young man is wanted for questioning in relation to the murder of the Unknown Spy's wife," McGuinness said. "He isn't going anywhere."

"Murder?" Toxique's father's eyes narrowed. "Indeed, it would be a wonderful thing, but I hardly think
that—"

"What *do* you think?" Brunholm said, striding into
the room. "That our leading detective is a liar?"

"I do not accuse any man of lying," Mr. Toxique said,
"but I demand corroboration."

"Danny can corroborate," Brunholm said smoothly,
"can't you, Danny?"

All eyes turned to the front door. Danny stood there,
his eyes moving from one to the other. The impulse to betray struggled with the need to be loyal to his friend.

"How can I believe Caulfield?" Mr. Toxique said.
"He has lied before."

"You are right," Danny said, "you can't trust me. I
can't corroborate the story."

"I don't believe it," Toxique cried to Danny. "The
Gift of Anticipation told me that you would back me. It's
never been wrong before!"

Danny shrugged, but McGuinness could see that his
eyes were glittering.

"Come on, boy," Mr. Toxique said. Toxique got to his
feet and without a glance at Danny followed his father out
the door.

"Danny!" Dixie cried, but he merely looked at her
without expression, turned and slipped away. Dixie went

to look outside. The door of the long black car stood open, its engine running. Toxique put his case in the back and started to climb in. Just as his father got into the front seat, there was the sound of running feet. It was Vicky the siren.

"I heard you were going," she said. "I just wanted to give you this back."

She handed Toxique a knife, a long thin blade with a raven-shaped handle.

"Where did you get that?" McGuinness gasped. "It was in my evidence locker."

"You're in a school for spies, Mr. McGuinness," Dixie said.

"It's the knife that killed the Unknown Spy's wife," McGuinness said, "but the chain of custody is broken now. It's been handled by someone else. It's useless as evidence."

"Here you go," Vicky said, handing it to Toxique. "I know it's yours." Toxique took it.

"The crime is unsolvable now," McGuinness said angrily.

"Unsolvable." Mr. Toxique looked at his son with new eyes. "Did you, son? Did you really commit your first assassination?"

Dixie held her breath. Toxique was too nervous to be a good liar, but he managed a half smile.

"A Toxique never admits to an assassination, even under torture," he said, "but I'm glad to have my knife back. Thank you, Vicky."

A grim smile creased Mr. Toxique's face.

"Perhaps I have been hasty," he said. "Devoy seems to have taught you something after all. You may stay at Wilsons. And allow me to offer you my hand."

Awkwardly the father and son shook hands. In her delight, Dixie disappeared and reappeared three times in rapid succession.

.

High above them, Danny and Mr. Devoy looked down on the scene from the window of the library of the third landing.

"You set that up, of course," Devoy said.

"It was no good my corroborating. A Toxique never gets caught. That would be worse than not carrying out an assassination at all. And Vicky owed me a favor."

"Where did you get the knife?"

"Les stole it for me. He doesn't thieve very much now, but he's still very good at it. He's gone with Vandra to see Daisy. She's come around a little."

"Toxique did not kill the Unknown Spy's wife, as you know," Devoy said. "It was Ness. He was afraid that she would reveal the Sibling Strategy and you would be forewarned about the girl you knew as Lily before you went to Morne."

"The Sibling Strategy," Danny repeated. "Pretending to be my sister."

"We are only at the start of a long and deadly conflict. There will be other treacheries."

There was silence. The fire flickered in the grate. A raven in the rafters stretched its wings and settled them again, its sharp little eyes alert. Devoy looked down at the ring on Danny's finger, the intertwined "S" and "G."

"There are other rings in the world, Danny," he said, "not just the Ring of Five. There are rings that mean loyalty, friendship, devotion, love. Rings that bind people to each other. Will you stay with us, Danny? Your mother and father were bound to this place."

Faces swam in front of Danny: Stone. Pearl. The girl who had claimed to be his sister. He went to the window. Vandra glanced up as if she sensed him, and her eyes met his for a moment. There were others out there too. He saw the siren Vicky and Brunholm in deep conversation at the edge of the shrubbery. They stopped talking and looked up, as if they too had felt his presence.

"You have the potential to be a great spy, Danny," Devoy said, "perhaps the very greatest."

"Or to be the greatest traitor in the history of spying," Danny said.

"That too," Devoy said. Danny looked down at his friends, then turned away from the window. He found himself staring into the Mirror of Limited Reflection. His eyes had changed; the brown and the blue were shrewd and knowing now. Treachery and loyalty in equal measure, and no telling which would win. Behind him the fire crackled and the raven shifted in the rafters. Danny knew that Devoy was at his shoulder, but only one face was visible in the strange mirror—a boy's face floating alone in the darkness.

About the Author

EOIN MCNAMEE was born in County Down, Northern Ireland. *The Unknown Spy* is the second book in the Ring of Five trilogy. He is also the author of the Navigator trilogy for children, and he is critically acclaimed as a writer of novels for adults, the best known being *Resurrection Man,* which was made into a film. He was awarded the Macaulay Fellowship for Irish Literature and has also written two adult thrillers under the name John Creed.